The Last Chapter

The Last Chapter

Guita Garakani

Translated from Persian by Sara Phillips

Garnet
PUBLISHING

The Last Chapter

Published by
Garnet Publishing Limited
8 Southern Court
South Street
Reading
RG1 4QS
UK

www.garnetpublishing.co.uk
www.twitter.com/Garnetpub
www.facebook.com/Garnetpub
blog.garnetpublishing.co.uk

This translation is based on the Persian edition first published by Caravan Books Publishing House, 2006

First Edition

ISBN: 9781859643037

British Library Cataloguing-in-Publication Data
A catalogue record for this book is available from the British Library

Typeset by Samantha Barden
Jacket design by Haleh Darabi

Printed and bound in Lebanon by International Press:
interpress@int-press.com

To Amir Ferydoun Garakani,
who wanted to evade his memories
and the recollection of his memories

All the characters, names and events in the story are fictional. Any likeness is a matter of coincidence.

All acts draw to a close and the actors eventually leave the stage, one by one, until the stage is empty. When the last member of the audience leaves, no one is left in the theatre; there are no actors, no audience and there will be no performance. One day a developer will arrive and demolish the theatre. Memories from all the plays and stories that have been performed there will be lost to the land, which bears no memory. But what of the destiny of the land itself, you ask? God only knows. A land that yields nothing holds no memories and, without memories, the world does not exist.

Tonight's show: The story of a man called Vaqar us-Saltaneh and his son Youssef.

Actors:	*None*
Audience:	*None*
The atmosphere:	*Desolate*

Actually, No! Wait! There is one person left: an actor who was in the audience; a member of the audience who was in the act ...

Prologue

The sun rose on Saturday just like on any other day of the week.

In that crepuscular hour the desert surrounding the city slowly began to take shape. The beams of light settled on the huts and modest houses, whose proprietors had left, well before sunrise, in search of work. The shaft of light progressed from the desert to the dusty narrow alleyways and, on its way, passed by the water-filled potholes and over the stones that had been scattered by schoolchildren tripping over them.

The shaft of sunlight reached the city, where it lit up its heart and main arteries. It passed by the newly constructed buildings, with stone façades that had not yet been dirtied by the city's pollution: buildings that had not been around long enough to bear witness to many tales. The shaft reached the older districts. It squeezed through narrow passages where the memories had departed with their creators. When the shaft reached the gentleman's house, it passed unscathed over the entrance before it descended through the branches of the trees and lit up the cobbled area in the garden, eventually reaching the main building. It passed through the closed windows of a house that still seemed to be asleep and then, reaching the second floor, penetrated through the thick drawn curtains of the study.

As Salman climbed the stairs, he wasn't expecting to encounter anything untoward. As usual he was up before dawn and was about to begin his routine of dusting, which started in the study because it was early in the week. When he opened the door an unfamiliar odour wafted towards him. It was the smell of cigar smoke mixed with something much more unpleasant; an odour that was somehow familiar yet that he could not quite place. It was difficult in the dark room to work out where the smell was coming from, so Salman went to the curtains straightaway. He pulled one of the thick green drapes aside, which allowed the light to pour into the dark room through the white net curtain underneath. Salman then drew back the curtains on both sides of the window completely and used the hook on the wall to secure them. He turned to face into the room to decide where to make a start. It was then that he began to see: his master was in the room. It looked as though he had spent the entire night there but not in the position everyone was used to. He was not seated behind his desk, as he invariably was when dealing with visitors. Master was sitting on the arm of his chair, which was positioned in front of the desk, and yet he had managed to face the desk while staring into space. His fingers were clutching the arm of the chair. His white hair, which he always wore combed back, was dishevelled now, with a clump scattered across his high forehead, as though he had run his fingers through it in a state of distress. But this was impossible; Master Vaqar was never distressed. He was always a composed and gracious man: he walked graciously, spoke graciously, sat graciously, and dished out instructions graciously.

Gracious or not, he would never spend the entire night in his study. Salman didn't know what to make of his master in his study at this hour. He had worked there long enough not to question his master's actions; he knew his master did as he pleased. Master had always been this way – he never felt he needed to satisfy anyone's curiosity.

Salman said hello, loud enough to be heard; then, since he didn't know what to do in such an unusual situation, he lowered his gaze and began to dust the room as usual. He thought his master would call to him, growl, ask for tea, even order him to leave the room and not bother him. But he didn't say a word. He did not call out to Salman; he did not ask for tea, or anything else. Salman approached his master. He had not moved, even when Salman drew the curtains. His head was resting against the back of the chair. His forehead was large, his cheekbones were rather prominent, his nose was straight and finer than most people's, his lips were pressed underneath his neat white moustache, and he had a strong and shapely chin – he appeared to be gazing at some undefined object in front of him.

Salman couldn't wait any longer. He stepped forward and asked, 'Shall I bring you tea, Sir?'

There was no response; his master didn't even move his head.

Salman tried again. 'It's the morning, Sir. Shall I bring you tea?'

Still no reply. Salman became concerned at this point. His eyesight was not good so he moved closer and narrowed his eyes to focus better. Master's face looked relaxed, with no movement. His hands ... Salman's eyes drifted down the arms to the hands. They were not just clutching the arms of the chair; they were tied to them with a piece of rope. Someone had tied Master's hands to the arms of the chair with a rope. Master wasn't reacting at all. His head didn't move. His chest was not going up or down. The man seated in the chair was an imitation of his master. It was a master-like doll whose eyes didn't see and whose mouth didn't utter any words.

Salman did not shout, nor did he cause a commotion. Since he didn't know how to react to what was sitting there in place of his master, he just stepped backwards, left the room and quietly closed the door. Once he had closed it his senses returned and he gathered all the might in his tired legs and ran. He ran the entire length of the hallway and reached the kitchen. He swiftly opened the door and then forced it closed behind him. He leaned against the wall and then looked at Sakineh and Qanbar agog. His visage frightened them. He was panting. Finally, he announced to them, 'Master! May the Lord lengthen his life! I think ... Master ... he ... he's not breathing!'

From that moment on, the house filled with people; first, family and relatives, and then the police. Perhaps the police came first and then the family; no one quite remembers.

Salman was right: Master was not breathing. His hands were tied to the arms of the chair but there were no marks on his body to suggest that there had been any resistance. Nor was there anything in the room to suggest a fight. One or more people had come to see Master the night before but they clearly had not come for money: as far as anyone could tell nothing was stolen; when they opened the safe, which was in the corner of the room, they found neat bundles of banknotes and documents sitting on both shelves, untouched.

Everyone who saw Master in his chair in that state was overcome with a sense of bewilderment mixed with dread. Perhaps a ghost had come to visit him to settle some issues from the past but they could tell nothing from the expression on Master's face. The only visible sign there of anything untoward was that his mouth was slightly open, as is typically the case with the dead, and slightly distorted. That was all.

The police searched the room. They searched everywhere: the drawers in the desk, under the carpet, every book on the shelves, every object in the room, but they couldn't find anything that offered any clues as to what had happened. It was as though Master himself had tied his own hands and then given in to death.

They only found one thing; it didn't have particular significance as far as the police were concerned but it startled the family. The expressions on their faces showed the same bewilderment and fright as could be seen on Master's face. There were two old envelopes in one of the drawers. They were worn and yellowed with age and each was tied with a ribbon as a result. One contained wedding invitations, but Master's wedding had never taken place. The other envelope contained letters from the girl who had been supposed to marry Master once upon a time.

Youssef, Vaqar us-Saltaneh's eldest son, died in the same house he was born in; the very house that became his after his father's murder, and who was himself murdered mysteriously some years later. No one had tried hard to find the murderer, which was perhaps for the best. A saga had drawn to a close with the second murder; the saga of Vaqar and his son.

The story of Vaqar and his son was quite familiar to the family elders but they wouldn't recount it to their children; they wouldn't even talk about it with each other. It was a secret, a secret that had been hushed up because it would be detrimental to the family's good name.

But discovery of the cards and letters had confused everyone. No one could believe that Vaqar's son had kept the invites for a wedding that had never taken place or letters that had been written by someone now long forgotten.

Chapter 1

Some people are like the sun; you can bathe in the glowing light and warmth of their affection. And if you err and gaze in their eyes you can become bewitched and fall into a hypnotic trance, in which the narcoleptic is doomed to settle; you will never be able to release yourself from the spell. The intensity of their light is such that your eyes can never see any other faces quite so clearly and you could spend the rest of your life searching for a face, the details of which you no longer remember; it is only the blinding light, the immense warmth and the unique charisma of this face which has stuck in your mind. However, none of these characteristics can ever direct you to your destination. You walk in the dark looking for a sun which now ignores you and has forever set in your life. Or perhaps that sun has departed your life so that it can rise to mark the dawn somewhere else, to give light to another traveller who has lost her way; and, without warning, the sun could leave her in the dark as well. This is the nature of the sun. It doesn't want to make you suffer; it just isn't there for you all the time. The wise traveller learns to make progress in the dark and relies solely on the faint light emanating from the lantern that she holds in her hand. She can only see the modest cobbled road under her feet. She doesn't fall in the potholes. She doesn't have any dreams. She is not in pain. But she who has immersed herself in the light of the sun sees, for one moment only, the wider landscape; all the flowers, the trees, the birds and the mountains; all of life's complex paths; the paths that all end up in dreams. And when her sun has set, she continues on her path regretting all that she *could* have had but now cannot. And this is the cycle of the story of love. Still, whoever finds her sun can't help but gaze in its eyes, at which point she will drown in infinite despair.

Youssef was Rana's sun. He wasn't like anyone else; not in life or in death. And Rana knew this, even when she knew little else about life. And when she gazed into her sun's eyes she had yet to learn about sunset.

Rana picked up the notebook from the desk and turned the pages, *a metal bucket with a hole but repairable ... two used copper sieves ... a metre and a half of rope ...*

A shadow crept over the page. Rana lifted her head; it was Youssef. He was laughing, just like every time he wanted to tease her. He tried to pull the notebook out of her hand but Rana clung on to the book at the other end. She had no intention of letting Youssef have the notebook; she wanted to read it first. There ensued a silent commotion over the notebook. Youssef won and finally got hold of it. Rana pulled a face. Youssef began to turn the pages and then let Rana have the book. He was still laughing. His quiet laughter made Rana laugh. She could never sulk for long when it came to Youssef. They were almost the same age; the same age and playmates. Whenever Rana went to stay with Auntie Malek, Youssef came too. Youssef was slender and scrawny and a little taller than Rana. His skin was darker and there always seemed to be a twinkle in his large eyes. He was noisy but composed. He could be docile but also ferocious; patient yet intolerant. When they played a game and something was not to his liking, he would just leave. Rana would then have to beg him to return and continue to play. Many times, though, she wouldn't succeed; if he decided to be stubborn nothing worked. Things would escalate quite quickly. There would be a flash of anger in his eyes. He would then purse his lips and leave. If they were in the garden, he would look down and then head back to the house. If they were indoors, he would leave without a word and end up in the garden. It was easier if they were out on the street because he would either walk ahead or walk behind, pretending he was looking in the shop windows. The situation would remain until he had calmed down and forgotten about the issue. But he never dwelt upon the subject; he never argued. He resented talking about what had upset him, though he exercised more patience whenever he was with Rana. They rarely squabbled, usually managing to compromise instead. They shared the consequences of their actions, whether it be reward or reprimand – they never betrayed each other by telling tales. If they were caught being mischievous they were both told off because no one could tell who the culprit was; it was assumed that they were both involved.

Rana asked, 'Are they still making *halva*?'

Youssef replied, 'They must be, otherwise Maryam wouldn't still be with Mother.'

Taj *Khanoum*, Youssef's mother, was Vaqar's wife and was a better cook than most. She had come over so that Malek wasn't left to do everything on her own. Ever since Mr Piran, Malek's husband, had passed away, the house was always full of visitors; the familiar and the unfamiliar – there was no privacy. Visitors came and went. The servants darted from one place to another offering tea to the visitors. Rana's hand was hurting now, having offered round the heavy tray laden with *halva* and dates. Malek remained seated but she would gesture to indicate to Rana who to offer the *halva* and dates to. Youssef helped out in the reception hall. He led the visitors in or out. He did all that youngsters in any household did to help out.

Malek and her late husband, Mr Piran, didn't have any children of their own, hence the need to have Rana and Youssef around. As soon as there was less to do, or just too much commotion for anyone to notice the children, Rana and Youssef would go into the garden to play.

Rana asked, 'Isn't Maryam going to come?'

Youssef replied, 'She's still with Mother.'

'Why?' To which Youssef shrugged and said, 'Perhaps she can't wait to have some *halva*.'

Maryam was Youssef's five-year-old sister. Her mother divided her wavy black hair into two plaits on either side of her head. Her black eyes always twinkled and were shadowed by long lashes, just like Youssef's. Wherever Rana and Youssef went, Maryam wasn't far behind: she always followed her brother. She didn't speak. She never made any noise. If she fell while playing, she never complained. Youssef had warned her that he wouldn't let her play with them again if she did. So Maryam tried not to make a nuisance of herself. She just wanted to be with her brother. To Rana, who didn't have any siblings, Maryam was like a walking doll; her presence didn't bother her. She loved her. Maryam was the little sister that she always wanted but never had. Rana didn't know yet that Vaqar was soon to take Youssef's little sister away from them. Maryam was not Vaqar's only victim but she was the first that Rana knew about.

Maryam never grew up. She remained Rana's young and amiable sister for ever. Rana always wondered what Maryam might have looked like had she grown up. She tried to picture her at different stages in her life: adolescence, youth, middle and old age. She wondered if Maryam would have remained the same beautiful girl after she had married and had a child. She would surely have put on weight, her hair would gradually have turned grey and her body would have lost its shape. She might have developed a double chin and perhaps little bags under her eyes. But girls tend to resemble their mothers as they grow older so Maryam would have been very lucky. Taj *Khanoum* was still a beautiful woman even though she was midway through her life and despite all that she had been through. In any case, Maryam didn't resemble her father, Vaqar, at all, thank goodness.

Youssef had two brothers as well; two younger brothers. They did not participate in his games and perhaps this was why she could not remember them well. As far as Rana was concerned they were two faceless little ghosts. Youssef, Maryam and Taj *Khanoum*, their mother, were the only ones that Rana could remember. The lines of their faces did not fade with the passing of time, rather they seemed to have been carved in stone, the stone of time; a stone that was hard enough to shatter the goblet of dreams.

Rana had yet to put the notebook back in its place; she was concerned that Youssef might take it and use it to tease her again. It wouldn't look good if the elders found out that they were laughing at Mr Piran. The cover of the notebook was black. Her aunt, Malek, had found it in one of the drawers in the desk when she was looking for the deeds of the land and the house first thing that day. The contents of the house were registered in the notebook in neat rows. Malek had bequeathed the notebook to Auntie and Uncle Sardari. Auntie turned the page, read a few lines, nodded and mumbled something with only one recognisable word: 'Idiot!'

Uncle Sardari arrived later that day and when he scrutinised the contents of the notebook he nodded here and there, admiring the blessed soul's attention to detail. Everyone else looked at it briefly before leaving it for the next person to browse. The last person to do so was Rana. Rana took the notebook and went through it thoroughly but she decided it was filled with nonsense, just like Mr Piran's conversation and the way he expressed his opinions. But then she shivered at her audacity to think that way about a family elder. If her Aunt Malek found out, she would be upset. Father would say that children were not to poke their noses into the affairs of grown-ups. Before any of them noticed her touch the notebook she shrugged, placed it back on the desk, motioned to Youssef and they both left the room.

* * *

It was already past two in the afternoon. The visitors had left. The household was taking a rest before the next wave of visitors arrived. Everyone on the late Mr Piran's list of relatives was supposed to be there by three in the afternoon so that the will could be read out. Malek, Mr Piran's widow, had used her headache as an excuse to retire to her bedroom. The only people in the room were Uncle Sardari and Auntie, neither of whom took a nap in the afternoon. Uncle Sardari had picked up a newspaper and pretended to read so that he didn't have to talk to Auntie, and she had bent over a book and turned the pages for the same reason.

Uncle Sardari made himself so comfortable in the deep large soft armchair that the newspaper covered not only his face and torso but also part of his thighs.

Auntie's walking stick rested against the arm of the chair she was sitting on. The only part of her hair that the black headscarf did not cover was the front section, a white mass; otherwise the headscarf with fine dark grey lines running through it was tied firmly to the back of her head. The dark colour of the headscarf seemed to hug the oval face, the beauty of which had not yet faded with the passing of time. The creases around her large and intelligent eyes made her gaze more intense. She had high cheekbones with a nose so small and fine that it was as though it had been carved from stone by a sculptress. Her walking stick was testament to the permanent pain in her legs – since it had flared up particularly severely a few months ago, no one had seen Auntie walk without her stick.

The reception room was dimly lit. The straw blinds were let down outside the windowpane and the thick curtains were drawn so that there were no gaps to allow light in. The air inside the room felt warm and humid. Uncle Sardari got one of the servants to switch on the fan that was suspended from the ceiling. Auntie was grumbling but Uncle Sardari ignored her and instead shifted so that he was sitting directly underneath the fan. The movement of the air lifted his white hair like the sails of a sinking ship. Auntie gave him a dirty look, as though her only hope was that the ship might sink and relieve her from the domestic tempests. They barely communicated with each other. Each of them belonged to a different branch of the family: he was the nephew of one of Grandfather's wives who had later married a grandson of Grandmother's aunt. The passage of time had witnessed him amass quite a fortune and build a strong position in the family, a position that meant that his approval was required in order to get anything done. Auntie, however, was the eldest daughter and consequently Uncle Sardari's only real rival. If anyone of the family wanted to marry their daughter off or was thinking of finding their son a wife, if anyone wanted to invest in a significant venture or end a family feud, they would go to Auntie. She seemed to know all the answers and have a solution to every problem. And, given that she was housebound due to rheumatism, she had time for everyone; for everyone except Uncle Sardari. She thought the only thing Uncle Sardari was capable of dealing with was the posthumous affairs of the dead. She would shake her walking stick in the air and chuckle, 'He's at it to bury everyone in the family. He can dream on, good luck to him! He'll take his dream of seeing me dead before him to his grave.'

The reality was that they had both lived longer than most and so had attended countless funerals. Now it was impossible to imagine a wedding or funeral without them. Choosing a ceremony or a date for a ceremony, or a venue for that matter, was impossible without first seeking their opinion.

The white chrysanthemums trembled in their large crystal vase on the table as the fan sent ripples through the air. The petals were not, however, lifting in the air like Uncle Sardari's hair; they just swung from one side to another, giving the impression that the vase could fall at any moment. Auntie called for Rana, who was in the kitchen. Hearing her voice, Rahman the servant appeared in the room. Rana and Youssef followed as well.

'Yes?' Rana asked.

'Rana dear, take this vase away please,' Auntie said, but before Rana could move, Rahman stepped forward and stretched out his arms to lift the vase and carry it away.

'There's no need,' Uncle Sardari protested.

'Take it away,' Auntie commanded.

'It looks better where it is,' he suggested.

'When the fan blows the vase over and onto the tray of halva, it'll look even better I suppose,' said Auntie, pulling a face. 'Rahman, take it away ...' she ordered. 'Take it to the dining room and leave it on the dining table.'

Rahman, who was still holding the vase, began to walk towards the dining table. The dining table had been pushed against a wall to the side of the room and had a large framed photograph of the late Mr Piran in the middle, with a thick black ribbon to the side. The table was dotted with various platters of *halva* and dates. Rahman placed the vase in the middle, next to the photograph and in among the various plates.

Uncle Sardari said to Youssef, 'Put Mr Piran's picture on the side table, Son, right there; we can't see it from here.'

Youssef picked up the frame and placed it where Uncle Sardari had asked him to. 'No, a little further to the side,' he said. 'A little more forward, to the front of Great Auntie's picture.'

No one, not even the late Mr Piran, had dared to touch the frame of Great Auntie's photo without first seeking Malek's permission. She was Malek's eldest aunt and had died young. The photograph was of a maiden of striking beauty with large, deep-set eyes, a small nose, and fine lips that seemed to press together – she was wearing large hoop earrings.

Standing next to Youssef, Rana pulled the photograph slightly to the back to allow room for Mr Piran's photograph. Uncle

Sardari said, 'That looks good! Perfect! It's quite easy to see it now.'

Mr Piran's photo frame was in Auntie's line of vision. She duly gave it a contemptuous look, shuffled in her chair and searched for her walking stick so that she could avoid seeing the picture.

Rana found the sight of Auntie and Uncle Sardari comical. She looked at Youssef and found that he too was forcing himself not to smile. They both decided to look for Maryam so that they could walk out, leaving the two steadfast rivals to themselves.

Mr Piran's photo frame was not usually placed near the other photographs; it was kept in a suitcase with the collection of family photographs. As a child, Abtin would sometimes climb into the suitcase containing the photographs, ransack it, and then ask Rana to promise to buy a few albums so that he could place all the photos in them. Rana did promise but the albums never materialised. The photographs in the suitcase were those she didn't wish to see. Abtin would put Mr Piran's photograph aside saying that he did not want that particular one in the album. 'There's no need for this one to go in. He doesn't look in a good mood here.' Rana couldn't bear the sight of Mr Piran's image either, because it reminded her of Youssef standing by the wall, smiling, in Auntie Malek's reception room. She would miss him so much, his happy and innocent expression, that her chest felt like it was about to burst open.

Mr Piran's black and white photograph showed a long-nosed and small-eyed man with very little hair. The black ribbon, marking the corner of the frame, was so wide that it made Mr Piran look as though he had a beret on his hairless head. The photograph had been taken when Mr Piran was a young man; it had been chosen carelessly and in haste for the funeral. The person usually behind such decisions was Uncle Sardari; he used a photographer acquaintance, someone of his generation, as old as himself and with poor eyesight – he could not focus well. For example, at the funeral of Rana's mother, Marjan, the photographer had accidentally enlarged a photograph of her husband, Nasrullah Khan, who was alive and well. The incident called for a few smiles except from Nasrullah Khan who, though not a superstitious man, considered the episode ominous. Auntie claimed that Uncle Sardari had photographs ready for everyone's funeral. Her claim had reached the ears of Uncle Sardari as well.

Mr Zaeem ud-Dowleh arrived before everyone else, clad in his top hat and tails; he believed that no major family event could take place without his presence. Auntie Mehr us-Saltaneh also made an appearance despite her lassitude and ailments. She was always mindful of what went through other people's minds and, since she did not want Malek to take offence, she had turned up. Vaqar, Youssef's father, arrived after the other two. After exchanging pleasantries he sat to the side keeping himself to himself but his small and cunning eyes watched everyone in the room like a hawk in search of its prey. The two cousins and a few others in the family felt an obligation to attend and hear the will read out.

The late Mr Piran's nephews and their wives were the last to arrive. Mirza Muhammad Khan, Mr Piran's eldest nephew, who was more than fifty years of age, was the first of them to step into the room. His title suggested that he had some pedigree but it was, in fact, one he had adopted of his own accord; he wasn't blessed with the best of handwriting either. His sisters insisted on the title, which meant that no one could bring themselves to call him otherwise. The rest followed him into the room, including Munir, Mah Leqa, Maheen, and even Mahmoud, who still didn't have a title because he was the youngest although already in his mid-forties. The daughters-in-law hadn't arrived yet. Assieh, Mirza Muhammad Khan's wife, a gracious and devout lady, had used her mother's illness to excuse herself from attending. Mahmoud's wife, who was younger than the rest and didn't seem to be on good terms with her in-laws, was nowhere to be seen. Munir's husband as well as Mah Leqa's and Maheen's entered the room one by one. Munir's husband was presented as the retired employee of an important organisation, but no one knew just which organisation. The other two husbands were supposed to be reputable merchants. They had a shop in the bazaar but no one knew what merchandise they sold or how they managed to do so well. Auntie believed nothing was straightforward with this family and didn't trust them – if they really were that well off then they would not be there, flattering their uncle. What the reality was God only knew.

The arrival of Mr Piran's nephews brought about more commotion: some stood up to greet them and then everyone settled back in their chairs while pleasantries were exchanged. The gloomy atmosphere gave way to smiles and then everyone began to chat quietly to his or her neighbour.

The tea tray went around followed by the offering of dates and *halva*. Condolences had already been exchanged on the day Mr Piran had passed away, as they went to bury the body and during the funeral.

Mr Piran's lawyer had invited everyone named on a list the deceased had drawn up when he was still alive. He had also made the point that the deceased had insisted upon Uncle Sardari and Auntie being present when the will was read out.

Malek was still resting in her bedroom. Her husband's long illness and the large number of visitors at the funeral service that had taken place in her home had exhausted her. Mr Piran was seventeen years her senior and when he died he had had no hair on his head, just like in his photograph, his small eyes being sunk deep in their sockets and his skin covered in freckles. His hands and the rest of his body were also marked. It was hard to imagine Mr Piran with a full head of hair and skin with no freckles or marks. Auntie said that he had looked the same even on their wedding night. He was the most unappealing groom she had ever seen. Malek, though, never complained about their conjugal life. Even in the latter years when the freckles had turned darker because of his malfunctioning liver and his behaviour had become increasingly unbearable, Malek still didn't complain. In his final years Mr Piran had disappeared into his own world more and more and hardly ever left the house. And when he did, he never told anyone what he was up to. Though he would never admit to it, the reason why they didn't have children was because he was impotent. He had divorced two wives on the grounds that *they* were sterile and unable to give him children. When he had sought Malek's hand in marriage he was still considered an eligible bachelor; a man in his forties with considerable wealth. Malek had not been that young either; nearly thirty. Her desire for a comfortable life with no financial worries, together with her fear of loneliness in old age coupled with rumours that she would never marry being mooted about her, were incentives for Malek to agree to the betrothal. After the wedding the couple had led a quiet life. Though Malek seemed complacent, after the first year dark rings began to appear around her eyes and the number of lines on her face increased. This was not surprising. Malek was Khanoum *jan*'s daughter. On her side of the family no one complained and everyone kept their affairs close to their chests. Even Auntie, who was privy to their secrets, didn't know everything, so the rumours were based on speculation. Illnesses only became public knowledge once the afflicted had passed away. Deaths, marriages, broodings and reconciliations remained behind closed doors. No one was brave enough to ask a question, nor did anyone dare intervene. Outsiders were at liberty to make assumptions but they couldn't say anything. The same applied to Malek's husband. Everyone was accommodating to the groom but no one, except the nephews who hoped to inherit some of his wealth, liked him; neither his contemporaries nor their children. It was therefore not surprising that no one was upset by his death.

Everyone was now waiting to hear the will. The family wanted to satisfy their curiosity about its contents, or, as Auntie said, to feed their interminable nosiness.

Mr Piran had liked writing his will and you could say that in the last ten years of his life he had pursued two principal hobbies; keeping a journal in the black notebook and writing his will. The black book was only for one purpose and that was to keep an account of everything. Mr Piran was a professional and experienced inventory maker. He would start his day by walking around the house and making a note of everything that was in it. He would then move to the shed at the end of the garden where, behind closed doors, he would make a note of all the objects inside the shed: three large pegs ... a metre and a half of used rope ... a pack of unused rope ... a bucket (with a hole but repairable) ... He would then move back into the house and register the contents in all the chests, the wardrobes and the cupboards; he would even make a note of the materials inside the chests. He carefully recorded the number of clothing items. He knew exactly how many shirts, how many suits and how many undergarments he had. He also kept a record of every tablecloth, bedspread and curtain, old and new. He made a note of the number of cupboards and chests, the stacks of linen in the airing cupboards, the clothes and materials that held mothballs in their folds, even the objects in the rooms. And, if he had time, he would go through the food cupboards as well as the kitchen drawers which held all the utensils – it was never-ending.

Once a month he updated his inventory just in case there were changes. If something that had been registered in the last list was missing he would ask Malek to explain its disappearance, but her explanations were not always plausible to him. He had repeatedly reminded Uncle Sardari not to listen to everything he heard. Whenever they had visitors, he would lower his voice as soon as Malek had left the room, saying, 'Well, one shouldn't just react to everything one hears because one hears so many things. Take my wife for instance. She whips up an excuse for everything. As soon as I ask her where something is she has a response ready. "Where's the pitcher," I ask her. "It looked too worn," she says; "I gave it away!" "Where's the rug?" "It looked too haggard," she says; "I've sent it for mending!" "Where are the copper pots?" "I have placed them all in the shed at the end of the garden!" She can say anything she wants but I don't believe everything that she says, do I?! ... No, certainly not. NO Sir, there's an account for everything in life.'

And he didn't care who his audience was, be they male or female, an acquaintance or a complete stranger. When Malek eventually returned to the room, she would encounter the puzzled expressions on everyone's faces, but she would merely smile and say, 'Mr Piran enjoys drawing up an inventory. That's what he has done, ever since he retired. It is actually a good thing to do. I can't remember everything and so nothing goes missing this way.' Following which she would offer the guests tea and pastries while maintaining her smile.

Mr Piran's other pastime was writing wills. He was, as a matter of fact, quite an expert in this endeavour as well. He was forever writing a new will and discarding the old one, never letting it be known what his old will entailed, or what changes he had made and whether anything new had been added. His nephews were always hovering around him like butterflies. They were confident that he would bequeath to them a portion of his assets. Malek's family, on the other hand, believed she would be the sole heir and would finally be able to lead a peaceful and trouble-free life without the man's demanding nature and archaic ways. And now there were many who were keen to stay in close contact with a soon-to-be-prosperous widow. While Mr Piran had been alive, her position had been little better than that of a respectable servant. But now, because of the position of this wealthy widow, a lot of people were eager to see her and offer her their sympathy. Which meant that although her social circle was of no consequence, they now had to offer her some sympathy. The only question that concerned Mr Piran's nephews – and they had already checked into the legalities should the need arise – was whether it was possible that Malek had already cleverly arranged for the transfer of the ownership of Mr Piran's assets into her own name.

Mr Piran's lawyer, Mr Etemadi, was the last to arrive. He was a slight man dressed in a dark blue suit with fine grey lines. With the buttons of his jacket done up he arrived flushed from the heat and looking as though he was about to explode, yet he didn't bother to undo his buttons. He even refrained from taking the cool sherbet drink that was offered to him; he seemed determined to look composed even in the most uncomfortable situation.

As soon as Mr Piran's lawyer arrived, Auntie sent Rana to call Malek. Malek was thus the last person to appear in the room. She looked plain in her simple black attire and she had donned a black lace headscarf. She seemed tired but not particularly mournful. Her expression was that of someone who had just lost a distant relation, or a neighbour who was not particularly popular. Her anxiety only became apparent when she kept rubbing her hands together.

Rana and Youssef followed Malek into the room and found themselves some chairs tucked away in the corner. Taj *Khanoum* did not attend as she needed to get on with the preparations for dinner and to supervise the household servants, but Maryam entered the room quietly and sat on Youssef's knee, her hair tied in plaits.

Mr Piran's lawyer did not take the tea offered either; instead he asked for a glass of water. He then asked the names of everyone in the room and made a careful note of some of them as though about to send a description to his deceased client. He worked in haste and looked impatient. His state of agitation was contagious, everyone else seeming irritable as soon as he had stepped into the room. They wanted him to get on with the will reading but he was determined to make certain that all was as it should be before starting: to begin with he wanted the children to leave the room. Rana, Youssef and Maryam remained, however, when Malek motioned them to do so. The lawyer decided to ignore their temerity, as though he didn't take himself too seriously. However, he was quite serious when he dished out his next set of conditions, which were met with vehement disapproval. Mr Etemadi placed a sheet of paper on the table and said, 'This list was prepared by Mr Piran while he was still alive and which he then left with me. He wished that only the people on this list remain in the room while the will is read.'

There was a commotion. Everyone spoke at once. A number of names were not on the list. Regardless of who they were – whether a family elder, or a son- or daughter-in-law – everyone present in the room at that moment felt they had a right to be there for personal reasons. They were decidedly unhappy. Zaeem picked up his silver-handled walking stick with his usual grace, nodded and left the room looking disappointed. Mehr remained pleasant and left the room with a smile saying that she could not stay any longer because she was not feeling very well. She said goodbye and left. Vaqar scanned the room with his small and cunning eyes, nodded and, before anyone said anything to him, also left.

Those who remained were now all talking at once and saying different things. The noise level was rising again when Uncle Sardari said, 'May I ask you please not to make such a racket. These are the deceased's instructions. We have to respect his soul and do as he asks. This is his last wish, my dears. Please be respectful.'

Someone said, 'You mean whatever he said must be done?' To which Uncle Sardari retorted, 'Of course! This is a will, not some game. The deceased is out of reach and we have to honour his wishes.'

Still in her armchair and with her chin resting on her walking stick, Auntie nodded in agreement. Uncle Sardari's retort and the rare case of agreement between him and Auntie seemed to have the desired effect, and those who had to leave the room did so quietly.

The warm air in the room felt heavy with humidity. Malek shifted herself in her chair. Rahman brought fresh tea and walked around the room so that everyone could help themselves; everyone except Auntie, who never drank tea. The lawyer placed his cup on the table and picked up his case. He then removed the papers from inside and placed them on the table. Munir's eyes welled up; she was Mr Piran's eldest niece. She sighed and said, 'Poor Uncle ...' Her sentiments were echoed by everyone else; they nodded in agreement as a sign of sadness, but they were so eager to hear what was in the will that they didn't look so mournful.

The lawyer, who was losing his patience, said quickly, 'The late Mr Piran showed huge concern over the contents of his will. He was adamant that its terms should be honoured as they are.' He then turned to Uncle Sardari and continued, 'Sir, he counted on you particularly ... Now, if you permit, I shall proceed.'

Uncle Sardari turned to Malek and Auntie, and said, 'With the ladies' permission ... ?'

Malek tightened the knot of her headscarf and nodded in agreement. Auntie also nodded and said, 'Certainly!'

Maryam shifted slightly and placed her head on Youssef's chest. She then fixed her eyes on the lawyer, who was perspiring because of the heat. He began; 'I, Muhammad Piran, have prepared my will herewith with clarity of mind and in good health, in the presence of my honourable lawyer, Mr Jafar Khan Etemadi, who has my confidence ...' following which the sound of Munir's wailing filled the room and her sisters followed suit. Uncle Sardari glared at Munir. Malek turned to Munir graciously and said, 'Munir *Khanoum*, if you would permit,' and then she turned to Mr Etemadi saying, 'After you ... Please continue.'

'I am not in debt to anyone,' Mr Etemadi continued, 'and if anyone claims so, please do not take any notice,' and everyone sighed with relief.

'And since my heirs, Malek *Khanoum* and my dear nephews, are all comfortably off, thank goodness, and have no need of my assets, my possessions shall be divided as follows ...' But there was hubbub in the room. Maryam, who had just closed her eyes to go to sleep, lifted her head from Youssef's chest and looked around with a startled expression. Youssef gently caressed her head. Mr Piran's nephews were audible now: 'Someone must have altered the will!'

'This can't be Uncle *jan*'s will ...'

Auntie, who was expecting to hear such comments, said, 'Let's hear the rest of the will.'

Uncle Sardari said, 'Wait ... wait ...' and then he turned to Mr Etemadi and continued, 'Please read ... Sir! Please go on!'

Listening quietly amid the racket, Malek just tugged at the corner of her skirt and then nodded to Mr Etemadi to continue. Mr Etemadi cleared his throat, had a gulp of what was now cold tea, and read on, 'Whatever my wife brought to my home from her father's house belongs to her. I have prepared an inventory of her possessions. The rest belongs to me and consists of land and properties. The property in Hassanabad and the mill, which I had constructed personally, must be sold and, after deducting one-eighth of the proceeds – the amount my wife is entitled to legally – together with the cost of the burial, funeral, charity, prayers and fasting, the remainder must be allocated as follows: one-ninth of my assets to be given to my nephew Mr Mirza Muhammad Khan Pirnazar so that he can spend it on charitable work under Mr Etemadi's direction.'

There was noise once again. Mirza Muhammad Khan said, 'Only one-ninth? For charity? Exactly which charity do I spend the one-ninth on?'

Mahmoud, who had not uttered a word up to then, said, 'Uncle *jan* had promised to give me some money so that I could finish the house! Where is it?'

Munir, who no longer looked tearful, began to talk as though she had a knot in her throat. 'So is this the gratitude for all the care I gave him?'

Looking increasingly impatient, Auntie said, 'God forbid, Munir *Khanoum*, I don't think you visited your uncle or sympathised with him because you were materially concerned about his wellbeing, did you?'

Auntie's sharp tone hushed Munir up. Mr Etemadi, who wanted to get on, rushed through the rest. 'The remainder of my assets must be distributed to various charities, under the kind and able management of Mr Ahmad Qoli Khan Sardari. I also ask that he, with the help of Mr Etemadi, see to the other items on the inventory, the distribution of which is not straightforward. The necessary instruction regarding the distribution of these items has already been discussed and, given our brotherly bond and long-standing friendship, I am confident that he will not spare any attention to detail in executing my wishes, in collaboration with Mr Etemadi.'

Uncle Sardari looked visibly elated having heard his name mentioned and given the importance of the task that was bestowed upon him. He got up and made a sincere declaration, 'May the Lord bless Mr Piran's soul ...'

Mr Etemadi said, 'I am not finished yet. Please remain seated. I need to clarify the fate of all the items on the inventory he's prepared.'

While settling back in his chair once again Uncle Sardari said, 'Yes, yes, certainly ...' Then, as though it had been choreographed in advance, Mr Piran's nephews all stood up together. Mirza Muhammad Khan said, 'We'll go and see a lawyer ...'

Mahmoud, in a tone that suggested he was close to tears, muttered, 'Someone has fabricated this will.'

Munir turned to Malek and said, 'Don't think we have not understood. It's all to do with you.'

'What has it got to do with me?' asked Malek.

'We shall find out in court!' retorted Maheen.

'For all we know,' added Mah Leqa, 'this isn't even Uncle's writing. You must have all done something behind the scenes!'

Auntie said, 'This is the late Mr Piran's will. It's between him and his lawyer.'

Uncle Sardari said, 'Please respect the dead. Let's wait and hear the rest.'

Looking furious, Mr Piran's nephews rushed for the door. They were in such a hurry that they were pushing each other, and Munir's handbag fell in the process. Maheen tripped over it and the sharp high heel of her shoe got caught in Mah Leqa's expensive *chador*, the one she donned for funerals and *sofrehs*. The incident left a big hole close to the border.

Maryam whispered in Youssef's ear, 'Is there a fight?'

'No, don't worry.'

Rana said to Maryam quietly, 'Do you want us to go to Mother?'

Maryam didn't wish to leave her brother. She declined the offer by shaking her head so vigorously that her plaits swung round on either side of her head.

Etemadi's voice filled the room, 'Ladies! Gentlemen! Please stay! I am not done yet!'

The commotion in the area near the door intensified. Mah Leqa was upset about the hole in her *chador*. Maheen stepped back and tried to pull herself together. Everyone else was in a state of disarray.

Maryam made herself more comfortable on her brother's lap.

Auntie said, 'Mah Leqa *Khanoum*! Munir *Khanoum*! Maheen *Khanoum*! Please be patient. Come and sit down.'

Uncle Sardari said, 'Mirza Muhammad Khan! *Sir*! Please go back to your chairs so that we can hear the rest of the will.'

Malek, who didn't budge despite all the insults, said, 'Please don't worry about your *chador*, Mah Leqa *Khanoum*. I happen to have a new one just like yours, which hasn't been touched. Please stay. I'll bring it to you before you leave.'

Mr Piran's nephews looked unhappy and returned to their chairs grumbling. Eventually they were quiet. There was a noise outside. Malek got up, closed the door and asked Etemadi to continue.

'The only matter now left to discuss is the inventory itself. The deceased has been quite specific with respect to these items. It is a written registry of everything in the house: "silver and ornamental plates that are part of bigger sets that include bowls, plates and trays (those which belong to me and are separate from my wife's possessions, which are mentioned in another inventory), six rugs, a suite of furniture (which was commissioned and purchased after the wedding at my expense and is therefore my property), two oil lamps that came from my previous home, a matching pitcher and platter, a Polish chrome samovar (this is in the closet in my bedroom and different from my wife's samovar, which is used when we receive guests), and a set of ..."'

The lawyer's calm and monotonous voice as he went through the inventory blended with the warm air in the room. There was no sound outside. Maryam rested her head against her brother's shoulder and her eyes closed again.

Malek's hand made a motion from time to time as she stroked her skirt. Her face was drawn, as though she were concerned that they could be overheard outside the room. Rana was looking at the pattern of flowers on the rug, or at Uncle's face. She was bored listening to what seemed like an endless list of items being read out. No doubt Uncle would bring in a second-hand goods dealer and sell them all at the same time for a nominal price, unless Malek had an alternative plan.

The lawyer read out the list of items in the building and then began to go through another inventory, which consisted of all the other items in the garden and storerooms: 'A metre and a half of used rope ... one rusty bobbin ... three large pegs ... one large copper pot (with a small hole) ...'

Uncle Sardari, who was growing impatient, interrupted Etemadi, which was in contrast to his usual polite manner, and said, 'Let's go through these later. Please have some tea.'

'We can't! We have to go through it now.'

'These are of no consequence. If Malek *Khanoum* doesn't mind, we'll bring in someone to buy the lot.'

'In that case, if you don't mind, I'll go through his personal possessions,' the lawyer continued.

To which Auntie said, 'Whoever comes to buy those will also buy the rest ... We may even put them all in a suitcase and give them away. The will suggests that Mr Piran was involved with charities. It's better this way.'

Etemadi protested. 'No, it's not possible. He's been quite particular about his personal possessions and he's asked that Mr Sardari allocates them according to his will.'

Uncle Sardari, who was keen to finalise the matter of the will, said, 'I shall, Sir. I shall definitely do so. It's of no consequence. Please have some tea.'

Malek stroked her face with both hands and said, 'Do have some tea.'

Etemadi continued nevertheless. '"My personal effects: a shaving kit (still in good order), a small pair of scissors (they are a little rusty but nothing else is wrong with them) ... nail clippers (slightly blunt but still functional) ... a knife to open envelopes, decorated with the outline of an elephant ... a diary (half of its pages are still blank) ..."'

Uncle said, 'Please don't trouble yourself any further, Mr Etemadi; we know all this.'

'So let me move on to the clothing items.' Etemadi seemed determined and, before anyone could argue, he continued, 'Three worn suits and five white shirts, all of which can still be worn; three new shirts, eight pairs of worn socks, two pairs of new socks, six worn vests, four new vests, six pairs of worn long johns, four pairs of new long johns ...'

Uncle was growing impatient. 'We're aware of all this.'

'The deceased has asked that the worn items be given away.'

Auntie responded, 'Certainly! We did say we would give everything away.'

'No Madam; that's the point. Not everything is to be given away. It is stated in the will that Mr Sardari must ensure that the new items of clothing are sold and that the proceeds are given to a charity.'

This startled Uncle Sardari and he asked, 'Are you seriously suggesting that I sell three shirts and four long johns?'

Malek said, 'We'll give them all away.'

Etemadi said, 'However you wish, but that would be against the deceased's will. Mr Sardari has to sell the new items and then send the proceeds to ...'

'I'll pay for them,' Uncle Sardari interrupted.

'As it happens,' continued Etemadi, 'he had thought of that as well. He was not prepared for money to come from the family. The items must be sold.'

Auntie, who had not yet forgotten about the episode with the fan and the photograph, turned to Uncle Sardari and, with a tinge of sarcasm, said, 'You did remind us that a will is a will and must be executed in accordance with the deceased's wishes.'

Mirza Muhammad Khan, Mr Piran's eldest nephew, spoke up. 'It is the case; a will is a will. But this will does not make sense; it's beneath us. Someone must've tampered with it.'

Etemadi, whose face was flushed with anger and the heat, declared, 'I have not touched the will, nor has anyone else!'

Maheen said, 'If no one's touched it, clearly Uncle wasn't feeling well when he wrote it. For him to insist that we sell the long johns while depriving us of our inheritance does not make sense at all.'

Mirza Muhammad Khan added, 'This is scandalous. It can't be. This point alone shows that something is not right.'

'Bravo!' exclaimed Uncle Sardari. 'It isn't right! It is absolutely not right!'

Mahmoud, who had talked least, got involved. 'What about the monies that Uncle had promised to give me to finish the construction of my home?'

Clearly enthralled by the turn of events, Auntie said, 'He'd definitely become forgetful. Just like forgetting that it was Malek *Khanoum* who paid for the purchase of most of the items in the house.'

Mah Leqa piped up, 'That's not the case.'

'The will is unacceptable,' declared Munir.

As though what everyone said did not concern her, Malek continued, 'We need to bring this to a close, Mr Etemadi.'

Uncle Sardari said, 'Yes Madam. But how?' And then he turned to Mr Etemadi, asking, 'What am I supposed to do, Sir?'

Auntie said, 'It's not a problem; you can just place the long johns in a plastic bag, make a trip to Lalehzar and give them to Mr Manon. Mr Piran used to shop from him. If not, just take them to the shop down the road, to Ahmad Aqa who, luckily, knows us. He can sell them. You can stay with him to ensure you're not ripped off.'

Uncle's face had now flushed with fury. He mumbled, 'For Heaven's sake ...'

Auntie, however, continued to look quite composed, 'But to sell the pegs ... let's see, how many of them? Three? Yes, selling three pegs, some rope and … what was the other one? … Ah, yes; the metal pan with a hole and the rest of the stuff, I am sure you can think of a way.'

Malek's tone was now admonishing: 'Auntie! Please!'

By now, Uncle Sardari was so furious that he drank the rest of his tea all at once in an effort to quash some of his anger. Auntie, who knew how superstitious Uncle Sardari was, continued remorselessly. 'You have always said that a deceased person's will must be thoroughly executed; otherwise the deceased will remain anxious and peeved with the heirs, and his dissatisfaction will catch up with them.'

Uncle mumbled another comment out of anger but did not say anything.

Etemadi said, 'In any case, Mr Piran did insist that every term of his will be executed.'

Uncle Sardari said, 'That's all true but selling undergarments is not my job.'

'He has actually thought of this as well,' Etemadi offered, 'and has stated that if you are not able to execute the will then someone else should be delegated to do so.'

Mah Leqa, who was still upset about her favourite chador being torn, said, 'Who do you suggest, may I ask?'

'Don't count on me,' muttered Mirza Muhammad Khan. 'Spending my one-ninth portion on charity is a perfectly adequate responsibility for me.'

Mahmoud, who looked quite irritated, said, 'I am very busy with the house project.'

'He wasn't specific about who should take care of everything,' observed Etemadi, which came as a relief to everyone. 'But,' he continued, 'he has left the land and property in Hassanabad, and the mill, to the person who is prepared to see to it that the will is thoroughly executed.'

Mirza Muhammad Khan quickly asked, 'Why has this not been mentioned before now?'

'This is stated in an addendum to the main will.'

Mahmoud said, 'The Hassanabad that …'

Concerned that Mahmoud would ruin everything, Mirza Muhammad Khan interrupted him. 'The very Hassanabad that Uncle so loved.'

'There's no point in continuing this discussion,' sighed Auntie. 'I don't think Mr Sardari has any intention of ignoring his obligation. The will of the deceased must be executed fully.'

Uncle Sardari said, 'Yes, but Madam, the wishes of the deceased must be sensible at the same time.'

Munir then raised her voice and, sobbing, asked, 'Are you suggesting that my beloved and innocent uncle had lost his mind as well?'

The sound of sobbing woke Maryam up. She looked harassed and her face was moist with perspiration. Youssef gave her a peck on the cheek and stroked her head.

Auntie was no longer interested in irritating Uncle Sardari. She was looking for a new line of attack. She thus turned to Mr Piran's nephews and nieces, and said, 'You did say the will wasn't quite right. Perhaps the poor soul's mind wasn't in a good state in the latter years of his life. He was unwell, after all.'

'Not at all!' exclaimed Mah Leqa. 'Not only was his mind perfectly sound; he was quite sensible as well. In any case, if you are all so willing to execute the will then why are you looking for excuses not to?'

Maheen said, 'It doesn't sound as though Mr Sardari wishes to execute the will. That's fine. My brothers are here and willing, and I am available as well. I'll deal with it. I'll sell everything and divide the proceeds as he has stated.'

Munir interrupted, saying, 'No darling, you're too busy. I'll deal with it.' Then, as she wiped her invisible tears, she began to wail, 'Oh Uncle, darling. I wish you were still alive so that I could look after you. You were so good. I wish you could see that I am going to execute your will as well.'

Mirza Muhammad Khan cleared his throat and said, 'My dear sister, such affairs are not becoming for a lady. Though it would be difficult for me to find the time to deal with a case like this I shall nevertheless undertake the execution of the will. I'll handle it. I'll sell everything as Uncle has instructed.'

Auntie was smiling now. 'It's not difficult at all,' she said; 'just put everything in a plastic bag and take it to the shop down the road, to Ahmad *Aqa*!'

Mirza Muhammad Khan, who found it quite difficult to deal with Auntie's poisonous remarks, retorted, 'I'll think of a way.'

Auntie said, 'If you personally see to the sale out on the street, displaying all from the pitcher to the pegs to the long johns and if you sell everything at the same time it would be much more economical and you wouldn't have to pay the shop owner anything.'

Munir said, 'Really! You seem to enjoy teasing my brother, Madam. This is not the time. No, my dear, I'll deal with it. You don't need to trouble yourself. I'll take everything and sell it all.'

Uncle Sardari asked in a bewildered tone, 'Are you suggesting, Munir *Khanoum*, that you are going to sell men's undergarments on the street?!'

'And what's wrong with that?' demanded Maheen. 'That's Uncle's wish, isn't it? But I don't think *you* should do it, Munir dear. Your legs bother you. I'll sell everything.'

Mah Leqa turned to the lawyer and said, 'I think I heard that Uncle did not insist on a particular person to sell these items, so I'll take it on. Why trouble my sisters and brothers? Bless you, Uncle. Bless your wisdom and common sense. Your Mah Leqa is alive and well, and she's not going to let you down.'

Mahmoud said timidly, 'I think I should deal with this because I am younger than everyone and not particularly busy.'

Munir said, 'Don't interfere!'

'I will sell the estate,' suggested Mahmoud, 'so then I will have all the money that I need to finish off the building work on my house.'

'You and your building work!' exclaimed Maheen. 'It's our beloved uncle's will we're talking about.'

Mahmoud said, 'Do you realise that if I don't build that house my wife will leave me and return to her father's home? She has said that she doesn't want to live in a rented property any more.'

' "My *wife*"!' exclaimed Mah Leqa. 'Don't meddle in our affairs!'

'Calm down!' urged Mirza Muhammad. 'I'll take this on.'

To which Maheen responded, 'What makes you think you can always boss everybody around?'

Mah Leqa said, 'Look what you've done, Maheen. Why don't you just keep quiet? And rather than lecturing us why don't you buy a replacement for the wonderful *chador* that you've torn apart?'

'Why?' Maheen answered. 'I didn't do it on purpose. Besides, I don't see any problem with it.'

'Are you suggesting the tear isn't a big deal?' Mah Leqa exploded. 'She tears a person's wonderful *chador* because she can't walk properly and then she wants to deal with a will!'

Munir said, 'You mustn't meddle. This is something that I should deal with. End of story!'

'Not at all!' said Mirza Muhammad. 'I'll sort it out.'

'If you could sort things out,' observed Munir, 'your life wouldn't be in such a mess. I suggest you keep your hands off this. I'll deal with it.'

Mahmoud piped up. 'I am available; so let me deal with the execution of the will.'

But Mah Leqa was having none of it. 'Sure! Nobody but you! You are not able to tell your right hand from your left! No, dear! I'll manage and I am right here!'

The argument was escalating into an angry hubbub. Everyone was talking at once and saying something different. And everyone kept putting each other under the spotlight: failures, setbacks, examples of incompetence and misfortunes were all lined up in a single file. The room was being flooded by the torrent of insulting words pouring out of the mourners' mouths. Auntie and Uncle Sardari, Malek, Mr Etemadi and the three children, two awake and one dozing, were the silent bystanders to what appeared to be a power struggle. Uncle Sardari was astounded. Mr Etemadi, who was used to such spectacles, had just about managed to keep his composure. Auntie was enjoying the entertainment that her meddling had caused. It was just Malek who was slowly losing her patience. She finally started shouting. Not actually yelling; she just raised her voice to a higher volume than usual – much higher. No one could remember her ever doing this before.

'Quiet!' she ordered, in a voice loud enough for everyone to hear.

Mr Piran's nieces and nephews turned and looked at her agog. In a more restrained tone Malek repeated the command: 'Quiet!'

Everyone obeyed. No one could even hear the sound of breathing. Maryam, whose eyes had welled up with tears, quietly wiped them away with the back of her hand.

Malek then retorted, 'Go back to your homes and once you've decided who is to execute the will you can contact Mr Etemadi. But I want you to leave! Now! Please leave my home!'

Munir, recovering from the initial impact of Malek's retort, shot back, 'You mean your ladyship's home? Which house are you referring to? We'll sell it. We'll sell everything. Uncle *jan* has instructed that everything should be sold.'

Malek, who had blanched at this point, said, 'Take your squabbles somewhere else. Sell whatever you fancy. Sell this house as well. Do whatever you want. But I am asking you to leave now.'

Mirza Muhammad Khan said, 'This is our uncle's house. We need to make a decision among ourselves …' but his speech was interrupted with the impact of Auntie's walking stick pounding on the floor. Her smile had vanished and her face had become as hard as stone. She uttered just one word: 'Out!'

Mr Piran's nieces and nephews looked at Auntie for a moment and then, as though they had seen a terrifying scene, they got up and withdrew from the room in a quiet flurry. The sound of the main door closing came. The door slammed again, suggesting they had not all left at once; maybe a few still remained behind. Or maybe the sons- and daughters-in-law had left after the main beneficiaries of the will.

Maryam whispered to Youssef and asked, 'Is the squabble over?'

Youssef laughed. 'Yes, it's over.'

Rana took Maryam from Youssef's knees and let her stand on her own feet.

Malek was still standing in the middle of the room after the last person had left. The room was dimly lit. It was getting cooler. Malek switched the light on. She called Rahman to bring her tea, asked Rana to change the water in the vase and then returned to her chair.

Maryam went and sat next to Youssef once again. She was brooding. Youssef wiped her tearful eyes and smiled at her. Rana lifted the vase and, before she left the room, looked at Maryam, who was now clinging to Youssef as though still apprehensive that the squabble might reignite.

Rana quickly filled the vase with water and returned to the room so that she didn't miss out on the next stage of developments. There was silence in the room. No one talked. Uncle Sardari straightened his hair, which had become dishevelled from the movement of air generated by the fan. Mr Etemadi placed his papers back in his case and prepared to leave but, before he stepped over the threshold, he turned to Malek and said, 'I'll keep you informed.'

'That's very kind of you but I don't wish to trouble you any further,' said Malek. She was her gracious self once again.

'It's my pleasure and no trouble at all.'

Auntie said, 'Yes. Do let us know the outcome. Let's see who will take on the task of selling the long johns.'

Uncle Sardari shook his head and mumbled, 'Bless his soul, he's whipped up quite a situation!'

Malek turned to the lawyer, who was standing at the threshold, and said, 'Do stay; we'll have some more tea.'

'Thank you. I've had some. I have a meeting to attend ...' He carried on talking as he left, words which no one could make sense of.

Uncle Sardari said, 'Poor man's scared to stay any longer.'

Auntie said, 'It wasn't that bad. The only thing that we never managed to establish was who would sell the pegs and long johns. I would've left it to Munir *Khanoum* personally. Now, that would be amusing.'

Malek looked at Auntie and smiled for the first time. Uncle Sardari smiled as well. When she saw the smiles, Maryam lifted her head, glanced at her brother and laughed. Youssef kissed Maryam's forehead. Rana pulled gently at one of Maryam's plaits, which Maryam pulled back out of Rana's hand with a grin.

When Rahman entered the room with the tea tray everyone wore a smile. A new group of visitors in mourning attire entered the room.

Malek adjusted her headscarf, composed herself and greeted the guests. As Mr Etemadi closed the main door, Malek was thanking the friends who had come to offer her their condolences.

Chapter 2

One, two, three, four …
One, two, three, four …

The masculine feet, clad in brown leather shoes, were making rapid progress on the uneven grey surface of the street.

The man was walking quickly as though in a hurry. He passed by a collapsed wall. A green shoot was growing amid the rubble and a few leaves had just begun to emerge here and there; in no time there would be branches and flowers. In fact there would soon be a proper garden; a garden suspended above the rubble; like the hanging gardens of Babylon, a triumph of the living over the dead.

The man would ordinarily come to a halt, take a look at the shoot, smile and then carry on walking. Now, however, he did not take any notice of the garden growing out of the remains of the collapsed wall. He was not paying attention to anything. He was young and tall, with a sunburnt face, dark complexion and windblown hair. He had pursed his thin lips and was looking ahead. Dressed in a dark suit, he was so well groomed that – save for the hair and anxious expression – he looked as though he were on his way to a formal dinner.

Someone touched his shoulder. 'Where are you rushing to, Youssef?'

Youssef stopped and looked at the man. He was hesitant, as though he didn't know what he should say. But he managed to blurt out, 'I've got work to do. I must dash.'

'Work? At this hour? Let's have some tea and catch up. You can go to work afterwards.'

'No. I really must go,' and then he left. He did not look back. If he had done so, he would have seen Rana standing at the window. He might have hesitated and returned and then everything would have been different. But he didn't; he carried on walking and didn't stop until he reached the sea ...

'Mother! Mother! I am leaving.'

The bowl slipped out of Rana's hands and fell in the sink. Youssef disappeared. Rana turned. It was Abtin.

'Did I scare you? I'm sorry!'

'Oh. No, don't worry, I wasn't concentrating.'

Abtin was standing by the kitchen door looking at Rana with concern. He was now taller than Rana; taller and stronger. He had dark skin with slanted eyes, unlike Rana who had large round eyes with transparent pupils and a fair complexion. As a child he had walked with Rana on the streets, looking like a lost soul who had been taken in by an East Asian woman. Many wondered and even asked Rana about the disparity between their features. Rana would smile and say that he mostly took after his father's side of the family. Her tone was such that it prevented further questions. At such times she would squeeze Abtin's hand hard, as though wanting to reassure him that no one would be allowed to take her little oriental away from her. Abtin's slanted eyes became even narrower on such occasions and he would cling to the woman whom people found hard to believe was his mother. He was anxious that people might ask irrelevant questions – questions that would not be answered – that would create distance between him and his mother. He was no longer a child. He now knew Rana was not going to part with him but in those early days he had been overcome with anxiety.

Rana reassured Abtin with her quick response. 'I am well; very well. It's nothing.'

'If you don't like this doctor, we'll go to another. My friends know a physician who …'

'It's not necessary. This one's a good doctor. I am taking the medicine as well.'

'I'll be home late tonight. Mahtab and her chums are meeting me after work and we are going out. Will you be careful? … Perhaps we should come and pick you up.'

Rana laughed, which accentuated the creases around her eyes and mouth. The creases gave warmth and kindness to her smile. She said, 'Oh for God's sake! Do go and leave me be. I am perfectly all right. Stop patronising your mother. Get on with your own life.'

Abtin laughed, 'Oh! Moody! OK, I'll go. Take care of yourself. If you need anything just call my office.'

'There's nothing. I don't need anything. Go! Go and get on with your work.'

Abtin hesitated by the door. He turned to Rana and said, 'By the way, when are you planning to get rid of all the junk?'

'Which junk?'

'All this: the photographs, the bric-a-brac and all the thousand-year-old junk.'

'Here we go again!'

'At least change the photo frames. And just let go of the rest. The house looks like a second-hand junk shop.'

'Mind your own business! Since you have mentioned it, go downstairs and clear up.'

'I wanted to do it on Friday, but you wouldn't let me.'

'It's too early now.'

'You see, you don't want to.'

'I just don't want anyone to touch Uncle's room.'

'That's it. You don't want anything to be moved.'

'We have to wait for a year to pass.'

'But there's not much time left before his anniversary.'

'Just leave Uncle's room to me; I'll sort it out. You don't know what must be kept and what must be put to one side.'

'Put aside and not thrown away.'

'That's enough.'

'Look Mama, next week is Uncle's memorial, is it not?'

'Yes, of course.'

'And you do want me to sort myself and Mahtab out, don't you?'

'Yes.'

'Well, before next week, the anniversary of Uncle's death, can you please sort out his effects and all the rest of your heirlooms, and I promise I'll clarify my situation.'

Rana thought for a bit. 'That's not a bad idea.'

'Not a bad idea? It is a very good idea and one that means *you'll* be relieved and so will I.'

'OK, let's see.'

'Look Mama, if you delay I'll have to get on with it myself, upstairs and downstairs.'

'Certainly not! You're not in a position to interfere in my affairs. Take a wife first and then you can do whatever you wish. You need to go now. Have a nice day.'

Abtin left grumbling but seemed content. Rana returned to the kitchen and, while she was there, heard the sound of the main door closing. Abtin, she felt, was too old to be living at home still and should have settled down well before Youssef had. His wife could then sort out their home as they wished and he could throw out whatever he wanted. But now was not a good time to do such things.

She picked up her tablets from the work surface, removed them from their foiled cells and tipped them into the palm of her hand. She picked up a glass of water and looked at the tablets.

Abtin had pushed her to see a doctor and had accompanied her on her first consultation, telling the doctor that his mother had become forgetful lately. Her responses to the doctor's questions had been bizarre and irrelevant, as though she were living in a different world.

The physician was quite knowledgeable and seemed to know how to respond sensibly to her answers. He had said that Rana was developing dementia and that she must be monitored closely. She would need to take medication and be tested regularly. In cases such as hers, the progression of the disease could be slowed down, preventing her from losing her entire memory too rapidly. He had asked Rana if she knew of anyone else in the family with the same problem. Initially Rana had said no. But when she saw Abtin's quizzical expression she had changed her mind and said 'perhaps'. She knew that the majority of her relations had suffered from poor memory in the latter years of their lives, the eldest ones in particular, though some had not been particularly old when they started displaying symptoms. For some, the problem had begun earlier. Abtin had interrupted Rana and given the physician an account of recurring episodes among various members of the extended family, thus contradicting Rana's version of events. The physician had then outlined characteristics of the problem and how to deal with it. He had said a great deal but Rana hadn't listened. She had watched many of her relations become increasingly forgetful. There was no cure. Nothing worked. One day their minds were sharp and the next they struggled to remember anything. Then, little by little, the day would come when they did not recognise anyone and were unaware of all that was going on around them; just like that. One day they were by your side and the next they had parted from you for good. They left without actually going anywhere. They had effectively passed away without troubling anyone with a burial.

The physician spoke and Rana looked at the objects on his desk. His practice was set in a dark and sad-looking room. You could hear the noise of the traffic outside, or the sounds of people calling to each other out on the street. Rana thought that if the person who had caught Youssef leaving – the one who called out to Youssef – if he had stopped him from continuing with his fast pace, perhaps everything would have been different now.

The physician had said that the dementia was hereditary in Rana's case but that it was still in its early stages. He had indicated that one could fight it, and suggested that Rana should take tablets to reduce the episodes and concentrate on establishing routines. In its early stages, he told her, the disease typically manifested itself in problems with short-term memory; forgetting the immediate present but remembering things from the past.

Neither the physician nor Abtin knew much about Youssef. They didn't know that images of him came and went in Rana's mind. They didn't know that Rana spent her days with Youssef. They didn't know that, every day, Rana followed Youssef through the streets of a damp and anguished city or that she lost him, every day.

The aunties had been the same. They had lived together, together but in the past. Their guardianship lay with Auntie. They lived in her house yet were distant from each other. They simply recognised one another. In those days, there weren't any physicians to give them colourful tablets and help them to find a way back from their private worlds, or to silence them completely so that they could never remember anything; neither the past nor the present. Certainly the notion of future didn't exist at all.

Rana thought that if the aunties had been there today, they would be fed a fistful of tablets and would sit on their chairs like ghosts, or spend the entire day in bed staring into space. Looking after them under such circumstances would be easy. But Rana's case was different. No one but her remembered the past. Everyone had departed; death or separation, it didn't make any difference. As far as Rana was concerned, going far away was as good as being dead. Those who had died had gone for good and those who had departed had departed for good. Only Rana was left behind, she and she alone. Now her brain was dying; it too was leaving her. The physician was saying that the medicine could postpone death; that it could put her memory back in order, calm her nerves and prevent worrying thoughts from permeating her consciousness and upsetting her. As Rana was leaving, the physician smiled at her and said, 'I promise you'll notice an improvement quite soon. There'll be no more forgetfulness and no more nightmares ...'

The physician sounded as though he was talking to a child. Who had mentioned the nightmares to him? Abtin; it must have been Abtin. Rana felt as though someone had invaded her privacy. As far as her son was concerned she had reached an age when she no longer had the right to her own nightmares; she had lived long enough to have earned some peace. The physician didn't seem to understand that some people never settled down and some questions were forever left unanswered, an undisturbed sleep eluding them for ever. Abtin didn't know that Rana had once tried to trap her scream inside herself with tablets, and in such a perfect way that everyone had forgotten what had happened a long time ago; perhaps the crisis she was currently inflicted with was nothing more than those hushed-up screams.

The physician was young. His aftershave was strong. He wore a light-coloured shirt and dark trousers and his tie was fastened in a tight knot. His tie was as bright as his aftershave; so bright in fact that it stood out in the dimly lit room. The walls of the room were covered with diplomas that had been written using distorted foreign letters and ratified by various signatures. Rana wondered what he would do if he woke up one day and was told that he was no longer a doctor; that he couldn't practise medicine, or make decisions for other people, or tell them how to think, how to dream or how to lament their memories? The physician didn't know anything. Rana could swear that he had never fallen in love and would never do so. He was far too successful to allow himself to become weakened by anything as mundane as human feelings. But she didn't ask any questions. She didn't dare. Previously, many years before, when she had been in another physician's practice, she hadn't asked any questions either; the physician had spoken a different language, insisting that the mind needed to calm down so that she could become a sensible person, just like all the other boring sensible people.

A while ago her eyesight had become blurred and she'd been unable to see very well; she'd thought she was going blind. She had kept it from Abtin for some time and hadn't bothered going to see anyone about the problem. She did not wish to face an unbearable reality. Later, when her eyesight became more of an issue, she did go to the optician. She was prescribed stronger spectacles; she was not going to go blind, she just needed a new pair of glasses. At the time that had made her very happy. Now, however, she didn't know which she preferred: going blind or losing her memory. The latter was worse, much worse than going blind, worse than any disease. If she lost her vision, she would only miss out on seeing the present. If she lost her mind she would lose the image of everything that she had stored in there thus far; everyone and everything from the past that she held dear would once again die in her worn-out mind. It was true that, before its demise, they would return to her more alive than ever. She would forget today and would remember the day before as though time had not passed, but this was only a spark – a fleeting revival before death; a last supper with all the people that she loved and those she had forgotten. How she resented that notion. And then it would all be over. All the detail that her internal world had constructed would be lost; a being without memory, without recollection; a black hole in the living world, dark, silent, without a past and without a future. The tablets would make her mind go numb. With the passing of every moment her internal world got closer to nothingness. It was as though every movement of the clock's hand accelerated the death of her mind.

* * *

Loyalty to one's past was just one of the family insanities. Uncle had not been prepared to part with his past. In all the years that he had lived far from his wife and child, and then alongside Rana and Abtin, he had remained faithful to the memory of those who were no longer present in his life. He'd always said that he would eventually follow them. One day he would sort everything out and then spend the rest of his life with them; with those whom he loved but who did not love him; with those who had left him – something which he had found it difficult to come to terms with.

She binned the tablets, drank the water and looked out at the street through the window. Not much was happening. She returned to the living room. The framed photographs rested on the round table in the corner of the room. She put them in order, something she did every day. Abtin talked nonsense; the frames were beautiful. They were old but there was nothing wrong with them. Abtin loved new and glossy objects. It was he who had chosen the frame for Uncle's photograph. It was a pretty frame made from a silvery metal which had the smell of something new, he said. He still didn't appreciate what beauty lay in the old.

She sat in Auntie's comfortable chair, which she had positioned so that she could face the photographs. Picking up Auntie's book, she placed it on her knee. *The Count of Monte Cristo*: the book's cover was made from brown leather which had become old and worn with the passing of time; it was so marked by water and tea that it was difficult to imagine how it had once looked. When Abtin was a child he had liked this book. Rana had read him the stories about a man who had wanted to change. Abtin had liked to hear about the Count's escape from prison and the subsequent tales of his fortunes and powers. But he would lose interest towards the end of the story. He never liked stories that didn't end well, just like he resented old objects. He wanted to replace everything. If she gave him free rein he would throw many things away, even the journal that had belonged to Rana's mother; in his mind most of her old possessions were disposable. What would he do with the clothes? He would no doubt throw them away as well. And one day, a day that was not today, he would get rid of Rana's clothes and *objets d'art* as well. In Abtin's world there was no room for the past.

When Rana didn't have much to do, she would spend the entire morning in that position looking at the photographs and remaining deep in thought. Abtin called it a family gathering. In the photographs, everyone was well groomed and looked healthy. They wore new and well-made clothes. They smiled at times but generally looked serious, their lips pressed together as they looked in the direction of the camera. The women's hair was often short. Auntie Malek's dress had been tailor-made with embroidery and lace-work. In one photograph, her mother had a small hat on with lace that reached her eyes. In another, there was a woman who resembled Auntie, sitting in her armchair. She had gathered her white hair behind her head. Her hands were clasped together and rested on her knees. She had turned her head towards the lens of the camera and stared at it with a haughty gaze. The photograph was taken outdoors in Auntie's garden beside the water feature, which was surrounded by geranium pots. Rana knew that if the photograph had not been so cropped one would also have seen the silk flower tree near the water feature. She didn't know the identity of the woman in the photograph. She had spotted it when rummaging through Auntie's effects, and had liked her haughty expression. She was familiar with everyone else. The eldest aunt, who had died young, had preserved her youthful looks and was positioned in the middle. In the black and white photograph, the green colour of her eyes was not apparent, nor was the red colour of her hair. Abtin found the resemblance to Rana quite unbelievable. When he was still a child he had repeatedly asked Rana who had taken the photograph and where it had been taken. He had difficulty believing that it wasn't his mother in the photograph. Everyone stood next to the eldest aunt or around her. Auntie Malek, Auntie, Moloud *Khanoum* and even Mr Zaeem ud-Dowleh. The most recent photo on the table was that of Uncle. It was Abtin who had placed his picture next to the rest of the photographs. Of all the family members, Uncle was the only one he had met and so he loved him more than the rest.

Rana would perch on the arms of Auntie's chair, gazing at the photographs, deep in thought. She would think for so long that she would eventually fall asleep in the chair, just as Moloud had done in times past. Rana had always felt there was something comical about Moloud falling asleep in that position; she would doze off after lunch whilst in mid-conversation; her eyelids would suddenly close and she would be asleep. She would smile while sleeping and Auntie would say, 'She's dreaming about Christ.'

Auntie had explained that Moloud had been quite beautiful as a young woman. Malek shared that opinion as well. But visualising Moloud in her youth was not easy for Rana; the Moloud *Khanoum* that Rana had come to know was an old woman with fine features whose left leg limped slightly when she walked, and whose dainty feet would be suspended in the air when she sat on a chair. She always wore a pair of earrings that had a diamond encased in a fine gold frame.

She also had an infallible belief in her priest, always talking about the priest from the small church she frequented and being convinced that the world was expecting Christ. She believed that everyone in the world was a practising Christian, irrespective of their actual religion or sect. In her world, no one lied, no one was corrupt and, more importantly, no one suffered any problems that couldn't be resolved. Even when her relations deceived her and effectively threw her out of her home, she never doubted their sincerity. When she had been told to pack a suitcase and leave her home, she'd accepted Auntie's invitation and lived with her. Later on she'd spent the rest of her life in a Christian old people's home, though arranging this had proved complicated. The people who ran the church home had claimed that there was no space for her, and Auntie had been losing patience over Moloud's insistence on living under the church's roof when they were not prepared to accept her. She'd decided finally to go to the priest in charge.

At first the priest thought that Auntie had come to renew her request that Moloud be admitted and he had been getting ready to refuse her again. But Auntie told him there was another reason for her call. 'I have just come to say to you that I have decided to change my will so that, after my death, all my assets will be bequeathed to the Soviet Union's Communist Party.'

The priest was horrified by such an unprecedented comment. 'You are a devout lady,' he'd said, 'so how could you say, let alone do, such a thing?' To which Auntie had responded, 'Because they value their old but *you* don't; not even someone who has spent a lifetime serving your church ...'

A week later, Moloud was delighted to be offered a place.

Auntie said that when the nuns moved around wearing their special habits, Moloud had felt that she was already in paradise and that the nuns were the angels. She said that no one felt more fortunate in life than Moloud.

Engrossed in her imaginary world Moloud led a carefree life. Rana agreed with Auntie; she had never seen anyone as content as Moloud. Her world could not accommodate evil; everyone and everything was good. She would even feel sorry for Satan,

God's fallen angel. Her sympathy for Satan, however, cost them dearly, especially Rana and Youssef. But it didn't make any difference as far as she was concerned. She only believed what she wanted to believe. Uncle, too, preferred to live in his own world. He never wanted to accept that his wife and child had left him. And he never believed that he would really have to spend the rest of his life far away from them. He always said, 'Everything will be sorted out, my dear, and I'll leave as well. Just a few more days as your guest and I will go and join them. But you must send Abtin to me, Rana. He's wasting his life here.'

And Rana would say, 'Very well. If you think you have the patience to look after this child then I will happily send him over,' after which she would laugh and so would Uncle, and Abtin would continue to dream about travelling to other countries. And he did so until he grew to adulthood, by which time Uncle had died and no one went anywhere.

Rana had not been around when Moloud was still a young woman, nor when Uncle had been a young man. In the same way, Abtin couldn't picture his mother as a young woman either. Rana shrugged. What difference did it make; neither of them was ever young. She may have even only dreamt about her own youth; the days when she was younger than everyone else. Perhaps she should also take a notebook like Mr Piran and jot down everything, everything that constituted her life. And then she could sum it all up and throw it away just as Abtin wanted; then she would become a proper mother, a mother without a past or a future, one who was the right age and lived only in the present. She would, from time to time, be able to go to the grave of those who had departed. She would give offerings and say prayers in their memory and then wait for her turn.

She should get a notebook, just like Mr Piran, and write everything down; a black notebook the colour of which consisted of all the other colours of the rainbow, a notebook that could hold every tale. Or she could begin to keep a diary and then leave it behind once she had departed, just like her mother. But Rana resented keeping a note of everyday events. She wanted to register only what really mattered to her. One could forget everything else. Anything that was not worth remembering had to be forgotten. One should preserve only those elements of the past that one could not bear to throw away; those memories without which life would be worthless.

Uncle had kept everything; anything that was a reminder of the past. Papers, photographs, paintings, the first shoes that his daughter had worn, even the large hairy monkey that had belonged to his daughter once upon a time and that had become patchy and worn, just like his memories. She had to go and tidy up her uncle's bedroom. She had to gather his effects. She had to give away what could be given away and keep what she had to keep. She had waited long enough because she was hoping that his wife and daughter would one day return and sort out his belongings themselves. But Abtin was right; they were never going to return. If they had wanted to come back they would never have left in the first place. The following week was Uncle's memorial, marking a year since he had passed away. Rana was going to put the downstairs rooms in order and Abtin had to settle down, as he had promised. Rana liked Mahtab. She was a nice girl. Abtin loved her as well but he had got used to a gypsy-like existence. He had assumed that Mahtab would wait indefinitely. But he was wrong; if he did not make a decision soon, he would wake up one day to find that Mahtab had left, for good. Rana knew that certain events could take place that were never supposed to. Now, however, she didn't have the strength to get up. She couldn't bring herself to descend the stairs, open the door and face the fruitless collection of objects from a lost past. As she thought about putting Uncle's effects together she imagined him standing next to her, shaking his head as though lamenting her actions. She didn't know what she should send to his wife and daughter. They had already taken all the valuables. They had not even left behind a single broken antique plate. The only thing they had decided to leave behind with Uncle was his memories, memories that they had forgotten. Rana sank further into the chair. She couldn't be bothered to get up. Her headache was troubling her. She closed her eyes.

Rana lifted her head to find Mr Zaeem ud-Dowleh standing in front of her. He was dressed in formal attire; top hat, tails, white shirt, tie; and carrying his silver-handled walking stick. He lifted his hat, lowered his head slightly and smiled. One could sense all the distant dreams in his smile. Rana had borrowed a nightmare from him that was more bearable than reality.

The eldest aunt was standing next to him with her untidy red hair and green eyes. If Abtin saw her he would notice that though Rana bore an uncanny resemblance to her great aunt, she did not have her hair or eyes. Rana's eyes were brown and her hair a rich chestnut. Her fine facial features, the shape of her eyes, her small nose and fine lips were her aunt's, but her complexion was softer. The only colour she shared with her was the fair colour of her skin. A group of ghosts was standing behind them. Rana forced her eyes shut and then opened them again. They had disappeared.

Perhaps the physician was right in suggesting that she should take the tablets. But Youssef … where was Youssef? Youssef was walking somewhere in the distance, wanting to reach the sea. There, near the sea, he would remove his shoes – first the shoes and then the socks. He would then put his feet on the soft sand of the beach and take his time walking towards the sea. He would walk towards the sea effortlessly, without any hurry, until no one could see him. He was walking away as though he had been invited to a soirée in the sea, a soirée of the gods of the sea, or, as Malek said later on, 'A soirée with no return.'

Rana ran after Youssef. She called to him. Youssef didn't seem to hear. Fishermen believed that the sea made people drunk, made them drowsy. They said that before one drowned one would feel sleepy; tiredness would envelop one to begin with, then one would feel as though drunk with the sea and start to forget everything as one let the sea possess one's body. One would give up the struggle and slowly become immersed in the depths of the water. They said that making one feel drunk and sleepy was the sea witch's craft.

Rana ran across the beach and felt the hardness of the shells on the soles of her bare feet. Youssef kept going. She felt the sting of the coarse surface of a starfish attach itself to her foot. She bent down and removed the starfish from her flesh. Blood began to flow. She lifted her head. Youssef was far away now; quite far; too far to know how much Rana felt attached to him.

Rana screamed, 'Youssef!' Her voice was lost in the tumult of the waves. A big wave came, twisted around her body and took her away. Rana was pulled from the shore by the waves. She called out again, 'Youssef!' but she gulped salty water down her throat. She struggled. A vortex pulled her down, down as far as the soft seabed. She was tired. She was drunk. She was asleep: 'Feeling drunk and sleepy were the sea witch's craft.'

Rana drowned in the sea witch's craft.

Rana fell asleep with the memory of Youssef, who was going further out to sea, and with the image of Mr Piran's black notebook lying on the sand where it had fallen, its pages fluttering in the wind.

Chapter 3

Uncle had a silver Jaguar.

He had bought it to please his wife when she was not supposed to leave him, when he had assumed his wife loved him. When he bought the car, he hung his daughter's pink satin soft baby booties from his mirror. When he died, the booties were still hanging from the mirror.

He loved his car. The silver colour had lost its gleam with the passing of time. The stitching on the seats looked terribly worn. The car had aged at the same pace as its owner. It was not clear which one needed more attention; the car or the driver. Uncle used to say, 'I need the car to get to my dialysis.' But the Jaguar lay in a state of disrepair most of the time. A few times when he left the hospital to recuperate at home the engine had been too stubborn to start. One of the problems that Rana and Abtin had was finding a garage to repair Uncle's car. While he was still alive he had dismissed Abtin's suggestion and refused to change his car for a simpler and more practical one. He had already lost everything without any resistance so he was not prepared to let this possession go as well. The Jaguar was a reminder of a glorious past, the only legacy that he wished to keep. The car was sold after his death and the money sent to his wife and daughter. The Jaguar represented all that Uncle dreamt of; the discoloured dreams of a man who wanted to live with passion. And, worse, a man who died still believing that he could indeed live with passion.

As far as Rana was concerned, Uncle's Jaguar was what remained of a ruinous innocence; she wasn't sad to sell it – keeping it agonised her. How could she take Uncle to a place which did not exist, to a warm and intimate future with a wife who was no longer in love with him? Uncle's Jaguar was a shattered dream which only existed in his bewitched mind, a mind that did not wish to accept that the sun had set in his life for good.

The rest of Uncle's effects were still there. Rana went downstairs around noon to sort out everything.

The house was quiet. Abtin's room was in its usual chaotic state. The sitting room was also in a state. When she opened the door to Uncle's room she was suddenly overcome with sadness; she could still smell him; the smell of medicine and aftershave. Rana always thought that if sadness had a smell, it would be just like that; it was the smell of loneliness, the smell of the sadness that hid behind a smile.

Abtin loved Uncle a lot. He was still quite small when Uncle decided to live with them. Uncle always thought he didn't have long left. He had already sold everything and was left with only one suitcase; a suitcase and the photographs of his wife and daughter. His wife wrote regularly asking for money: money for their daughter's school, for summer and winter clothes and extracurricular activities; money for a new coat for their daughter; money for a new car for her graduation. His wife said living abroad cost a lot of money. She needed money to sort everything out, to pay a lawyer so that he could join them. His wife bought a house in the foreign country and sent him a photograph. It was a large two-storey brick-covered house. The window frames were white and she had drawn a line around one of the windows upstairs and written on the back of the photograph, 'Your Room'.

Uncle showed everyone the photograph saying, 'This is our house. This is my room.' And then he would investigate every avenue in an effort to procure more money to send over to her.

Every year, he would buy a new diary just before the New Year and then send it to his wife, together with a number of presents, as though wanting them to live in synchrony with him. And every year his wife would write in a New Year's card, 'You'll be with us this year.'

Every year Uncle would tell Rana just before the New Year, 'Next year I'll spend the New Year with them.'

The record of *I am going* played until a few days before the New Year. He would never let it be known that he had lost hope. Instead, he would keep himself busy with Abtin and help Rana prepare for the arrival of the New Year – he would thus wait for another year hoping his wife and children would be with him when the equinox marking the Persian New Year took place. And after the equinox had happened he would say, 'Well, this is the last New Year I am with you. Next year you'll miss me ...'

But in those last days, he seemed to realise that there was no likelihood of his leaving. He told Rana a few times, 'This last chapter of life, my dear, is bitter, so bitter ...'

When Abtin was younger, he believed in the story of Uncle's eventual departure, but as an adult he couldn't bear it. He would tell his mother, 'How long is he going to go on believing in their lies? Why doesn't he want to understand that they don't want him to go over?'

Rana would only shrug her shoulders and say, 'They're mad, all of them,' and would not react to any more of his complaints. Abtin was not aware of the family insanity. He was certainly not aware that Moloud's simple mind would result in huge losses. He had not seen Zaeem's silver-handled walking stick. He had only heard about Auntie Mehr from time to time. Abtin didn't know much about shattered dreams and losing hope. He did not know how Auntie Malek had lost everything she owned except her pride, without batting an eyelid. He did not know that losses or failures sometimes happened for no good reason. In the world where Rana and Uncle lived, everyone was a loser, just like their fathers and mothers and their fathers and mothers before them. There were only three rules: silence, complacency and wishful thinking.

Rana could barely remember what followed the reading of the will. There were no major changes immediately afterwards and the house continued to run as usual. Every day Malek received family, friends and acquaintances who came to pay their respects. After a week the number of visitors diminished although there was still the occasional visit out of curiosity, fuelled by the rumour going around about the will. Malek would not speak about the terms of the will, nor did she allow anyone else to discuss it. But various rumours were circulating behind her back. Everyone knew that Mr Piran had stated in his will that even the house that Malek lived in should be sold, but no one believed that Malek would let everything be taken from her so easily.

No one had seen Uncle Sardari since the will had been read. He had used a bad back as an excuse to stay indoors. Auntie believed he was frightened that Mr Piran might have prepared other wills. Vaqar had sent word that he would not attend any further gatherings due to the hostess' unpleasant manner. Zaeem had told Mr Sardari that he had felt so belittled the last time that he, too, could not bring himself to attend any future meetings. In reality, however, he didn't feel 'belittled' for long. Only Mehr seemed to ignore the first episode and kept coming back to Malek's home to see how she was keeping.

But something else had happened: a hidden bond had developed between Auntie and Malek. Auntie claimed that, because of her age, it was too much effort for her to make the journey to visit Malek regularly so it would be better if she just stayed with Malek. Malek never said anything but she seemed content with the situation, particularly because Auntie's presence quieted the gossips and prevented many unwelcome visitors. No one wanted to be on the wrong side of Auntie, particularly when Auntie was clearly on Malek's side. A week after Mr Piran's death, a memorial was held, without the attendance of Mr Piran's nephews and nieces – they had sent word via Mr Etemadi and a few other relatives that at the end of the mourning period Malek had to leave the house so that they could execute all the terms of the will, one of which was to sell the house. They had said that if there was anything missing from Mr Piran's inventory, they would take Malek to court.

The messages had upset and angered Malek but, rather than becoming irritated, Auntie had sent a message back via the lawyer stating that they need not concern themselves, because she was determined not to let anyone squander the long johns. She had also added that she had decided to stay on in the house so that she could keep an eye on things in general and the long johns in particular! When Auntie spoke to Mr Etemadi his face was quite a sight; to begin with, he had thought that Auntie was teasing, but when he realised that she was quite serious he was speechless and asked Auntie whether she really intended for him to pass the message on. Auntie said with her usual poise that they had to hear her exact words.

As instructed, Mr Etemadi had communicated Auntie's message to the opposition word for word. The message was testament to her fury and meant that Mr Piran's nieces and nephews didn't dare approach the house.

Nothing had changed in the house except for Auntie's presence becoming permanent, along with Rana, Malek's niece. Even before Mr Piran's death Rana used to spend a great deal of her time with Malek. But now she was always with her.

Nasrullah Khan, Rana's father and Malek's cousin, had been planning to remarry before Mr Piran died. Everything had been arranged but Mr Piran's death meant that the wedding was delayed. Nasrullah's wife-to-be was the only daughter of a reputable merchant who had been widowed the year before. Rana didn't know much about her father's new woman. She wasn't familiar with her; not that she meant much to him anyway. She had never felt close to her father. Her father had been married before he married Rana's mother and he had children from his first marriage as well. As far as Rana was concerned a father was someone who paid for the upkeep of the home and kept an eye on everything, often from quite a distance.

Nasrullah's planned marriage concerned Malek more than anyone else. She wasn't against his marriage; she considered it a natural thing. But she did not wish her niece to be at the mercy of strangers. On the other hand she didn't know what to do about her own situation either. Contrary to what people believed, Malek wasn't wealthy. The major part of her family's fortune had been spent on the treatment of her eldest sister, Marjan. Marjan's illness and death had been the most significant event in Malek's life. At times she had thought to herself that if Marjan had not married, if she had not fallen ill, if her illness had not been so serious … there were so many ifs that never led to anything because everything that shouldn't have happened had happened. She often thought Marjan's stubbornness had unwillingly ruined her life and her family's happiness.

Abtin returned home late. Rana had spent the entire afternoon sorting out the papers and photographs. The week before, she had taken some of Uncle's belongings upstairs. His photographs and notes had got mixed up with hers and now she was concerned that something had gone astray. She thought that she might have forgotten something, left something important somewhere, and that it might subsequently get ripped up by mistake or thrown away. Rana had carefully kept every sheet of paper and every photograph. Before her, Malek had done the same and perhaps Auntie had as well. Now it was difficult to tell who had worked the hardest to preserve family mementoes. Rana had become familiar with many members of her extended family through the photographs and notes she had kept. She had memorised as much as she could with a mind that was fast deteriorating. She had preserved Youssef's image in her mind but couldn't remember anything about her mother. For her, Mother was just a name along with a bunch of photographs, notes and letters. She didn't know much about her. She also had difficulty remembering her grandparents. Her image of them was based on what Malek had told her; their house, the water feature in the middle of the garden, the wooden structures that were placed under the trees in the summer months, the manners, habits and memories from that time. Rana had stored Malek's recollections and made them her own. She was so familiar with that place and those people it was as though she had lived with every one of them. She forgot at times which recollections were real and which were borrowed. And this went back to the period of the onset of her memory troubles.

But she knew one thing quite well. Her grandfather had always opposed the match between Father and her mother, just as her father had been opposed to her marriage to Youssef. Her mother was not as accommodating as her. She had done as she wished. Rana was different from her mother; she spent so much time thinking about others that she forgot what she wanted for herself. Perhaps she had even forgotten what Youssef's wishes were. Now, she wasn't sure any more whether Youssef had ever really wanted to marry her. Perhaps Youssef was like Abtin as well; he didn't know what he wanted. He searched for something that did not exist and he sidestepped things that ought not to be avoided. She had read somewhere, 'One always trips when one is escaping,' but couldn't remember where. She did not like the word 'trips'. There were other words that could be used instead but it didn't make any difference. One cannot escape one's destiny. One has to face problems and solve them. Today it dawned on her that, whether one realised it or not, one could not resolve every problem in one's life. Youssef escaped from his father; he escaped from her; he escaped from life; and nothing changed. Now her mind was throwing away her only treasure, her memories, or perhaps it was her dodging them rather than facing them, quite unlike her mother. Her mother did not evade destiny; she went after it, faced it and gave in to it.

Mir Seyed Hassan Khan, Malek's father, had opposed Marjan's marriage to Nasrullah from day one. Nasrullah was his brother's eldest son, but family feuds had meant that the two brothers did not speak. The majority of feuds were because of the Mir's sister-in-law, Assieh. She dominated her husband and later on her children. But the Mir wouldn't give in to her powers. Assieh's domineering nature and the Mir's resistance meant that the two brothers were slowly driven apart and their children grew up away from each other. Because of his bond with his father's side of the family Nasrullah resumed relations with Uncle and his family years later. When Nasrullah stepped into the Mir's house, he was an eligible man some fourteen or fifteen years older than Marjan. He already had two children and had just divorced his wife. Shokuh, Nasrullah's first wife, was an unbearable creature, but the stigma of divorce was hard for the family to bear. There had been no divorces in the family up to then and no woman had left her husband except the great aunt who had lost her mind, and her excuse was considered a valid one.

The Mir used to say, 'Marriage is an agreement but one that cannot be terminated. You either don't get married or, when you do, please do not, heaven forbid, consider divorce.'

But Marjan wouldn't pay any heed. Nasrullah was always well turned-out; he wore well-made suits and a tie. He was neat and punctual. He worked for the Ministry of Justice so he also had a good job. He was a generous man who sometimes spent more than he should. He was convivial and as far as Marjan was concerned he was the only man who deserved her love. Everyone in the Mir's home adored him. And since he spent most of his time with them after his divorce, Marjan fell in love with him. The Mir found it hard to believe that his darling eldest daughter could succumb to such a weak sentiment.

The Mir had three sons – Yahya, Murad and Ali – and a younger daughter – Malek – as well as Marjan. Ali, the youngest, died young and no one knew the cause of his death. He developed a fever one night, went to sleep and never awoke.

Malek told her that Ali was sitting on the window sill the night he died and that he had kicked her, she who was two years his senior. Malek yelled out; the Mir reprimanded Ali; Ali didn't take any notice and kept kicking Malek; the Mir eventually lost his temper, got up and struck Ali on his back. The impact didn't seem that severe but Ali burst into tears. He became feverish and died the same night. The Mir never forgave himself. When they returned from the cemetery he sat by the flowerbed and said, 'O my early morning star, how late you dawned and how early you set!' but he never saw his star again.

Whenever Malek recounted the tale her eyes filled up with tears. It would then take Rana some time to change her mood. Malek had repeated what her father had said so many times; whenever Rana looked up to the sky she would feel a close bond with every star she spotted and later she would come to realise that she could see all those whom she had loved but had died in the same early morning star. They rose late and set early. When Youssef left, Rana felt as though all the stars in the sky had been extinguished at once. She never said anything to Malek but after Youssef was gone she never looked at the night sky again.

Ali had passed away some time ago. The Mir didn't speak of him any more but he no longer paid any attention to Malek or her two brothers. They didn't seem bothered by it either. The boys played together. They were full of energy and if the opportunity arose they engaged in some studying as well. It was mainly their mother who attended to them. Malek, now the youngest, never caused any trouble. She followed her mother wherever she went as though she were her shadow. But she kept herself busy and never asked for anything or stirred up any trouble.

Marjan was much loved by her father now that Ali was gone. He had lost his own mother when he was a child and he always said that Marjan resembled her. And Marjan, whether it was because of that resemblance or for some other reason, had become the centre of attention and affection in her father's life and the light in their home.

The Mir's other passion was his library. After Ali's death he spent most of his time in his library. He hung a framed calligraphy work of a couple of verses that read:

The hopeless desires
are the hapless chalice that is unfilled.

The library became the Mir's sanctuary. It kept him away from the tumult of the outside world. He worked hard to compile his collection. Sometimes it took months to receive a particular title and on occasions he had to turn to friend and foe to find some of the more obscure books. Despite his meagre income he never spared any money when it came to acquiring books. As far as his wife was concerned only idle people read books. But she knew her husband could not part with his library and so she never teased him about it. The library was a small room at the bottom of the garden; it was the Mir's area. It was the only place he never let the children enter. He took it upon himself to keep his library clean. Once a week he would dust every book and then place it back on the shelves. Neither his wife nor the old maid were allowed to enter the room, even to clean it. The only people he welcomed into that room were his close friends. When he returned home from his office he remained in his library until the small hours, reading and taking notes.

Marjan was the only other person who could enter the room. No one objected. Everyone knew that Marjan was allowed to remain in that room as long as she wanted and take any books she liked. The Mir had taken it upon himself to teach her to read and write. He even taught her calligraphy. Whenever Marjan was tired of reading, her father would dictate a piece to help settle her down. And sometimes, when he read, Marjan would lie by his feet like a cat and go to sleep. Her father would then lift his head from his book and embrace his sleeping daughter, kiss her hair and her brow, and then take her to her bed. Marjan was, in a way, her father's companion.

The Mir's wife never complained. She somehow managed to come to terms with her husband's unusual ways. She had bigger problems in her life: she had to run the house and look after everyone. She was the first to wake up in the morning and the last to go to bed at night. And when it came to meals she was the last to sit down. She would sit on the veranda in the early evening in an effort to keep her asthma at bay; it was a source of discomfort. Her biggest concern, though, was her sister. She had a very beautiful sister – the cherry on top of the cake icing – who had married the son of a distinguished man. Her sister had large green eyes, long wavy red hair, a small nose, a fine mouth and a neat row of white teeth. She had been such a young bride that she had resembled a doll. The wedding celebrations stretched over a few days but it didn't take her long after the wedding to return to her father's home for good. No one knew what had transpired. The bride didn't say a word either. In fact she never spoke again as long as she lived. She wouldn't talk, wouldn't eat much, wouldn't change her clothes and wouldn't wash. She was washed, dressed, fed by others and then left to sit in a corner. She would show no resistance, nor move of her own volition. She had become a living doll who sat and stared into space. No one knew what went on in her head but they could somehow sense that she had a preference for her sister, the Mir's wife, though there was nothing in her manner to suggest this. The Mir's wife took it upon herself to deal with the affairs of her incapacitated sister. Hoping that her sister's condition might improve, she had brought her into the Mir's home. The Mir was not very optimistic but his good nature meant that he allowed her presence, just as his wife showed understanding over his library.

The children called their mother's sister Great Auntie *jan*. Auntie *jan* did not have a name. No one ever called her by any other name and she never responded to any questions. She didn't seem to need a name. Years later, when the Mir and his wife passed away, when all those who might have known Auntie *jan*'s real name passed away, Malek tried to find out what it had been, but she couldn't: her name and her soul were both lost.

Auntie *jan* only once reacted to the world around her and that was when the library caught fire. Everyone had been asleep when the smoke rose up through the windows. It was the smell of smoke that woke everyone up. When they realised what was happening, everyone tried to put out the fire. The neighbours rushed in to help. The Mir tried hard to save his books. His hands were badly burnt but it was useless: his books perished; all of them.

Everyone was so busy extinguishing the fire that it took them a while to realise that Great Auntie *jan* was standing in the middle of the garden with bare feet and with her hair dishevelled, sobbing silently. Her face was wet with tears and her long red hair, which was spread over her shoulders, looked even redder in the reflection from the fire. When she was taken back to her room she did not put up any resistance but she kept looking at the burning ruin that had once been a library and crying.

After that night, the Mir's wife would occasionally find her sister's silent face wet with tears. The Mir could no longer bear the sight of the tearful woman because it was as though he saw his books in every tear that she shed – every time she cried the Mir quietly left the room.

Rana had heard Malek tell her the story many times; so many times, in fact, that she thought she could see Great Auntie standing in the middle of the garden at midnight with her bare feet and dishevelled hair, crying over the burnt library. Rana had added the bare feet to the story: Great Auntie wouldn't have gone to bed with her shoes, and with no one about to put her shoes on for her, she must have been barefooted.

After the episode of the fire, the Mir became like Great Auntie; he didn't talk to anyone for some time afterwards. He would sit in the same spot deep in thought. When he saw his wife looking at him anxiously he would sigh and say that he had a headache and then would ask the children to look through the window to see whether it was cloudy or not.

The Mir resented the fact that there were two things in life that terrified him: sin and clouds. He was terrified of committing a sin because he held a profound belief that heaven and hell were in this world and whenever you sinned you would receive your punishment during your lifetime. He resented the clouds because whenever there were clouds in the sky he developed a headache. The relationship between the Mir's headaches and the clouds was such that whenever he was sitting in a corner and had a headache, he would ask the children to look through the window to see whether it was cloudy or not. And the children always responded positively. He would then remain in the same position until the clouds disappeared, at which point his headache would improve. After the library burned, his sense of loss compounded the rest of his woes. He kept wondering which of his sins deserved such punishment but, since he could not think of one that was grave enough, he decided that he must be paying for one of his ancestors' sins; his losses were his retribution for their sins, as were the headaches on cloudy days. Perhaps one of his ancestors had broken someone's heart on a cloudy day or had committed something grave that his children had to pay for. He never managed to find out which of his ancestors was the culprit. Before Marjan's wedding, he thought losing Ali, the burning of his library and the perishing of his books were the worst events in his life.

After the fire saga, the father and daughter's reading sessions ceased. The Mir no longer called Marjan to come to him to talk about literature. He didn't even give her writing practice. Marjan's efforts to attract her father's attention proved useless. Marjan was now a daughter just like any other; a daughter who saw her father from time to time and with their relationship limited to simple pleasantries. In reality, the burning of the library and Marjan falling in love and getting married had so depressed the Mir that he had forgotten about his darling daughter. It was too late when he realised that the trauma of losing a flower was more painful than losing an entire library of books.

Before the library caught fire, Marjan had read the entire collection. Father and daughter would debate for hours on end. Her father's only regret was that Marjan was not a boy. 'If she were a boy, she could achieve anything in life, but I can't see the same potential in the others.'

Given her determination Marjan always managed to accomplish whatever she wanted. The Mir could never resist giving in to his daughter's wishes. Marjan was very like her father but no one knew where her obstinate nature came from.

Malek always mentioned to Rana that her mother was quite stubborn. She said, 'Too stubborn, and the stubbornness brought her trouble in the end.'

Everybody else thought the same. They said, 'Bless her, Marjan *Khanoum* did whatever she fancied. She didn't take orders from anyone. You shouldn't be like her. It's not nice to be so unruly.'

Malek was concerned that Rana might grow up to be like her mother. She didn't want Rana to be obdurate. She wanted her to listen to other people and discuss matters with those who had more experience. She wanted to teach Rana to be sensible. But all this was before Rana fell in love; before she saw Youssef again. In those days she had yet to learn that there would come a time when she had to make up her mind and stick to her decision. In those days she had yet to learn that she had lost before the game had even begun.

It was Marjan who chose Nasrullah. She did not discuss it with anyone; she didn't even speak to her mother about it. When the romance began no one knew about it. When Nasrullah went to Marjan's father and sought her hand in marriage the Mir did not leave his room for a few days. There were no religious or moral impediments to the match between his daughter and his nephew but his gut feeling was against it. He believed that a man who had already divorced a woman was capable of doing so again. Marjan, however, was deaf to everyone who was against the union. Although she never interfered, mother and daughter talked a few times and the hope remained that the mother could change her daughter's mind. Then there was the correspondence between father and daughter. The father wrote a number of long letters filled with guidance and advice to his daughter and she responded with similar, lengthy letters. They each had their own reasons for and against the match. He believed that a man who was already divorced with two children was not a suitable husband for his pampered maiden. Nasrullah would be better off marrying a widow who was prepared to accept the complexities of such a life and, Father reminded her, the major part of Nasrullah's fortune had to be spent on the children from his first wife. He also warned her about the rumours that would inevitably circulate. He did not wish his daughter to become the subject of gossip suggesting that she had wrecked another woman's marriage. The age gap was also large. The Mir was too reserved and gracious to comment on the unsavoury temperament of Nasrullah's first wife and the possibility of his daughter falling out with her.

Marjan wrote in her letters that a match between cousins was bound in heaven and this was sufficient to stop people's tongues wagging. Nasrullah was a modern man and would be able to provide a good life for her as well as for the children from his marriage. As far as the age gap was concerned, she reminded the Mir that he himself was twenty-five years older than her mother and yet their relationship didn't seem affected by the difference.

Marjan and her father saw each other a great deal during the day but they never spoke directly to one another. At family gatherings they kept up appearances and behaved as they always had. The only change in their routine was that Nasrullah didn't visit any more. The younger children never found out about the tumult that lay behind the calm façade of the adults. Such was the way in their family; a code of conduct that was rigidly adhered to for years to come.

After a few months had passed and Marjan hadn't changed her mind, her father finally gave in. The in-house correspondence stopped and the Mir said to her mother that if Marjan was still determined to marry her cousin then he consented. The mother looked into the father's eyes and found in them the same anguish that she had seen the night the library had burned. She tried to use her charm to lessen his suffering but it was no use. Marjan's marriage meant that the library was once again burnt and his books had once again perished.

The night of the wedding, the Mir's wife helped her sister put on a pretty dress. She combed her long red hair and tied it back with a pearl-covered ribbon, but again it was useless: Great Auntie spent the entire night in a corner crying silent tears. The Mir, who still saw his burning library in her tears, lost his composure; before the bride left, he pulled his wife aside and said, 'Look how she cries; this doesn't bode well. This match will not last.'

His wife responded, 'You sound so gloomy. The poor thing doesn't realise what she's doing. She doesn't say anything either.'

'Yes, she does. She says much more than anyone else. Look at her tears. These tears talk.'

'Perhaps she's just remembering her own wedding.'

'Maybe.' And then he sighed, and added, 'I do hope some good comes out of this.'

He was right. Almost from the start, Marjan and Nasrullah's marriage succumbed to arguments and squabbles. They were never happy. Marjan had enjoyed a sheltered upbringing. She was used to her father's affection and gentleness. Nasrullah was not in the business of sweet-talking his wife, nor was he at home much. He spent most of his time travelling. Marjan became fed up with his absences and he became bored with Marjan's nagging. Assieh, Nasrullah's mother, who had not forgotten the deep-rooted family feud, didn't approve of the pampered bride, so she only inflamed the situation further.

Marjan's first two babies died, for different reasons, and her mood deteriorated as a result. The situation then escalated. Whenever they were together they couldn't stop arguing. They decided not to speak unless absolutely necessary so that they did not end up arguing. It was then that Rana was born. Her arrival brought back a period of calm. Nasrullah loved his daughter and tried to spend more time with his wife and infant. But this didn't last. Assieh kept criticising everything Marjan did. Marjan grew weaker and became more irritable. She couldn't bear her situation any longer; she complained about being in pain all the time. The physicians couldn't find a cause for the pain. Someone suggested that she visit the warm spa waters, but that was mainly to calm her nerves more than for anything else. Nasrullah took Marjan to the warm spa waters. Everything was fine again for a while. But one day he came home and said that he had to go away on business. Marjan didn't trust him so they ended up arguing. The trip had a bitter ending. They both returned home angry and hurt and from then on they were never at peace with each other. Every word, every action, caused more bickering. Marjan did not trust her husband. She thought that sooner or later he would leave her. She believed her mother-in-law would find another wife for her son and remembered her father's words and his caution about marrying a divorced man. Nasrullah couldn't put up with a pampered cousin who wanted to read poetry all the time and talk about the imaginary events in the world of books. Every day that passed saw them become more distant from each other and Marjan's health deteriorate. When her condition became grave Assieh claimed that her daughter-in-law had developed paranoia. She told everyone, 'Poor thing, she never had a decent brain, she's just like her aunt so it isn't that strange. A lot of them are insane in that family. This one is just another example and it was my son's bad luck that he got stuck with her!'

One day, when Nasrullah was away travelling, Marjan took one-year-old Rana and returned to her father's home. She had told everyone that she was unwell but the reality was that she didn't get on with her mother-in-law. When Nasrullah returned and found that his wife had left, he was so upset that he issued an ultimatum stating that unless Marjan returned he would not go and visit her. Marjan, however, was no less stubborn than her cousin and decided never to return to Nasrullah, remaining instead in her father's home for the rest of her life. She was quite unwell and her condition deteriorated rapidly thereafter. She spent the last two years of her life living with her family until she died. Marjan's illness and death was a terrible blow to everyone. Her father sold all his possessions to pay to find a cure but it was to no avail. Her stomach became terribly bloated. Her skin had become yellow. She was in pain and no physician was able to make her feel better. In the end she was mostly unconscious but she would wake from time to time and ask for her husband. She was told that he was away and couldn't get there. This was true; Nasrullah could not get to Marjan because it was winter and there had been a heavy snowfall and the roads were closed. Marjan was desperate to see her husband. The last time she opened her eyes and spoke was when someone arrived and asked how she felt. Marjan asked after her husband and was once again told that heavy snowfall had blocked the roads. She sighed and then recited a verse that said, 'If the friend languishes after the patient's state, tell him not to worry, she's still breathing.' From then on she never spoke again, not even to ask for anything; she waited in silence and, as she waited, she died.

By the time Nasrullah finally arrived Marjan was dead. It was too late. He shed many tears and then picked up Rana and left. Rana didn't wish to leave her aunt. Their parting was hard but her grandmother thought it was better that way. She believed that the child should remain with her father so that he did not forget about her.

Malek, who was still a young woman, had spent her entire life dedicated to taking care of her sister. And now her niece became the focus of her attention. It seemed from then on as though Malek spent her life waiting to see Rana. She was always waiting for her. Rana spent a substantial part of the year with them, including the entire summer. Nasrullah was aware of how much they loved Rana so he never objected. Frequenting his wife's home didn't seem to make him uncomfortable – there were no hard feelings between him and them. There were no arguments or disagreements. Maintaining relations with the family mattered more than anything else. The Mir loved Nasrullah. He didn't consider him the cause of his daughter's illness and death. Whenever they talked about Marjan her mother would say, 'Fate dictated it be so. Just like her brother Ali, Marjan didn't have a large share of this world.'

Her husband would then say, 'There *is* no fate … we are paying for the sins … not our own sins but the sins of others. We are not paying for the sins that we have committed but ones that we know nothing about.'

The great aunt died soon after. No one could tell whether she had noticed Marjan's death or not. On the day Marjan passed away, she was standing in the middle of the garden with her uncombed red hair, watching the birds that had perched on the wall. When she died she didn't say anything, nor did she seem to put up a struggle. She lay in bed for two days and died on the third day. After her death her sister found one of her pre-wedding photographs and placed it on the mantelpiece. It was a black and white photograph. The girl in the photo had large dark eyes with a small nose and thin lips that were pressed together. Her hair was parted in the middle and tied back, although a few strands had broken free and were falling down her forehead. There was a hunted look in her eyes, as though she were a terrified deer that had been forced to stand still. The photograph was of a girl who did not have a name.

After Marjan passed away the house felt cold and silent. Everyone pined for Rana to arrive and fill the house with the sound of infantile chatter and girlish laughter. As soon as the boys, Malek's brothers, Yahya and Murad, came of age, they used a myriad of excuses to leave home. They married soon after and got on with their lives. Malek, who had witnessed her sister's bitter fate, kept rejecting her suitors. The Mir, who had never paid any attention to this particular daughter, didn't seem bothered whether she married or not. His wife, though, quietly resented all talk of marriage until one day she woke up to the fact that Malek was getting on in years and so she decided to encourage her to marry her last suitor, Mr Piran. Malek took her aunt's photograph with her to her new husband's home and placed it on the mantelpiece. Malek started to develop the same haunted expression in her eyes but she had one source of happiness in life and that was Rana. Rana was growing up into a beautiful young woman. Though her eyes and hair were dark brown, her resemblance to her aunt was so uncanny that it terrified Malek. It was as though the girl in the photograph had been reborn. Malek thought that was indeed the case, but without the green eyes and unruly red hair this time. The light brown hair was tame and her eyes were sparkling and bright.

Mr Piran put up with Rana some of the time. He didn't want to share his home with a stranger and since he could not have children of his own it upset him to see Malek cherish Rana. Malek had to arrange to see Rana on the days that her husband was not around and, when she saw her, she inhaled her aroma, played with her and felt that all her wishes had materialised. But she also knew that her happiness would be short-lived. She had to put up with living far away from her and knew never to complain.

Now that Mr Piran was dead and Nasrullah was about to remarry, he had no objection to leaving Rana with her aunt. There was no impediment to Rana staying in the house any more, except that Malek was homeless. As the end of the forty-day period after the funeral approached, when a memorial service would be held, Malek grew more and more anxious and unhappy. She didn't know what to do or where to go. She did not wish to approach her brothers and spend the latter years of her life in their homes. She didn't have any other home to go to either. Rana had to go back to her father, and Malek had to think of a solution for herself, but she did not know what that solution could be.

Chapter 4

Rana had not planned anything lavish for her uncle's memorial service. She wanted to spend the money on those who were in need and then hold a small gathering and invite her uncle's friends; a small but becoming dinner was not a bad idea. It was an idea that would have no doubt pleased Uncle; he always liked dinner parties. Rana could make his favourite dishes, a comforting thought. Yes, she would hold a dinner. She would invite his friends and prepare the food that he liked. If she did this, everyone would know that Uncle was still present in Rana's house. Rana did not want Uncle to leave her home. The true years of being at 'home' were those that he had spent in that house with his nurse, Rana, and her son, Abtin. She could do the same every year; she could hold a similar gathering. And she was certain that her uncle would turn up with a smile, and rise from his chair, just as he always had when he knew a visitor was about to arrive, even if he was suffering from an illness. He would take a shower, get changed and attend to the visitor looking content. His manner was such that no one ever noticed his yellow complexion or his bloated tummy; he was the most convivial person on earth at such times. When Malek had lost her home she still had many years to live. The household that gave her shelter in the end became her true home for the rest of her life. Uncle, too, found his spiritual home there after he had been driven from his own house. Rana didn't want Uncle to lose his spiritual home, even after his death and now, before she succumbed to complete dementia, the whole family could be together under the same roof, in her home. When something terrible happened, everybody preferred to be together to forget life's horrors. Togetherness was a way of forgetting about fears.

It was twenty days after the momentous day when the will had been read out that Auntie went to see Malek. It was some time in the morning. Rana had gone to visit her father the previous night. There was no one in the house. Malek was sitting on the floor in the sitting room rummaging through the different pieces of material that she had randomly collected in bundles in the chests over the years. The sun shone through the window, spreading its light on the flower pattern on the rug. Malek was sorting the old from the new. What she felt she could use she put aside, folding the rest in another pile, ready to give away. She didn't know where she was going and it was possible that she would settle in a place where she could not keep too many things with her; too many things which might become a burden. She wanted to give everything away, and had to do so before Mr Piran's nieces and nephews arrived. She had no intention of leaving any of her belongings behind for them. So absorbed in her thoughts was she that she didn't notice Auntie's presence in the room.

Auntie moved quietly to sit on a comfortable chair and observe Malek for a while. Malek eventually sensed the weight of Auntie's gaze and turned to look at her. She was at first startled but soon composed herself, nodded, said hello and smiled.

Auntie said, 'Well, Malek *Khanoum*, what are you planning to do?'

'I don't know. I really don't know.'

'You can't go on forever not knowing. If you keep delaying, the long john sellers will turn up. You need to make a decision before they arrive.'

Malek frowned and said, 'Yes, I have to make a decision.'

As though reading her mind, Auntie said, 'You don't wish to go to your brothers' home, do you? That's ridiculous.'

'I will have to if I can't think of an alternative solution.'

'Everything has a solution. One only has to think straight.'

'I have a small income. I've thought of renting a place.'

'Not a bad idea. What would you do with Rana?'

Malek's eyes welled up with tears and she said, 'I don't know. I think she has to go back to her father. I can't take care of her as well, given the state of my finances.'

'Rana doesn't wish to leave.'

'I have no choice. I am homeless; I can't accept responsibility for someone else as well.'

'It's not as bad as you think,' said Auntie, which prompted Malek to gently wipe a tear from the corner of her eye saying, 'It *is* bad, very bad.'

'Don't tell me you're worried about those heirs?' This forced Malek to smile and say, 'I am worried about them as well. Mr Piran knew his nieces and nephews quite well. He knew their greed would bring them here to plunder the house so that they could get hold of Hassanabad.'

'I say to hell with them. They can do whatever they want.' And then she looked around and continued, 'This is not such a wonderful place after all.'

'It would've been sufficient for me. I could begin to live however I wished.'

Auntie mellowed her tone and said, 'Let's do something else, my dear Malek.'

'What else?'

'Look, my house is large enough. The children didn't live sufficiently long to inherit it. Given the state of my legs, I only use a couple of rooms. There's no one else in the house so only the servants seem to get the use of it. There is just me left; me and the aunts, who will also need looking after one day. I never knew such a large house would one day feel like a prison. If you and Rana come and live there, the house will come alive once again and I shan't be alone any more.'

Malek was quiet. She couldn't believe what she had just heard. This was the most generous offer anyone had made to her recently. Actually, the only offer she had received. Auntie was right; her grounds were too large, the largest and grandest in the family. On them were three gardens planted with trees and three houses. There was a kitchen at the end of one garden with a row of rooms for the servants. Both Auntie's sons had developed typhoid and passed away when they were still young. Her husband had also passed away soon after. She had been living on her own for some time now. But this was the first time that she had complained about being lonely.

Looking back now, Rana thought that Auntie had not been as lonely as she claimed. Any family member or friend who needed somewhere to stay ended up in her home. These houseguests might stay for a short period or sometimes they became permanent residents. Rana had continued with the same tradition; whoever needed a home could come and stay with her any time. She called her guests Auntie *Khanoum*'s guests. Uncle was one such guest.

Before Rana and Malek arrived, Auntie's houseguests were the other aunts. Auntie did everything she could for them. She accommodated them with as much comfort as she was able. They were attended to with a great deal of care. But their presence did not cheer Auntie up. Uncle's case, however, was not the same; he made Rana laugh and was a source of entertainment to her. He told her stories about other countries and shared his memories. Despite his illness he was a charming companion. As long as you did not get tired of hearing his wife's name mentioned over and over, you could spend hours talking to him.

Auntie treated Malek's silence as dissent, thus saying, 'I know it won't be easy to tolerate an old woman, but I shan't be a bother to you and Rana. You can have your own space and live the way you like.'

'My goodness! I would be delighted to accept your offer but I don't wish to be a bother to you. Besides, what would people say? What about the family?'

Auntie, who had found her good humour once again, said, 'They can say whatever they wish. You don't have to pay attention, do you? Besides, no one has ever dared mind my business.'

'Do you think Nasrullah Khan would agree to Rana staying with me under such circumstances?'

'You're so naive! Of course he would! He's getting married again and doesn't want other women about. Even if he does disagree, you leave him to me. I'll deal with him. But for now be gracious and accept my offer and leave the rest to me.'

Malek smiled and said, 'If it's no bother, of course I shall.'

Auntie smiled and said, 'Thanks! I was dying of loneliness.'

Malek became concerned. 'What shall we tell the others?'

'For Rana's sake we'll just tell Nasrullah Khan. Leave it with me.'

'What about the others? They all ask me what I am going to do. What shall I tell them?'

'Whose business is it anyway? Just get everything ready. While I am here, sort out the furniture and your belongings. I'll arrange for everything to be collected.' Auntie then leaned on her walking stick and rose with difficulty. Looking at her with gratitude, Malek also rose. She had never imagined she would find such a strong ally. She kissed Auntie's face and said, 'Thank you.'

Auntie, who was once again wearing her humorous mask, said, 'On the contrary, it is me who should be grateful to you for saving me from loneliness. I have a lot to do. Call Rahman.

We need to send a message to the house so that the rooms can be arranged how you want them to be. I think the quarters to the southern side of the garden might be most suitable for you. In fact, why don't we go there tomorrow so you can see the house and choose whichever part of it you wish so that, if anything needs repairing, we can sort it out before the forty-day memorial period is up.'

Malek asked, hesitantly, 'You're not suggesting tomorrow, are you?'

'Certainly, we do actually have quite a bit to do. We can't just sit around.'

'I am just concerned that they might say she couldn't even wait for the shroud to dry up.'

'Let them say so. It is up to the deceased and his shroud. It would be much better than staying here and being bossed around by his nieces and nephews.'

When she heard the reference to the nieces and nephews, Malek's face looked drawn; they were going to turn up sooner or later. They would come and take everything. She did not wish to be there when they came. So she said, 'You're right. Tomorrow sounds good.'

'So, we'll leave in the morning and return before noon.'

As Auntie was leaving the room Malek felt calm. She had only to consult Nasrullah and secure his agreement so that she could take Rana with her to the new house.

Chapter 5

When Rana woke up in the morning she still felt tired. Abtin had kept her awake till late, giving her a lecture about the benefits of socialising. Rana had to change her life-style. She had to venture out more often to visit her old friends. She had to take steps to protect herself from depression, which was the outcome of loneliness. Abtin was concerned. Rana was aware of this but couldn't do anything about it. It was always the same; it was as though wherever she went she was carrying a shadow with her; a shadow that kept her away from the others. If she kept a safe distance from everyone, she wouldn't get hurt. The phrase 'You don't miss what you've never had' kept running through her mind. She preferred not to have many things so that she wouldn't suffer their loss. Perhaps this was something that she had learnt when her mother had passed away while she was still quite young, or when she had left her grandmother's house and moved in with a father whose presence was virtually nonexistent. There were times when Rana doubted whether she had even had a father. She had no recollection of him from her childhood. As far as she was concerned he was more like a respectable guest; the master of the house; a lofty position that did not require him to get involved in trivial matters. It was perhaps easier to think of Zeus climbing down from the top of Mount Olympus than of Nasrullah leaving his ivory tower.

Whatever the reason, Rana protected herself from even the possibility of getting hurt, although she was not always successful. She did not distance herself from Abtin. Although Abtin mainly spent his time outside the house and away from her, their relationship was not affected.

And Youssef ...

She did not put any distance between herself and Youssef at all. There were no shadows between them even though Youssef was unpredictable. He could spend hours sitting in a corner, staring into space pondering and then suddenly think of a terrifying joke and ransack the entire house with his playfulness. But whatever he did Rana was sure of one thing; he would never hurt her; never upset her. Rana felt a certain security when she was with him, which made any sense of distance between them disappear.

She felt the same with Malek and Auntie as well, although the security she felt when she was with them was different from the warmth she felt in Youssef's presence. She could, however, rely on her aunts, which in itself meant that any gaps between them were bridged. Living with them had slowly taught her to drive away the shadow that she felt between herself and the others. Later on, when life became a nightmare, her shadows returned and once again found refuge in her. But, until then, Rana had managed to live without keeping too great a distance from the people around her.

Malek and Auntie quickly began to get their plan moving.

Before she did anything else, Malek sought Nasrullah's permission for Rana to continue to live with her. She did not need Auntie's mediation. She then went to Auntie's house. She chose the building situated on the southern side of the garden. The rooms were swept clean and put in order. Malek's belongings were packed up and sent over to Auntie's house. After the forty-day memorial had been held, Mr Piran's nieces and nephews went to his house to arrange for the furniture and objects to be sold. Malek no longer had anything left in that house to prompt an unpleasant encounter with them. As they arrived, Malek picked up her handbag and, without saying a word, left the house. They collected everything and took it away with them, giving the impression that they were going to sell it all. They even unhooked the lamps in every room. Uncle Sardari, who had remained in the house on behalf of Malek, reported to Auntie later on: 'The only things they did not take were the walls and the doors. And that is only because they were not strong enough to do so; otherwise they had no qualms about removing absolutely everything.'

Malek's move was quick and painless. Having saved herself the nightmare of another encounter with Mr Piran's nieces and nephews, Malek now seemed composed and content. Rana liked the new house. Her father was thinking of getting married. Rana didn't know her father's new wife very well and did not feel particularly close to her father either. As far as she was concerned her father's marriage was neither a bad nor a good thing. She liked being with her aunt. Auntie's house was a new environment to explore; the new order of things coupled with new people to mix with kept her occupied. Malek and Auntie both took charge of managing the household. They seemed to have an unspoken agreement with respect to the division of tasks. Malek dealt with chores that needed close supervision, such as shopping, cooking and all that had to been done outside the house. Her duties were not simple: she had to keep an eye on a number of servants who had been with Auntie for many years but now had little to do. Malek had brought Rahman with her. He dealt with security in the house and the shopping. She asked Sarvar, Auntie's personal maid, to oversee the general household chores. Sarvar was the main channel of communication with the rest of the servants. But the chief decision maker was still Auntie. She was also the official guardian of her sisters, who rarely left their rooms.

Auntie's house was like the heart and soul of the family; it was a place where important family decisions were taken.

The house was quiet in the mornings; there were generally no visitors, although occasionally one might come along by chance. Auntie spent a good part of the morning in her own room. She read, did her embroidery, went over the accounts or wrote letters. Malek decided about lunch and dinner in the morning. She attended to the household routines and often took Rana for an outing, sometimes to do some shopping or sometimes to visit family and friends. Auntie used the discomfort in her legs to avoid socialising. Her sisters' day effectively began at midnight; they slept during the day. They retired to their bedrooms at the same time and woke up at the same time. They conversed with each other about subjects that only *they* knew about. When they got up at midnight, it was as if their day had just begun. They made tea, laid out the breakfast and got ready for a lunch that only they knew about. And they would drop whatever they were doing just before dawn, when fatigue would take over and they would fall asleep in their chairs. Then, they would briefly wake up just before noon, hardly able to remember all the nocturnal arrangements for lunch that they had made.

The first thing Sarvar did, every day, was to attend to the chaos in the kitchen. She cursed. Rahman, the manservant who sympathised with the entire universe, would rush to help her to put everything in order so that she would become less abrupt; she seemed to take everything out on him. And when she was too tired, she would grumble in Auntie's presence.

Sarvar would say, 'I wish they were up in the daytime and went to bed at night. At least I could keep an eye on them.'

Auntie would glare at Sarvar and say, 'They need to feel at home. They are not children. They can live however they wish.'

'I wish they were children. They're worse than children.'

Auntie would scowl, which would stop Sarvar from talking further. She would brood and go about her chores cursing. Auntie would then turn to Malek, shake her head, smile and resume her own work.

Visitors would arrive at different times throughout the afternoon; they anticipated visitors beginning to turn up from mid-afternoon onwards. They were usually family members, friends or acquaintances, who came on any pretext. They were often gone by early evening, although one or two usually ended up staying for supper. Zaeem and Mehr were regular visitors. Since Malek's arrival, Uncle Sardari used Malek and Rana as an excuse to visit regularly.

Zaeem lived next door; as Auntie's late husband's cousin he was a permanent presence among the visitors. After his wife passed away, Zaeem lived on his own and every afternoon he would arrive in his tails, his white-collar shirt and tie, his top hat, and would be carrying his silver-handled walking stick. He always said that he came over to make sure everyone was well. But it was widely known that he wanted to escape his loneliness. Zaeem's smudged collar was testament to his loneliness. It had become quite dark with dirt, having not been washed for some time. It was quite clear that the servants did not look after him as they should. His eyesight had deteriorated as well and, worse still, he had become absent-minded. One day, after he had been engaged in his favourite pastime, gardening, he arrived still wearing his gardening headgear even though the rest of him was formally dressed. On another occasion he arrived carrying just the engraved silver handle of his walking stick – the wooden part was nowhere to be seen. Zaeem loved his top hat and reminded everyone whenever he could, whether true or not, that he had purchased the hat during his last visit to Europe. He claimed that it had been made by one of the most renowned milliners in the world and that only three people had one like it: him in Iran, Churchill in England and Stalin in Russia! Zaeem, who considered himself an expert in agriculture, had one magnificent dream: to breed a seedless medlar. He was adamant that he would eventually succeed, having carried out countless experiments, and he was certain that the world would be in awe of his great mind. He would then sigh, shake his head and stare into space as he imagined people taking off their hats to him in praise and as a mark of respect.

He used to use the title of *Mamalek,* meaning 'of Estates', as a suffix to his family name, rather than *Dowleh,* which suggests 'of government'. Once, during a gathering, Uncle Sardari, who could no longer bear Zaeem, said to Nasrullah, 'Did you know that the title of *Mamalek* has been changed to *Dowleh*?'

Nasrullah stepped in, saying, 'Thank God; a nation has been spared such disgrace. Sod the *Dowleh*!'

But Nasrullah's temperamental nature had not driven Zaeem away from family gatherings. He put Nasrullah's sarcasm down to playfulness and so didn't get upset. Moreover, he was delighted that his daughter was now living in Auntie's house. Zaeem felt that the family was closer this way. And he could seek out Nasrullah's company more than before, even though Nasrullah didn't care for such company.

Mehr was another regular presence in Auntie's house. A slight lady with fine features, she was popular because of her docile nature and gracious manner. She was an only child and thus thoroughly pampered. Having settled down quite late in life, she had lost her husband quite early. From then on, she had lived alone and didn't mind it either. She had suffered so much from her husband's family during her short-lived marriage that she believed her husband's death was the only luck that she had encountered in life. Mehr seemed to show a certain empathy with the dead. She always remembered those who had departed. She referred to them as 'so and so, bless his soul', but she made an exception when it came to her late husband, about whom she said 'God curse his soul', which gave him a prominent position among the dead. Auntie couldn't see why Mehr held such a grudge against her late husband. She believed he had been no better or worse than any other man, but no one was courageous enough to say such a thing in Mehr's presence.

Once Malek and Rana settled into Auntie's house, Mehr was the first to visit. She kissed Rana and said, 'Rana darling, Marjan *Khanoum* asked me to give you a kiss and tell you that she's very happy that you're with Malek *Khanoum* and Auntie.' She then turned to Malek and said, 'She sent her regards to you as well, and thanked you for all that you are doing for Rana.'

The only person who was surprised to hear what she said was Rana, since she was not familiar with her strange character. Mehr was quite fascinated by her own dreams. Every afternoon she arrived and would draw everyone's attention to her dream from the night before. Her dreams were as harmless as she was. For instance, if the anniversary of the death of someone in the family were approaching she would always have a dream in which the deceased expressed satisfaction at his or her new life. The only complication was the actual message that the dead sent via her: the deceased who appeared in Mehr's dreams often made requests to mark their anniversary, asking that certain conditions be observed; she passed these instructions on to the family. As long as these requests did not go beyond what type of donations were to be given to which charities and how much, there were no complications and everyone would honour the request, to avoid breaking Mehr's heart. But occasionally she stepped over the line: although kind and something of a dreamer she would sometimes inflict a heavy burden upon the living. At such times, everyone would try to avoid meeting her demands, but in such a way that they did not hurt Mehr's feelings. She dreamt about everything. If anyone was thinking of arranging a match for a daughter or trying to find a wife for their son she would announce that she had dreamt about the match. The same applied to illnesses and unexpected accidents. She always claimed that she had dreamt about everything. She also insisted that she had already discussed the dream. If someone became unwell she would say she had seen it in a dream and that she had also dreamt that they were going to get better soon.

Her dreams solved all problems and cured every pain. Since everyone knew it was useless to argue with her, no one troubled themselves to prove to her that she was wrong.

Auntie, though realistic and devoid of superstition, was the only person who exercised patience and understanding over Mehr's dreams. She claimed, 'The whole family's mad but everyone's madness is different. Hers happens to be in this form. God bless Mehr us-Saltaneh! She's the dead person's telephonist. Imagine if she had turned out to be like Vaqar us-Saltaneh; what would we do then?' Auntie wasn't amused by her own comment, nor did it amuse anyone else. Vaqar's tale was quite different. No one liked talking about him much. He wasn't like anyone else. He was polite, well-mannered but aloof. Wherever he made an appearance the atmosphere would change; bodies would go stiff and smiles would vanish; everything would turn cold and lifeless just like him. Rana felt his presence made the air in the room freeze. Vaqar's house was referred to as the stoning tower. Though his wife and children were at liberty to come and go and to visit their relations, he never wanted anyone in his house. A great many tales were told about his absurdities and his abnormally parsimonious nature. Rumour had it that he lent money and charged interest; that the larder in his home was locked and the key resided in his pocket. Every morning he weighed the dried food and then passed it to his wife. Yet, despite his reputation, everyone believed that as the heir to the great Vaqar, he was one of the richest men they knew.

Fathullah Khan Vaqar Saltaneh, son of Kazem Khan and his beautiful and very-much-loved wife Zibandeh, was the sole heir to his father's fortune. Kazem's children had all died before they reached the age of five. Fathullah's birth had coincided with Esmaeel's death, the fourth and most loved child.

Mehr mentioned that when he was born he was fragile and sick-looking; no one thought he would survive. She said that she had heard it with her own ears from the children's wet-nurse that as soon as the ominous sound of the baby spread throughout the house it was as though an owl was hooting. Esmaeel, who had been playing and was looking perfectly healthy up until that moment suddenly began to cough, after which his complexion grew dark and he died shortly afterwards. Whenever Mehr came to this point in the story she was very intense. She would then blow air around her, hoping the bad omen and misfortune would be driven away.

Malek found the story nothing more than an apocryphal tale with no beginning and no end. Esmaeel had been alive and well until Fathullah was one. Then he had become ill. Rumour had it that he had developed diphtheria. Medicine was of no use and the child perished. But the younger brother developed a reputation as the bearer of bad omens. Malek had heard this from her own mother and everyone knew that she never lied. But, in any case, Zibandeh resented the new baby. The only person who paid attention to him was the baby's paternal grandmother, Saltanat.

According to Mehr, Saltanat resented Zibandeh to such a degree that even if Vaqar had been Satan himself (which he was) she would have been attentive to him only to irritate her; she used every opportunity to use the child to criticise her daughter-in-law to her son.

Despite Nasrullah's resentment of Vaqar, he was not bothered about the bearer of the bad omen, although he believed that the creature was not a normal human being. He said that when Vaqar was a child he never drank tea. He would, however, demand his share in dried tea-leaves and sugar cubes. He would then wait until his dried tea-leaves were a bagful and he had collected a sufficient number of sugar cubes to achieve the volume of a sugar cone, after which he would give both to the officer in charge of buying property and, in return for a pack of tea and a sugar cone, Vaqar would take the items to the corner store and sell them. He'd still been a child when he'd begun to lend money to members of his family and charge interest. Once, he even took old furniture out onto the street and laid it out to sell it.

Everyone was familiar with these tales. Every time there was mention of financial difficulty, everyone remembered Vaqar and retold the tale from the beginning to the end. They knew that many family members had had to turn to him, at least once, to raise funds to save themselves from financial embarrassment, repaying him years later with hefty interest. Vaqar liked what he did: not only did his own capital grow; he also had everyone at his mercy and could manipulate them however he wished.

Nasrullah was immensely resentful of Vaqar. Whenever Auntie noticed that he was angry she assumed that he must have become one of his victims, given that he was generous and prone to overspend. In any case, she did not know the actual number of Vaqar's victims or the extent of his wealth.

Uncle Sardari used to say, 'He is the richest man in the family.'

Zaeem believed there were only two people in the whole of Iran who could match his wealth.

Auntie, however, was convinced that he was so mean that the most impoverished people in the country were effectively richer than him because, despite his wealth, he lived like a dog.

Rana never participated in the debate. She was too young to question, let alone keep up with the adults. She would just listen. Youssef was not merely her best friend; he was her only friend. Given that they were related, Rana saw a great deal of Youssef. But she had never been to his home. She had occasionally seen his father at funerals and weddings. Rana tried to visualise the house in which Youssef lived. It was a house that had once belonged to Youssef's grandfather; a damp and dilapidated building that continued to deteriorate. Vaqar would stand on its threshold weighing his beans with his small scales and then give them to his wife who stood next to him with her head tilted, while carrying a child. She peered at his hand and couldn't have looked more miserable. Rana couldn't see Youssef in such a dreadful family portrait. Youssef was neither standing by his mother's side nor was he to be found anywhere else in the building. The pride that emanated from Youssef's eyes, his sudden bursts of happy laughter and his unexpected and at times risky jokes about his home, were contradictory to the desultory image that the family members portrayed.

Vaqar's wife and children were viewed differently from the man himself; everyone loved Taj *Khanoum* and her children. As far as Auntie was concerned, Youssef, Vaqar's eldest and Rana's childhood friend, was the family's darling. She felt he was superior to the rest of the children. Sarvar believed the reason behind the affection was Youssef's uncanny resemblance to Auntie's eldest son. She said that whenever Auntie caught sight of him she would remember her poor child.

'Youssef is a lovely boy,' Auntie said. 'His mother's also gracious. They are captives, herself and her children. Poor Taj *Khanoum* didn't have much luck; in fact no luck at all ...'

She went on saying that everyone in the family owed a debt to Taj *Khanoum*. And that everyone should feel embarrassed: all of them were full of hot air and none had done anything to prevent such a match. Save from the psychoses, this was the only area in which Auntie felt that the family suffered. Perhaps she had good reason to believe so.

Chapter 6

Mrs Rassouli, or Mrs *Lashouli* as it sounded when she pronounced it with her heavy Russian accent, had been another regular presence. She came over to Auntie's home once or twice a month and, each time, she stayed at least a week. She was a beautiful Russian woman who had married an Iranian businessman many years before. Rumour had it that when he first set eyes on her fine facial features, saw her fair complexion and her large, deep blue eyes, he admired her serenity and fell head over heels in love with her. Mrs Rassouli's father was a teacher. Her family weren't happy with the match but they had accepted it in the end. The young couple had returned to live in Iran after the wedding and had a son, whom they named Teymouran. They lived a good, comfortable life for many years but unfortunately Mr Rassouli went bankrupt and died in poverty. Of all the riches he had accrued, the only things that they were left with were a modest house, a number of pieces of chrome cutlery and an elaborately patterned set of china. An accomplished seamstress, Mrs Rassouli used her contacts and began to make clothes for the wealthy.

Occasionally, when she was faced with particular financial obstacles, she would supplement her income by selling a few personal items as well. In spite of the challenges she faced, she managed to raise Teymouran and he eventually settled down with a wife and obtained a home of his own. By then she was living on her own, although she spent a great deal of her time at her clients' homes. Wherever she went she stayed at least a week and, while she was there, she would mend and renew various garments and change the style of others so that they were once again fashionable. She would even alter mothers' dresses to make them suitable for their daughters' use. Mrs Rassouli was a pleasant and polite woman but she never mastered the Persian language; she couldn't even pronounce her own name properly. Instead, she taught her clients Russian and German and occasionally some French.

Mrs Rassouli's visits always gave rise to an air of anticipation. With every visit she brought fresh gossip; news about marriages, squabbles, illnesses, trips and bankruptcies – she knew it all. She knew who was about to get married, who had what gown made for which social event, and who had fallen out with whom and over what. Auntie always had a lot of work for Mrs Rassouli, and with Malek and Rana now part of the household the volume of her work increased exponentially. Whenever she arrived Auntie would pull out her treasure trove of fabrics and let Malek and Rana choose which ones they wanted for the new gowns that Mrs Rassouli would be commissioned to make. Auntie always wore black and had done so ever since she had lost her sons; she rarely thought of having something new made. Whenever Mrs Rassouli suggested to her that she consider something different she would say, 'I am past new dresses. It's Malek *Khanoum* and Rana's turn.'

Auntie never spoke of her sons' deaths. She talked about them as though they were still alive. If you listened to her conversations you would think that they were away on a trip and might arrive home at any moment. But, once, Rana had seen her alone in her room, turning the pages of an old leather-bound book with one hand and wiping a tear from the corner of her eye with the other. Rana had gone to tell her that lunch was ready but she didn't know what to do; she stood still at the threshold of the room. She had been about to turn quietly away when

Auntie had lifted her head and seen her. Somewhat abashed, Rana quickly said, 'Lunch! Auntie Malek asked me to tell you that lunch is ready.'

Auntie smiled, stretched out her arm and proffered the book to her, saying, 'Come my dear. Take this book. It's *The Count of Monte Cristo*. A beautiful story. It belongs to the children. When they were young I used to read it to them. Take it, you should read it.'

Rana took the book and became so engrossed in its pages that she read a third of it that same night. The rest took only a couple more days. Auntie would occasionally ask her, 'Where are you in the story?', and Rana would tell her everything that she had read thus far. Auntie loved the story. Later, she would ask Rana to read it to her, saying that she did not have her spectacles. When Rana read *The Count of Monte Cristo* aloud to Auntie she listened with her head down, and if Rana stopped reading she would lift her head and Rana could see a new expression in her eyes, as though she had been transported to a different world. At such times Auntie would say, 'The children were both quite fond of this story.'

One day, when Sarvar was in a good mood, she had told Rana about the illness and subsequent death of Auntie's sons. Sarvar had been a young woman when she had first arrived at Auntie's home. The boys had been healthy then, but had developed a fever when they returned from a visit to the village where their father's properties were located. The fever was identified as typhoid and the appropriate treatment was started but, by the seventh day, the children's complexion had turned yellow, they had become delirious and they were no longer able to recognise anyone. The physician believed that they had succumbed to jaundice.

The boys' nanny sat at their bedside reciting a prayer over and over, and making them repeat the words after her. The physician prescribed flute music to be played in the boys' room at night, so a master flautist was engaged to play. The music had a calming effect on the boys and reduced their delirium.

The physician had also given other instructions, which were all carried out, including dipping the children's feet in a pan of warm water in the early evening in an attempt to lower their fever. Tragically, two weeks after the initial onset of the disease and just before dawn, one child after the other drew their last breath and passed away.

From that point on Auntie became resentful of the village where the boys had caught the disease and hated the sound of the flute. She could not bring herself to listen to the instrument being played ever again. Her husband passed away shortly after, so Auntie lived with just her memories; the memories she never spoke of but which appeared to be hiding somewhere between the pages of the tale of the Count of Monte Cristo.

Auntie's sense of loss was a secret that she diligently kept from everyone else. But Auntie harboured other secrets as well. Whenever Mrs Rassouli came to visit, she always brought a parcel with her. The parcel was wrapped in a piece of *termeh*, an old-fashioned and intricately woven cloth, which had a gilded paisley pattern woven into it. Sarvar would quietly take the bundle to Auntie's room and place its contents, whatever they were, in the wardrobe. Auntie never spoke about the parcel or what it contained and neither did Mrs Rassouli. However, Rana and Malek noticed that Mrs Rassouli received money whenever she delivered the parcel: Auntie would also give Mrs Rassouli another parcel before she left, together with a bundle of banknotes, and say, 'I don't need to give you the instructions, do I?' To which Mrs Rassouli would smile and say, 'Not at all. Mrs *Lashouli* will take care of it.'

Malek never asked about the parcel but one day, after Mrs Rassouli had left, Rana, who was more inquisitive, asked, 'Auntie *Khanoum*, what's inside the *termeh*-wrapped parcel?'

'Nothing. Nothing of importance.'

Malek glared at Rana but Rana ignored her and asked smiling, 'If it's of no importance then how come no one is supposed to know about it?'

'Who said that no one should know about it?'

'Well, because you never open the parcel when other people are around. And you never say what's in it. So perhaps you don't want anyone to know what's inside.'

'Go to my room and bring me the bundle that is wrapped in a checked cloth in the first drawer inside my wardrobe to the right. Bring it here. Everything is in there.'

'It really doesn't matter,' Malek said, feeling somewhat embarrassed. 'She's still young and just couldn't keep her curiosity under control.' After which she turned to Rana, and scolded, 'Don't poke your nose into grown-up affairs!'

Auntie said, 'Let her be, Malek *jan*. It doesn't matter.' And then she turned to Rana and said, 'Rana dear, go and bring the bundle here. I want Malek *Khanoum* to see its contents as well.'

Rana got up and swiftly went in search of the secret bundle. Auntie's room was a forbidding place and Auntie rarely gave permission for anyone to enter her room without her. Now that Rana was looking around Auntie's room in the daylight everything seemed extremely ordinary: there was a Russian bed, which was narrower than the usual sort of bed, an armchair with a small table by its side, and a wardrobe, which appeared to be made from the same wood as the headboard. The wardrobe had carvings on one door and a large oval-shaped mirror on the other. Rana looked at herself in the mirror. Her hair fell around her face and her eyes twinkled with happiness. She looked like a curious and naughty child. She was suddenly very self-conscious. She didn't dare open the wardrobe at first but when she heard Auntie's voice calling to her from downstairs asking, 'What's going on Rana?' she pulled the door open. At the bottom of the wardrobe there were four drawers arranged in pairs, side by side. She had forgotten which drawer she should pull out. She held her breath, closed her eyes and pulled out the first drawer that came to hand. It was the correct one; the bundle with its check-patterned wrapping lay inside. She picked it up. It wasn't heavy. She then quickly returned to the sitting room. She placed the bundle on the table and studiously ignored Malek's glares. Auntie undid the bundle and out tumbled a number of *termehs,* all made from chiffon, silk and velvet with extraordinarily beautiful embroidery and stitching with seed pearls. The patterns looked as though they were dancing on the materials. The flowers were intertwined. The branches were twisted around one another. Thick gold threads and fine silk ones sat alongside the small gleaming seed pearls, each of which was a different shape. The surface of the table had suddenly turned into a garden filled with imaginary flowers and unbelievable patterns.

Malek couldn't help but say, 'These are so beautiful!'

Rana asked, 'Who do they belong to?'

Auntie laughed and said, 'They are yours. When you get married you can take them all.'

'You promise? All of them?'

'You can have everything.'

Malek pulled a face and protested, 'Rana, stop being so childish!'

'I don't need these,' Auntie reassured her. 'Rana can have them all.'

Rana said, 'If you don't need these, why does Mrs Rassouli keep bringing you a fresh bundle each time she comes?'

Rather than responding to the question, Auntie picked up one of the pieces with pearls sewn on it and placed one side of the material on Rana's shoulder, letting the rest fall across her body. Then she said, 'Because you're very young and you will need many new and colourful dresses. Let's see if you can use this in your new dress.'

Malek, who was going through the pieces of material, looked intently at each piece and said, 'What hands could create such work? What workmanship! Where does Mrs Rassouli find these?'

Auntie said, 'You are quite right. She's unique,' and then went quiet. Sometimes, while she was talking, Auntie would suddenly lapse into deep thought and a faraway look would cross her eyes; she would be off in a distant place that nobody but herself could see.

Rana was looking through the different materials and admiring their beautiful patterns when she peered at Auntie. The look in her eyes was as distant as those times when she was reading the story of the Count of Monte Cristo and thinking about her children. Rana rose, held the pearl-strewn material across her chest and looked at herself in the large sitting-room mirror. If Youssef could see her in a dress like that he would be stunned. Perhaps he would even find her comical and then refuse to speak to her for the rest of the day, just like the day when Rana had worn a glittering dress to a wedding reception. Youssef had told her that she looked like a grown-up woman and then kept his distance from her for the rest of the evening. Youssef was like that – one could never tell what he was thinking – but Rana was certain that if she wore such a dress, no matter what Youssef said or what he did, he would also find her astonishingly beautiful. Her thoughts made her laugh. What difference did it make whether Youssef found her beautiful or not? Youssef was a child just like her; a child, a playmate, a friend ...

Auntie looked at Rana and smiled. She said, 'Zari must be getting married one of these days. Mrs Rassouli was saying that they're getting ready. I think this material with the pearls would make a very becoming gown for you to wear to the reception.'

'Are they really planning a wedding?'

'I don't know. They haven't said anything. But I think something must be going on.'

Auntie didn't say any more that day. Malek and Rana didn't ask any further questions either. Malek was frightened that Rana's needless interrogations might have upset Auntie. And Rana was wondering why Zari had never told her about her wedding.

Chapter 7

The sound of laughter woke her up around midnight. It was a happy sound, the sound of a soft and ringing laugh.

It was the sound of Zari's laughter. She recognised the tone. When she opened her eyes she saw Zari standing at the foot of her bed and smiling at her. She had not thought about her for a long time. Zari had died years ago; she couldn't recall how many years had passed since her death. She had died before everyone else, before she had had the chance to grow old, just like the great aunt. But now she was standing there staring at her with her large hazel eyes, but her hair was not soft and brown as it should be. Her hair was now red, just like Great Aunt's hair had been; the colour of fire: red and wild. She was wearing a long dress that resembled the gowns worn by princesses in fairy tales.

Rana sat up in bed and stared at Zari. She then closed her eyes and rubbed them with the backs of her hands. When she looked again, Zari had gone but the sound of her laughter still hung in the air. The window was open, allowing the wind to tug at the curtains. Perhaps Zari had entered and departed through that same window, riding on a winged horse, just like in the fairy tales she had told. Perhaps she was en route to a big heavenly reception and she had come to pay her a visit as she passed by. And perhaps Rana was losing her mind rather than her memory. Perhaps it wasn't even an important issue. Maybe Zari had just come to see her, or maybe she had come to take her with her, even …

* * *

Zari was the youngest daughter of Kazem Khan, a reputable carpet merchant who lived next door to Auntie. The Khans were long-standing acquaintances; a quiet family who kept to themselves. Mobashereh, Kazem's wife, was twenty years his junior yet they were a devoted couple and rarely apart. Kazem often had to go away on long business trips so he took his wife with him. As the youngest, Zari was usually left behind. Whenever her parents travelled, she was looked after by the servants and the nanny; the latter was an old woman now. If the trip became extended, she would go and stay with her older siblings. When she was at home she would see a lot of Auntie. Rana met Zari for the first time at Auntie's house. And though she was a couple of years younger she became a good audience for her tales. Zari had Rana over on most days. To begin with Rana looked forward to these visits but later she became bored with Zari.

Kazem's house was large. No sounds emanated from it for the greater part of the year: the sitting-room doors only seemed to open when the proprietors returned. Zari wandered through the large and spacious rooms every day without doing very much. She sat in each chair and imagined herself as an adult, travelling far and wide and then returning home and filling all the chairs with visitors. She would thank her imaginary visitors and talk to them about the distant places to which she had travelled and the strange things she had seen in those foreign lands. She would talk about the long journeys she had taken, the strange animals she had seen and the fabulous palaces she had visited. She would speak of the sumptuous parties she'd attended, the handsome princes who'd fallen in love with her, the lavish gifts they'd given her and their melancholy faces when their offers of marriage were refused; and of riding through unknown lands on their horses. She didn't want to break people's hearts and remind them what tedious lives they led. She had told Rana everything and, when she spoke, her eyes had twinkled. Zari was a dreamer but Rana found her company charming, perhaps more so than anyone else she knew. It felt like Zari's dreams clung to the doors and the walls; it was as though they lit up the room. The glory and magnificence of her imagination changed everything and it broke the monotony of her routine life.

Zari's body was as dainty as her dreams. As Malek put it, 'The child is as fragile as a strand of gold thread; she is a waif.'

She did have a waif-like body. She was tall and pale with large hazel eyes, a short but fine nose, thin pink lips, soft straight dark brown hair and long, slender fingers; Rana thought such fingers were really only useful for weaving intricate dreams. When she spoke, she waved her fingers in the air, held imaginary hands and smiled at faces that were invisible to Rana. When she laughed, she revealed two neat rows of white teeth. Her laughter had a pleasant ring to it, a resonance that Rana never heard in anyone else's laugh. Rana never forgot the sound of Zari's laughter. She tried to forget it but she could not. She heard it time and time again. And years later she recognised a brittle quality in that laugh that she had not previously noticed.

Zari was the first person, from among all the people that she knew, who had tried to determine her own destiny, and she had done so with her own very particular brand of obstinacy. Whenever she decided upon something, she became single-minded and ignored everyone else; they did not matter to her. She pursued her dreams relentlessly. She wanted to live on her own terms. She said, 'If we have to live according to everyone else's wishes then it would be better to die.'

Rana found Zari quite an odd character. One minute she felt she understood her and her quirky ways, and the next she felt she didn't know much about her at all – she couldn't make head or tail of what she said. Rana was at pains to identify what had prompted Zari to be so rebellious. She lived in the same house as her parents and although they travelled often they always returned. Rana did not have a mother and only saw her father two or three times a year. As far as she was concerned, Zari's life was not as bad as she thought it was.

Auntie, though, did not find Zari's life quite so satisfactory. She said, 'Kazem Khan and his wife are quite thoughtless. They ought not to leave a child alone in such a big house all year round.'

Always looking on the bright side, Auntie Mehr commented, 'It's not a problem. She has her nanny there with her as well as her sisters and brothers. Mobashereh *Khanoum* needs to keep an eye on her husband. Even when they are at home, Zari's day-to-day care is the nanny's responsibility anyway.'

Auntie said, 'In any case it's not right; the situation is far from satisfactory.'

Zaeem would sigh and say, 'Her ladyship is right; being left alone for long periods of time is not right; it isn't right at all,' following which he would brush some invisible dust off the sleeve of his jacket.

Malek did not know much about Zari and her family so she did not contribute to the discussions about them; but she could see the gravity of Auntie's concern.

Shortly after Rana and Malek arrived to live in Auntie's house, Kazem Khan and his wife set off on yet another long trip and, as always, they asked Auntie to keep an eye on Zari. From the moment they left, Zari practically lived with them. Rana would spend her days with Zari, listening to her tales and laughing at her dreams.

Zari was fifteen years of age and Malek thought that her parents would soon marry her off. They had done so with their other daughters at a similar age and they had also found wives for their sons early. Auntie believed that her neighbour didn't want her children at home. Mehr thought, however, that Mobashereh was too busy helping her husband to amass a great deal of wealth so her children were naturally not at the forefront of her mind. Malek thought Auntie was right. Rana, though, didn't understand any of what they talked about; she only understood and believed that Zari would never give in to marriage because she harboured too many dreams.

Great Auntie's photograph sat on the mantelpiece. Malek took the photograph with her wherever she went. Zari had told Rana on the first day they met that she resembled the girl in the photo but, as always, Malek quickly said, 'It seems that way because it is a black and white photograph. Great Auntie *jan* had green eyes and red hair. She didn't look like Rana at all. No, not at all!'

Zari did not comment but, when they were alone, she told Rana once again that she did look like the girl in the photograph and that the colour of her eyes and hair didn't make much difference. Zari wished to learn more about the girl in the photograph but Rana didn't know much and Malek would say little more. Zari said that the girl in the photograph looked sad. Rana didn't think that she looked particularly sad but she did think she looked somewhat on edge. But Zari said, 'Nobody's eyes would look so melancholy if they weren't sad.' And then she once again asked about the fate of the girl in the photograph. She asked so many questions that Malek finally said, 'Great Auntie *jan* was much loved. She got married. It didn't go well. She returned home and spent the rest of her life with us.'

But Zari didn't seem convinced. Whenever she came over she would spend time standing in front of the photograph. She looked at the girl in the picture and insisted on knowing more about her. In order to rid herself of Zari's questions, Malek removed the photograph from the mantelpiece, saying she had to change the frame, and placed it in the wardrobe in her room. She only returned the photograph to its rightful place later, after Zari's death. When Malek was putting the photograph back on the mantelpiece, Rana felt she regretted not having answered Zari's questions properly. Neither Rana nor Malek said anything. From then on, no one removed the picture from the mantelpiece but then no one asked after the fate of the girl in the photograph either. After Zari's death, Great Auntie's photograph seemed even more melancholy and terrifying than before; it was as though Zari's dreamy gaze had blended with the dark and deep-set eyes in the picture. The transformation was so convincing that she soon forgot that Zari had light brown eyes and dark brown hair. She started to remember her with green eyes and red hair. Only two things hadn't changed in her mind and that was Zari's waif-like body and the resonance in her voice. The character of Zari's voice belonged to the wavy red hair that spread across her shoulders and was tossed in all directions by the wind, and to the flaming eyes that danced in the night – neither of which she had actually ever seen.

It was towards the end of the month when Zari's parents returned. After their arrival Zari's visits to Auntie's home became less frequent. They had their own visitors each day. Rana missed Zari but Malek told her that they were busy and that she should not impose herself. When Rana insisted to see her, she would just say, 'A lady doesn't go to people's homes uninvited.'

Rana was fed up with what she was constantly being told, and still insisted to see Zari. She then asked Malek to allow her to invite Zari over to their home instead. Malek agreed and they sent Sarvar with the invitation, but Zari apologised, saying that she was too busy, so couldn't come. Rana was hurt but didn't show it. She felt something was about to happen and waited to find out. Finally, early one morning, Auntie made the happy announcement that Zari was getting married. Rana smiled but felt something was not right. She wanted to speak to Zari. Sarvar, on finding Rana deep in thought, said to her, 'Don't be sad; your turn will come.'

The idea of a wedding was entertaining and kept a host of different people engaged. Initially, Mrs Rassouli was sent for so that she could make new dresses. She used the material with the seed pearls to make a gown for Rana to wear. Rana's gown had a tight bodice with a long skirt that was puffed up by a gathered underskirt. On the front part of the skirt, and on the shawl that covered Rana's shoulders, the pearls revealed the outline of a flock of birds – birds that looked as though they were flying. Rana's gown was so beautiful that she was certain Maryam would scream with joy and Youssef would not dare to mock her. She couldn't wait to put it on. She fretted over her hair and how it should be styled to suit her gown. She would stand in front of the mirror, gather her hair behind her head with one hand and then let it fall loose again so that it spread across her shoulders in a wave. She tied her hair on top of her head with a ribbon, then untied the ribbon and then sought to tame only the lower parts of her hair. She would then divide her hair into two and hold it on either side of her wondering and uncertain face. Her desperate gestures showed that she could not decide what to do with her hair. She finally announced that she wanted to have it cut very short. That way she would not have to think about how to style it. Her decision was met with Auntie Malek's vehement disapproval. Malek went beyond that and forbade her even to stand in front of the mirror and think about what to do with her hair. In the end Rana never found out how it should be styled to suit that gown because she never wore the dress. The wedding did not take place. Zari died before the wedding.

Zari's intended husband came from a very good family. His father was a carpet merchant. He had studied abroad and had just returned so his family had decided to find him a wife. Everything seemed to be going well. Zari's parents were planning to travel again in a few months so they wanted the matter to be finalised sooner rather than later. In Kazem Khan's house, wedding preparations kept everyone busy. Zari came over to Auntie's house once but she didn't speak much. Mainly, she seemed to be in her own world. She didn't respond to any of Rana's questions about the groom; she just said that he didn't look like a prince. He didn't even resemble a person who had studied abroad. He looked more like a young assistant who worked in her father's office. She didn't know anything about the date of the wedding. She didn't want to talk about the wedding but didn't say anything about her dreams either. Before she left, however, she said to Rana, 'One day they'll realise that I am not like my sisters. I shan't become a wife to any of these creatures, even when I am dead ... Lucky you. Your aunts are very different from my mother!'

At the time Rana didn't quite understand what Zari meant. What difference would it have made anyway? She saw Zari a few more times but her friend kept her distance from Rana. She had become quiet and aloof. She wouldn't come over and spend time with Rana; on the rare occasions she did, she would visit briefly and then leave.

Rana said to her aunt, 'Zari has become strange. She's either become full of herself or is somewhere else altogether.'

Malek said, 'I don't think so; she's just thinking about her future. This is normal.' And then, with a smile to Rana, she carried on, 'Your turn will come as well. You'll be just the same.'

Youssef would smirk and make faces, showing his approval for what Malek said. This would drive Rana mad with rage but she couldn't say anything in the presence of the grown-ups. She had to wait until no one was paying attention and then deal with Youssef. She could kick him in the shin or make him trip over her foot.

Two weeks before the wedding, when Mrs Rassouli was helping Rana try her dress on for the last time, and was telling her how beautiful the wedding gown was going to be, with its gorgeous pearl work, Mehr asked with her usual naiveté, 'Is she actually happy with the match?' Her question was so unexpected that everyone was taken aback. It had not occurred to anyone that Zari might oppose the match. Marriage was not something that children thought much about. It only concerned the adults; they were the ones who made the decisions.

Auntie's reaction to the question was mixed with annoyance, 'Why shouldn't she be? She's got to settle down some time, has she not?'

Mehr shook her head and said, 'She needs to be in agreement. *I* wasn't. Lord knows, I wasn't. Bless his soul, he wasn't either. He said as much at the time, as well.'

Sarvar, who was always around, said, 'Please don't talk in such a negative way, my lady. It's much better this way, better than being homeless and lonely.'

Mrs Rassouli, while busy marking the side of the gown with pins, said, 'They'll get used to each other.'

Mehr shook her head anxiously once again. She didn't say anything but she was not convinced. Malek changed the subject. It was much later when they realised Mehr had been right. Perhaps the dead had sent her signs. Zari's parents had to ask Zari personally.

Zari didn't have much time to get used to the groom; two weeks before the wedding, the sound of wailing rose from Kazem Khan's house. It was early in the morning. Sarvar was taking a cup of tea to Rahman, who was sweeping and watering the tiled parts of the garden. Malek had the teapot in her hand in the kitchen, and was pouring tea into the glass tumblers, when Sarvar made such a sudden and noisy appearance in the kitchen that Malek's grip on the teapot became loose. The teapot fell and shattered into pieces on the work surface.

Auntie, who looked displeased, asked, 'What on earth is going on, Sarvar? Why are you behaving this way?'

'I swear to the Almighty, something has happened, my lady!'

'Obviously something's happened. Because of your madness the teapot is now broken!'

Meanwhile Malek, who was busy wiping up the spilt tea with a cloth, said, 'Why are you jumping to conclusions, Sarvar?'

'You've no idea what's going on in Kazem Khan's house. We can only hear the sound of wailing and sobbing. Someone must have just died!'

Malek said, 'It might be Kazem Khan's mother. I heard she wasn't feeling very well.'

'No, my lady, it must be something else; something much worse.'

Auntie put her weight on her walking stick so that she could get up. She said, 'Why don't you go over and check what's going on while Malek *Khanoum* and I get ready.'

Sarvar donned her chador and left. Malek and Auntie were still getting ready when Sarvar returned. She looked in a daze. 'Zari *Khanoum* has died!' She had heard the news from the servant. 'Zari *Khanoum* had a heated discussion with her father last night. She said she didn't want to get married.' The nanny found her body when she entered her room in the morning. Her complexion was darker than normal, as though someone had strangled her. The servant sobbed, saying Zari had taken poison.

Rana was informed later. No one wanted to say anything to her. When she came down the stairs to have breakfast she found the house quiet. She couldn't see Auntie, or Malek. Sarvar was sitting in the kitchen weeping continuously.

The mourning period for Zari didn't last long, the commotion and noise swiftly being brought to a close. They said she had developed a fever overnight and died in the morning. When Auntie returned from the memorial service she was furious. She said, 'The groom's family were very upset. They were left with heavy bills for a wedding which isn't going to happen now.' Rubbing her painful knees with one hand, she continued, 'No one cared for that poor girl. Not even her mother ...'

Auntie spent the rest of the day in her room. Whenever Rana passed by the room she saw Auntie leaning against the arm of her chair holding *The Count of Monte Cristo* open in her lap, but her mind was clearly elsewhere.

From then on Auntie never mentioned Zari's name again. If she had to talk about her she would just say, 'Poor thing!'

The news of Zari's death brought Mehr to Auntie's house. Zaeem arrived as well. Mehr was visibly upset. She kept wiping her tears, saying, 'Didn't I tell you that the girl must be in agreement? Didn't I say that her opinion mattered? There you go! They now have to visit the poor thing's grave instead. See? Instead of a wedding gown she'll be covered in a white shroud and the rest of them will be in mourning attire.' And then she put her wet handkerchief aside, pulled a fresh one out from her handbag, and went on, 'I was anxious a week before this happened; just anxious without knowing why. I knew something dreadful was going to happen.'

Auntie snorted in annoyance. 'No doubt you dreamt about it the night before!'

'Yes!' Mehr responded, 'Yes! I did dream it! I saw my mother in my dream the night before! She was in a state. She was crying. She said that I should forgive her for marrying me off without asking me. But I have to say, I didn't know then that my mother was really worried about that poor child ...'

Auntie mumbled, 'Thank God you dream about everything.'

Mehr, who didn't hear what Auntie said, asked, 'Did you say something?'

Malek stepped in quickly. 'Auntie said dreams are such bizarre phenomena.'

'Yes,' added Zaeem, 'dreams are truly bizarre.'

Rana and Youssef were both badly affected by Zari's death for some time afterwards; they were both depressed. Youssef hadn't known Zari very well, but he still wanted to know why she had done it. At times, when the grown-ups were not around, Rana and Youssef spent hours talking about Zari. Youssef bombarded Rana with questions. What sort of a girl was she? What had upset her to such a degree? If she so resented marrying this man why didn't she talk to her parents about it rather than commit suicide? Why didn't she seek refuge in Auntie's home? Why didn't she ask Auntie to speak to them on her behalf? Everyone knew that if she had done so no one would have dared to marry her off without her consent. Youssef considered suicide the most unintelligent and worst solution. Why did Zari choose the worst solution? Rana didn't know the answer to Youssef's questions; and no one else did either. Malek only said, 'Zari left because she didn't want to stay.' Auntie said, 'May God put a curse upon the one who's brought about such a tragedy,' and since Youssef and Rana did not know who that was, their questions remained unresolved.

Rana couldn't sleep well after that. Zaeem was right in saying that dreams were strange phenomena. Zari was alive in Rana's dreams. She would visit her every now and then. She visited her the night before Rana was going to get married. Her eyes were filled with tears. In her dreams, before Rana got to her wedding, Zari turned and left. Rana woke up. She was short of breath. She knew she was mistaken.

Zari seemed to appear at melancholy times; the night before Rana was going to see Youssef again, for the first time after his return, she came to her in her dreams. She didn't look happy. The eyes were hers but the red and dishevelled hair was Great Auntie's. She had caressed Rana's face with her fine fingers. Rana opened her eyes. She had seen Zari. She was smiling. But her eyes were sad. Rana couldn't hear the ringing tone in her laughter. And this was exactly the same as the night that Rana was going to see Youssef again after many years ...

CHAPTER 8

Abtin had to settle down.

He was almost thirty. If he continued to delay it would be too late. Rana thought about this as she was dusting Mahtab's photograph. Abtin had met Mahtab during his first year at university and, ever since, he had been thinking about whether he should get married or not. Whenever Rana mentioned it, Abtin would avoid answering. He knew his mother resented his indecisiveness.

His excuse had been Uncle's illness and the demands of nursing him. Uncle wasn't Rana's uncle. He was her cousin on her mother's side; Yahya Khan's son. His kidneys had stopped functioning the year before so he had to have dialysis three times a week. But nursing Uncle was not a real excuse for Abtin because Rana took care of him.

Uncle resented any reminder of his illness; he didn't like anyone expressing concern when he had to go for dialysis. Occasionally, he would speak sadly about a patient who had died during the process; about patients whose hearts couldn't take it any more, or who couldn't tolerate the machine breaking down and the problems resulting from this, and so would leave. He would say, 'Yes my dear, that's the way it is. Sometimes one cannot stand things any more. Sometimes ...'

But he did put up with it because he wanted to be with his wife and child.

One night, after Uncle's wife and child had left, Rana and Abtin took him back home; they were returning from a family dinner. The car came to a halt in front of the house. Uncle got out of the car with difficulty, feeling heavy. He didn't feel well at all. His complexion looked darker than ever, his tummy was quite bloated and he stooped. It took him a while to take the key from his small bag and open the door. Opening the door took a few minutes as well, but he finally managed it. He then turned to Rana, smiled and gave her a not-to-worry-you-can-go-now wave.

Rana left but she was concerned. Concerned about a man who had lost everything and who had opened the door of a house where no one was waiting for him any more; a dark silent house where he drowned in solitude. After spending the entire night crying she decided that, whatever it took, she would have to convince Uncle to live with her and Abtin. She would use her own loneliness as an excuse and suggest that if Uncle were to move, he wouldn't need to keep his house any longer. If he got rid of his bric-a-brac now, he would not have to worry about selling it in a hurry just before he left. Uncle agreed to live with Rana to help her. He sold what was left of his belongings so that he could leave promptly and finally arrived at her house with only his favourite possessions. In fact, he lived out the rest of his life with Rana and Abtin. Uncle had not departed like Mr Piran; he did not leave behind a long list of his effects in a dark notebook.

When Uncle had fallen in love, he had been just like Rana's mother: he wouldn't listen to anyone. He said that was what he wanted and that was that. The family elders had opposed his marriage but Uncle had hosted a sumptuous wedding reception and dedicated his life to his wife from that day forward.

But when he became unwell his wife had said to Rana, 'I've looked after him this far, but from now on his family must take care of him.'

Now, whenever Rana told Abtin that he had to take a wife, Abtin would say, 'And why should I; so that I end up like Uncle; so that I can dedicate my entire life to someone who will eventually leave me? No, Mother. I am not going to. I want to find someone whom I trust; someone who's truthful. Someone who is honest about who she is.'

What he said irritated Rana; she thought Abtin was just avoiding the responsibility. He didn't want to grow up. He didn't want to make a decision, and Rana resented people who could not make decisions. Such people ruined everything. It didn't matter how good things were. Hesitation made for lost opportunities. Youssef had been the same. He had been hesitant. He had always been hesitant. He made tardy decisions which were wrong; wrong decisions because he had waited too long to make them. He made bad mistakes because he would not take timely action.

It was a quiet spring morning and the sun had filled the room with light. The room had just been dusted and the doors to the reception room had been left open for ventilation. No one was expected. Everyone was busy when Rahman found them and said, 'Taj *Khanoum* and Youssef Khan have arrived.' Auntie and Malek were surprised by the untimely visit. Even Rahman seemed surprised.

The visitors followed Rahman into the room, where Auntie greeted them with open arms. Everyone liked Taj *Khanoum*. They admired her patience and tolerance. Youssef followed his mother in. Rana was unsettled when she saw Youssef; his eyes were red, as though he had not slept well for a few nights. He didn't look at Rana, nor did he smile. Rana had never seen him look so depressed and be so quiet.

Taj *Khanoum* removed her coat, sat down and rested her handbag against the foot of her chair. She removed her colourful silk headscarf and touched the blonde hair, gathered behind her head, to ensure it was still in place. Then, when Auntie asked after her, she suddenly burst into tears. It was as though she had been waiting for the question. Everyone was quiet for a while afterwards. No one knew what had happened. Youssef placed a gentle hand on his mother's shoulder and asked her to try and calm down. His mother attempted to compose herself. Rana ran out, following a gesture from Auntie, and brought Taj *Khanoum* a glass of water.

Taj *Khanoum* took a gulp, placed the glass on the low table before her, and said, 'Auntie *Khanoum*, Malek *Khanoum*, you know that I have tolerated this man for many years now and I have never complained. But now I've reached the end of my tether. I don't know what to do about this situation ... Maryam's perishing ... and this man ... this '*jalad*' ...' and then there were more tears.

Auntie asked, 'What's happened? What's the problem?'

Youssef said, 'My sister is not well and ...' He swallowed his tears as well as the rest of the sentence.

Auntie's colour changed. Ever since she had lost her sons, her face would change expression on hearing that a child was unwell, as though she were dealing with her own children's illness once again. Rana, too, looked perturbed after hearing about Maryam's illness.

Malek asked, 'Where is the child?'

'At home,' Taj *Khanoum* responded, 'with her brothers. That godforsaken man won't let us call a doctor, nor will he allow us to take her to a doctor. He says that nothing is wrong; that she'll recover.'

Auntie asked, 'How long has she been unwell?'

Youssef said, 'She's been feverish for ten days now ...'

It began to dawn on Rana why there had been no sign of Youssef for so long.

Taj *Khanoum* turned to Auntie and said, 'She looks yellow and weak. She doesn't eat anything. She's burning up. I beg of you, do something. I suggested to him that I call a doctor; he said he didn't have the money. He said these things were expensive and asked if I wanted to ruin him? I said I'd pay for the treatment, but he snapped back at me that he had known from the start that I had saved money from the household expenses and hidden it away. He then locked us in the house, which is where we have been for the past two days, and went out. His excuse for leaving was that he is fed up with my moping. Youssef somehow managed to break the lock and then I thought of coming here to beg you for help …'

Rana had never seen Auntie so angry. She was so pale it looked as though the blood had drained from her body. Auntie leaned on her walking stick as if to rise, and told Rana, 'Call Rahman. We have to go to Mr Vaqar Saltaneh's house.' She then turned to Taj *Khanoum* and said, 'First, we are going to deal with the child's treatment. Then we'll think of a proper solution for you and the children. Enough is enough.'

Seeing that Auntie intended to go to the house personally, Taj *Khanoum* became hesitant. 'Perhaps it wouldn't be appropriate for you to come, Madam. I just wanted to ask you to send him a message … I am frightened of what might happen if he finds you in the house … God forbid he should become disrespectful towards you …'

Auntie snorted. 'In this family no one has the guts to do such a thing. Don't upset yourself. This scandalous behaviour must be stopped at once.'

Auntie called Rahman and instructed him to call on Dr Tashchian and take him to the Vaqar residence. She told Rana to remain at home and to help Sarvar to prepare a room for Maryam to rest in. Auntie and Malek then left together with Taj *Khanoum* and Youssef.

While Rana was preparing Maryam's bed, she thought about Youssef's penetrating sad look; she wanted to help them in whatever way she could. She made the bed using the nicest linen and placed some flowers by the side. Then she opened the windows and ventilated the room. By noon everything was ready. Rana took a last look around the room and felt something was missing. She suddenly remembered *The Count of Monte Cristo* and placed the book by the vase; she could read the book to Maryam. The aunties passed by the room a few times and looked in at Rana in disbelief. They didn't recognise her. They enquired suspiciously, 'Excuse me, Madam, do we have any guests?'

Rana said, 'A young and sick guest.'

One of the aunts turned to the other and whispered, 'I told you that this guesthouse is not a safe place. Something's not right with these people. They are turning this place into a convalescent home.'

The other one told Rana, 'Rather than doing this you should change the linen in our bedroom; otherwise we'll lodge a complaint about you. We'll have you sacked.' She went on grumbling, 'Bless our own maids. They knew their job. Not like this careless girl. We'll complain.' And then they left in a huff.

Rana was motionless. She was baffled by the encounter. Shaking her head to clear her mind of all negative thoughts, she smiled and returned to her own room. She looked at her reflection in the mirror. Her hair was all over the place and she wasn't dressed appropriately for the occasion, so she got changed. She combed her hair and tied it with a ribbon, then looked at her reflection once again. She didn't look too bad. She told herself that she did all this so that her appearance wouldn't embarrass Malek when their guests arrived. But she knew deep down that that wasn't the only reason for tidying up her appearance.

Sarvar was fortunately too busy to pay attention to what Rana was up to. With Rahman gone, she felt helpless and had to cook lunch for an unknown number of people as well as stock up the cupboards with enough food to last for a few days. A sick person in the house meant an unknown number of visitors. Everyone would come to see the patient. If they came in the morning they would stay for lunch and if they came in the afternoon they would stay for dinner. The serving in between lunch and dinner was separate. Rana preferred not to go to Sarvar. One could not talk to her at such times.

Auntie and Rahman returned home late that afternoon. Taj *Khanoum,* Youssef and Maryam were not with them. Malek had stayed behind in Taj *Khanoum's* house to help out, so Rana wanted to find out what the problem was. She kept asking questions. Auntie said, 'The doctor didn't let us move the child. He said she was too weak. The treatment, he told us, should have been started much sooner.'

'You mean to say that Maryam's quite unwell?'

'She's not well at all. In any case, we should leave it in the hands of the Almighty ... Tell Sarvar to bring us some tea.'

'Wasn't Mr Vaqar critical of you and what you have done?'

'First of all, he wasn't in. Secondly, I sent word to let him know that I was going to visit his wife and children and that, having done so, I found his daughter to be quite unwell. I informed him that I had called the doctor and that I would continue to do as I saw fit from then on.'

'How come Auntie Malek stayed?'

'It wasn't a good idea to leave Taj *Khanoum* and the children alone. I know that man. Whatever he does and however he behaves, he likes to keep up appearances. It's impossible for him to cause any problems so long as Malek *Khanoum* is in that house ... at least I hope that's the case ...'

Rana asked indecisively, 'When will Auntie Malek return?'

'I've said that when the child begins to feel better they should bring her over here; perhaps tomorrow or the day after tomorrow. I'll go over again tomorrow.'

'Can I come as well?'

'What for? It's not a party!'

'I know ... I just ... I wanted ...'

'Goodness gracious me, you have such curiosity! Very well, I'll take you with me. For now go and ask Sarvar to come here; she has to prepare some food for us to take tomorrow. The poor things have nothing in their house. Everything's locked in the larder and the key is in that beast's pocket. It's a disgrace. Truly a disgrace ...'

Rana woke up early the next day. She had some breakfast before doing anything else and then waited for Auntie in the room downstairs. The night before, the aunties had ransacked the kitchen so Sarvar was busy clearing up the plates and pans and complaining. When Auntie came downstairs, Sarvar rushed towards her and said, 'Ma'am, you really need to sort something out for the lady aunties. Get them a nurse. Get someone to check on them. This is infuriating. Look what they did last night! Heaven knows, I can't take it any more ... If things carry on like this then I'll go back to the village!'

The 'I'm going back to the village' was Sarvar's usual threat. It was perhaps her wish, even. But, deep down, she knew that she wouldn't last even two days in the village, because she had grown used to the comfort of Auntie's house. She managed everything; everything except Auntie, who no one dared to cross or question. But whenever she talked of going back to the village it meant that she was really furious.

Auntie said, 'Give it a rest, Sarvar. This is not the time. Just pour some tea.'

Sarvar was still angry. While pouring the tea she yelled from the kitchen, 'Ma'am, they've crippled me; they've ransacked everything. Nothing's in its place. Seems they wanted to make pickles last night. When I came in here this morning I saw that they had chopped herbs but strewn them all over the floor. And then they just left it that way. It was chaos. I've been clearing herbs and vegetables since early this morning. Rahman's been here twice now to take rubbish out. I can't believe their energy. They don't seem to get tired, ever … Please, Ma'am, you need to think of something …'

Auntie wasn't listening. Her mind was somewhere else. In the end she just said, 'OK, OK. That's enough Sarvar. Get some lunch ready. Ask Rahman to come. I want to go to Malek *Khanoum*.'

Rana was relieved. Auntie was in such a bad mood that she'd been concerned Sarvar's moaning might drive her over the edge and cause her to explode, the prospect of which made everyone apprehensive.

Rana, Auntie and Rahman arrived at the Vaqars before lunch. The house was much bigger than Rana had imagined. It had a large garden with tall old trees. The paved part of the garden was covered with dried leaves. The sound of the crows that nested high in the trees filled the garden, adding to the gloomy and melancholy atmosphere. The main building was situated towards the back of the grounds. The mansion had tall windows and a number of verandas. It was one of those homes that had been built to accommodate many inhabitants and host countless social events. But the social events were no more and the only inhabitants left were a small family who occupied a handful of rooms. The cracked walls and chipped paintwork were manifestations of an almost deserted house. But right in front of the main part of the mansion there was a flowerbed – a small cultivated patch of ground with a number of beautiful and colourful flowers. The flowerbed was in stark contrast to the depressed atmosphere of the household. Rana discovered much later that it was Youssef who had created the flowerbed to cheer up Maryam. It was the children's only hobby and, since it didn't cost much, Vaqar did not object. The children had planted the flowers and looked after them as well.

Rana's eyes searched for Youssef, but it was his mother, Taj *Khanoum*, who came to greet the guests personally. Her husband, Vaqar, was not in. Maryam was resting in the sitting room by a window that overlooked the garden. When the sun shone through the window its rays reached the middle of the room, which was simply furnished except for a few items of antique furniture. The room was otherwise tidy and clean; there were no signs of chaos. Malek was sitting by the sick child's bed. Taj *Khanoum* went to prepare some tea. Malek said that Youssef had spent the entire night with his sister and had just gone to get some sleep at his mother's insistence. The sight of Maryam, looking frail and with a yellow complexion, lying in bed coughing all the time, soon made Rana forget her excitement over seeing Youssef. Auntie said that the child's condition had improved but Rana sensed that Auntie was lying, which was unlike her. There was something in Auntie's face and tone that seemed unfamiliar; despite her composed manner she appeared to be intensely worried. Malek looked anxious as well. So anxious, in fact, that Rana began to wonder whether she had adopted the same look when she had nursed her own sick sister. The physician had been to see Maryam first thing and had left some instructions. He had particularly asked for the younger children not to be allowed to come too close to her. Malek had sent the children to a different part of the mansion and specifically told them not to come near the patient's room. Maryam was having difficulty breathing. She struggled to inhale and exhale and in between her gasps there were dry coughs which sounded sharp enough to tear open her chest.

The physician had not allowed anyone to move Maryam. He said that the air outside would worsen her condition. Maryam's hair was wet with perspiration. She looked pale and her lips were dry and chapped. Rana had never been so close to death. She thought that this must be when she might be able to see the angel of death stand by the patient's bed. And she was scared at the thought.

Taj *Khanoum* entered the room with the tea tray and, a little later, Youssef arrived as well. His eyes were red from lack of sleep. He sat next to Maryam, kissed her forehead and held her hand. Rana looked at Youssef. He bent over his little sister in such a way that it looked as though he was trying to hide her from death's eyes. He caressed and stroked Maryam's hair and whispered, 'Little lady ... little lady ... you'll get better soon.' Auntie had a knot in her throat when she looked at them. Rana saw her turn her face away so that no one would see her tears. She, too, looked away so that she didn't make Auntie feel uncomfortable. It was then that she noticed the tablecloth; a small but heavily embroidered piece of material covered the table that had been placed next to the wall. Rana had seen the same intricate workmanship before. She looked around at various parts of the room. The handicraft on the cushion covers, what lay on the arms of the chairs, even the embroidered piece that lay on the tray; they had all been done by the same person. These were the same style of work that Mrs Rassouli brought to Auntie, in the *termeh*-wrapped bundles. When Taj *Khanoum* noticed Rana looking at the needlework so intently, she said, 'Whenever I'm not busy I make these.'

Auntie looked at Rana, who now knew another of Auntie's secrets. She said, 'Rana dear, no one is able to create such beautiful work in silk.'

Rana said, 'These are stunning.'

Malek said, 'I am not so gifted, Taj *Khanoum*. You should teach Rana *jan* your craft.'

Taj *Khanoum* smiled and said, 'God willing, when Maryam recovers I'll teach Rana *jan*.' And then she picked up an embroidered cushion cover from the top of a chest that sat in the corner of the room and handed it to Rana. The embroidery on the cushion cover depicted a house on top of a hill with a brook flowing past it. Behind the house there was a tall mountain covered with trees that stretched as far as the foot of the mountain. For the most part the embroidery was done in a golden thread much finer than the rest.

Taj *Khanoum* said, 'This is for you Rana *jan*. I like this one a great deal. I made most of it with my own hair. It dates back to when I was a maiden with two long plaits on either side of my head.'

Rana was overcome by this kind offer and didn't know what to say. Malek and Auntie insisted that Taj *Khanoum* shouldn't part with the cushion cover because it was too generous a present for Rana. Maryam then had a sudden attack: she couldn't breathe and had turned blue. Youssef called to his mother. Taj *Khanoum* rushed towards her child, looking terrified. She held her head, patted her back and poured spoonfuls of a herbal concoction into her mouth. Auntie asked Rana to dissolve some powdered starch and bring it to her while Malek prepared a vapour bath. Youssef held the little girl. He held her head so that she could breathe in the steam. Maryam finally calmed down. She lay on her back and began to breathe noisily and with obvious discomfort. No one was thinking about the cushion cover any more. Everyone was sitting somewhere quietly and watching the little girl.

Malek and Auntie stayed the night with Taj *Khanoum* but Rana returned home with Rahman. On the way home, Rahman dabbed at his tears and kept murmuring a prayer. Rahman was a stocky man who came from a village but he was the most kind-hearted creature that Rana had ever met in her entire life. He was considerate towards everyone. Each morning he would place some food for the ants so that they did not go hungry. He even put food out for a mouse, just outside the hole he had discovered, rather than getting rid of the creature. He said, 'So that God's beast does not go hungry.' His actions enraged Sarvar and she complained about him, but to no avail. That was the way Rahman was. It was hard for him to see Maryam in such a state and, while he gave in to the Almighty's will over such matters, he couldn't understand it most of the time. Rana felt depressed. Rahman's tears made her feel even more miserable.

The sound of Maryam's laboured breathing still resonated in her ears. It was pointless to prepare a room for the patient; she had lost all hope of the patient ever leaving the house.

Maryam died the next day and the funeral took place soon afterwards. The whole family attended. Rahman had called upon each family member first thing in the morning and delivered the news. Vaqar attended the funeral. He murmured a prayer and left. He didn't seem much affected. Someone commented, 'He's so in control of his emotions.'

Someone else was sarcastic, 'Yes, quite in control!'

As Maryam's body was lowered into her grave, Youssef wasn't looking; his eyes were focused on his father. There was an odd look in his eyes. Rana had never seen such a hateful gaze before; it was a mix of hatred, fury and determination, and it made her shudder. Youssef then looked at her and Rana met his gaze.

After the burial everyone went to Vaqar's house. The first group arrived before Vaqar himself did. Sarvar and Rahman had come to help out. They took the tea tray around but there were no sugar cubes. Sarvar whispered to Taj *Khanoum* that she couldn't even find a sugar bowl. Taj *Khanoum* wiped her tears with the palm of her hands and said, 'He's bound to come back soon; the sugar is in the cupboard and he's got the key.'

Her face was moist with tears.

Auntie's fingers were going through the rosary beads. She was cursing quietly and then, in a whisper so that no one else heard, she asked Rana, 'Call Rahman to come over. Ask him to go and get whatever they need.'

The act of not calling a doctor, not receiving guests at the funeral and then serving them tea without sugar cost Vaqar dearly: a week later, his wife and children left the house of melancholy. Auntie masterminded it all; she reassured Youssef and Taj *Khanoum* that she would support them in any way she could. She told them not to worry about finding a home or how they would manage their lives. She promised to sort everything out. Everyone knew that when Auntie said something she meant it. The rest of the family stood behind Taj *Khanoum* as well. Their attitude towards Vaqar changed completely. Up to that point the stories of his parsimony had provided them all with some amusement, but not any more. He was a man who had made his family suffer and had brought about his own child's untimely death. No one wanted to see or even talk about Vaqar. Everyone tried to pretend that they were not blood relations; that they did not even know the man. When his wife and children left him, no one said anything. No one talked behind Taj *Khanoum's* back or wondered why she had left her husband. She simply took her children's hands and left Vaqar's home for ever.

Chapter 9

Sorting out Uncle's effects and tidying everything away took much longer than Rana had anticipated.

She spent every day in the rooms downstairs; it had not occurred to her that Uncle might have accumulated so much whilst he had lived there. She gathered up all the clothes first. This was hard; the clothes still bore his smell and made her think that he might enter the room at any moment and ask why she was ransacking his belongings. It didn't feel as though he had left their lives. Rana felt like she was waiting for him just as she had always done on those evenings after his dialysis. At such times she couldn't help but wait for him. He would come home, drink a cup of tea, eat a bit of bread and cheese, and then, once he felt revived, talk to her about the day's events; he would talk about the unstable state of the country, theft and corruption, and the danger of another war. They would chat on and on until he reached his usual conclusion, 'This place is no place to live my dear. Thank goodness my wife and child are no longer here. I am leaving as well. I am only still here because I feel sorry for you and this boy. You've become stuck here. We must all leave. I am leaving and whether you want to or not, I am going to take you with me as well. I shan't let you stay ...'

And Rana would agree and say that she'd definitely leave with him, but she knew that neither of them was going anywhere.

Uncle had placed his wife's pictures everywhere around the house. After his death, Abtin collected up as many photographs as he could find and put them away in the cupboard.

Rana looked out through the window. The sun had almost set and the street was congested with people. She didn't know anyone, not even the neighbours. The passers-by were strangers; she thought about all those people who passed by her home throughout the day, none of whom came to see her. She thought that everyone she knew had now gone. Only Abtin was left behind; only he had delayed leaving.

She now knew that people left for different reasons. Taj *Khanoum* had left her husband because she didn't want her remaining children to share in Maryam's fate. Youssef had left his father because he wanted to support his mother and brothers. If Vaqar had loved his wife and children then things wouldn't have reached such a desperate state; the story would have been completely different and, in it, Rana would not have lost the man she loved. She would have spent her life with someone who was everything she ever imagined wanting and her story would have found a happy ending, just like Zari's dreams. But Vaqar had been what he was; he poisoned everyone around him with his vengeance and hatred. He did not forgive anyone who disobeyed him and he had Satan's patience when it came to exacting his revenge.

The room that Rana had made ready for Youssef's little sister became Taj *Khanoum's* bedroom. The children and Youssef also found rooms in Auntie's house. Rana seized every opportunity to help Taj *Khanoum* and to console her, and then she spent as much as she could of her remaining time with Youssef. Youssef was quiet. Rana used any pretext she could think of to start a conversation with him and to prevent him from thinking too much. It was quite hard at the beginning; Youssef would keep changing the subject. He avoided socialising with other people and spent most of his time looking after his mother and brothers. Rana thought of the enlivening flowerbed in that depressing house and decided to make one herself to keep

Youssef engaged. She asked him to help her. The flowerbed was a good idea. Auntie allowed them to create one wherever they fancied. They chose a spot in front of the water feature, where the flowers had been withered for some time. Changing the soil in the beds, planting the bulbs and tending to the sprouting flowers kept them both busy. At first Youssef showed reluctance in the project but at some stage during the course of the ensuing days he started to go to the flowerbed enthusiastically. Rana and Youssef would spend hours working in the garden without exchanging a single word. Rana's cheeks turned red from the sun and Youssef's skin darkened. The grown-ups didn't dwell upon their relationship. Malek, who had experienced loss, shared their grief, and Auntie, for reasons known only to her, was content to see the two grow increasingly close.

Taj *Khanoum* and the children were comfortable in Auntie's house but they still felt like guests. Taj *Khanoum* was concerned about Vaqar at the beginning; she didn't know what he might do. She thought she would hear from her husband but there was no news. He didn't turn to anyone to act on his behalf and to beg his wife and children to return, nor did he send messages to them. For him it was as though they did not exist any longer. It seemed as if he was actually happy that they had left of their own accord. Perhaps he thought that a lack of money or need of shelter would force them to return eventually. After some time had elapsed, everyone reached the conclusion that Vaqar had washed his hands of his family. Many were surprised by his attitude and searched for a reason, but Auntie believed that he would not do anything because they were no longer a financial burden to him.

Their presence made Rana happy. She could now spend as much time as she wanted with Youssef; she didn't have to wait to see him any more. She saw him every day and they were together all the time. Everyone had grown used to seeing them together; even the aunties, who didn't pay much attention to the world outside their own, had almost come to accept their friendship. It seemed that the situation could continue. Everything was going well until Taj *Khanoum* announced that she was soon going to leave Auntie's house. She was tired of residing temporarily in other people's homes and wanted to arrange a proper home of her own for herself and her children. Malek and Auntie tried to convince her to stay with them but Taj *Khanoum* had made up her mind. Despite his age, Youssef was prepared to overcome any problems in order to look after his mother and brothers.

The thought of their departure perturbed Rana; she had become used to having Youssef around. Their shared grief over losing Maryam had made their friendship more profound. Now, Rana didn't wish to be far from him, even for a moment. Auntie didn't want them to leave either; ever since Taj *Khanoum* had mentioned leaving, Auntie had scowled and spent even longer in her room than before. At times Rana caught sight of *The Count of Monte Cristo* left open on Auntie's knees without being read while Auntie gazed into the far distance for long periods of time. But the situation didn't last. Zaeem suggested that Taj *Khanoum* and her family take up residence in the opposite mansion in the grounds of his own home. The mansion had once belonged to his late brother and it had spacious rooms with large windows opening onto the grounds.

No one knew whether Auntie had played a role in the proposed arrangement, but Rana knew that it was impossible for Auntie not to have been involved somewhere in the process. Zaeem's house was next door to Auntie's, which meant that they were not going very far at all. Taj *Khanoum* accepted the generous offer. Youssef then said that he wanted to go out to work, but Auntie wouldn't hear of it; she wanted Youssef to study. She had high hopes for him.

Zaeem did all he could to make Taj *Khanoum* and her family feel comfortable. Before they moved in, he undertook all the necessary repairs and sought Taj *Khanoum's* opinion about the alterations, so that everything was carried out in accordance with her wishes. When they were ready to move, everyone in

Auntie's house worked together to help, and Auntie took it upon herself to equip them with everything that they needed for their new home. Rana kept going from one house to the other, doing as much as she could to help them. Taj *Khanoum* said that the Lord had sent Rana to fill the void left by her little Maryam so that she wouldn't suffer her loss so much.

After Taj *Khanoum* and her children settled into their new home, Rana spent most of her time there. Malek started to become concerned. She asked Rana to lessen the frequency of her visits, which Rana agreed to for a couple of days before resuming her habit. She would find any excuse to go to their house or to drag them over to Auntie's house. Auntie was content. She loved Youssef immensely and didn't hide her feelings.

Taj *Khanoum* taught Rana embroidery. Rana wasn't a bad pupil but she found it hard to sit still and settle to putting her needle in and out of the material. She liked being active and preferred to follow her own path. Learning embroidery, however, was a way of spending more time with Taj *Khanoum* and Youssef.

Mrs Rassouli still came over with her bundles of embroidered material for Auntie. Blissfully unaware that Auntie was her client, Taj *Khanoum* spent most of her time creating beautifully embroidered pieces; works that brought in money to help them as a family.

But it wasn't long before Vaqar sent word that he was now prepared for Youssef to work with him so that he could earn money to support his mother and siblings. This would have meant that Youssef could not continue to study, which didn't seem a problem as far as his father was concerned. At first no one gave heed to Vaqar's offer but, one day, Youssef announced to Rana that he had to give up studying and that he was planning to accept his father's offer of a job. When Auntie heard the news she shook her head, sighed and began to think what she could do.

The next day, Auntie invited Taj *Khanoum* to her house and, with Malek in the room as well, they spoke for a while behind closed doors. They didn't allow Rana in. When they emerged, it looked from Taj *Khanoum's* eyes as though she had been crying. As she was about to leave she said, 'Please allow me to speak to him,' and then she left.

Rana tried hard to find out what had been said behind those closed doors but it was hopeless. Neither Auntie nor Malek revealed much. Youssef didn't say anything either. Rana sensed something was about to change.

A week later, Rana realised what was going on. Auntie had proposed to send Youssef abroad so that he could continue with his education and she had said that she would take care of all the expenses, both his and his family's. Youssef wouldn't accept the offer but Auntie insisted on sending him away from Iran. Rana demanded to know the reason behind such a decision, so Auntie told her, 'You're still young. You don't know Vaqar. This man was behind his own father's death. The degree of vengeance and rancour that he harbours is enough to make one shudder. Youssef needs to be as far away as possible from his father, otherwise he'll destroy his life as well. He'll destroy everyone's life.'

When Auntie made a decision, it had to be executed. Rana sat in the recess by the window in her bedroom and wept. She had lost her mother and had been so young at the time that she wasn't even able to remember her any more. She saw her father no more than three or four times a year. Zari and Maryam had both died. Youssef was the only person who held her hopes, yet he too was leaving. Youssef was going somewhere that Rana didn't know anything about; he was going to a world far away, a world that was very different to the one she lived in.

Rana's crying brought Malek to her room. Rana didn't know why everyone was so frightened of Vaqar; why even Auntie avoided him and was apprehensive about his bitterness and anger. Perhaps it wouldn't be a bad thing for Youssef to work for his father; at least it would mean that he could stay. He would eventually inherit his father's wealth. Perhaps that would be best.

Rana could be with her best friend and Taj *Khanoum*, who was still grief-stricken from the loss of one child, would not be far from the son who was her closest companion and support.

Malek lost patience with Rana's weeping and tried to console her, but couldn't. She was sitting by the window and looking outside. Malek paused and looked at her. Rana didn't turn her head.

'Rana, don't you want to have supper?' Malek asked.

'No!'

'In any case, come downstairs. Taj *Khanoum* and the children are coming to dinner tonight.'

Rana turned to her aunt, looked at her and said, 'What difference would it make whether I was there or not?'

Malek said, 'It does make a difference,' and she came closer. She encircled Rana in her arms and said, 'Don't be in a huff. Youssef must stay far away from his father.'

With a knot in her throat, Rana asked, 'Why?'

'This man will destroy his life. Just as – bless his soul – Youssef's grandfather destroyed his son, Vaqar's, life and taught him how to hate.'

Rana murmured, 'Perhaps he won't be that bad ...' but she swallowed the rest.

Malek tightened her arms around Rana and said, 'He is that bad and he will be bad for Youssef. Hatred hides in people; it grows quietly and every time it shows itself it becomes more profound. Hatred is innate and doesn't allow any love to grow.'

Rana remembered Youssef when he had looked at his father during the funeral. She had seen the hatred in his eyes; a profound hatred; hatred that she now knew he had inherited from his father; hatred that Auntie wanted to immunise Youssef against.

Rana had dinner with everyone. She didn't complain about Youssef's departure any more. But her grief wasn't diminished either. She became quiet and didn't talk much. She tried not to show how his leaving broke her heart.

Auntie arranged everything her own way. She contacted a friend who lived abroad and asked him to become a guardian to Youssef. She then summoned Vaqar one day and spent half an hour talking to him while no one else was around. And when Vaqar was leaving, she saw him out, something she never normally did. She was still leaning against her walking stick long after he had gone, as though she were looking at something in the distance.

Rana was hoping Vaqar would not give his permission for Youssef to leave the country, but that was not the case; he had given Auntie complete authority. However, no one knew what he had received in return.

Auntie was informed that an acquaintance of hers was leaving Iran with his wife and children, so she asked him to take Youssef with them. She requested that they take Youssef to the friend, who was to become the boy's guardian. Rana never imagined everything could be arranged so quickly. She didn't even have the opportunity to say goodbye to Youssef. One day Youssef was there and the next he was gone; just like that. He left in such a way that it was as though he had never been there in the first place. When he was saying goodbye to his mother he didn't mention Rana; he just left the flowerbed to her and then he was gone.

After Youssef had gone everything changed. The pace of life slowed down. Auntie spent most of her time reading and thinking. Malek rarely left the house. There was a drastic reduction in the number of people who came to visit. The house was quiet. Rana began to feel lonely and bored. The house was filled with the ghosts of those who were not there; it was filled with memories that could not be forgotten and didn't bring calm when remembered. Rana saw shadows lurking everywhere; shadows and the dark. It was as though Youssef's departure had made the sun set forever on their home ...

Chapter 10

When she opened the door she found Mahtab standing there with a box of pastries in her hands.

It was raining.

Mahtab was drenched.

Mahtab said, 'Sorry for knocking so much but I thought you weren't in. Were you sleeping?'

'No, no. I wasn't sleeping. I was sitting. Just sitting ... Come in. You're completely soaked! Come in quickly!'

Rana was right. She didn't think she had been sleeping but perhaps she had just forgotten. She certainly hadn't heard the doorbell ring. She didn't know what had compelled her to open the door. All she knew was that she had got up for no reason and felt that she had to open the door. Finding Mahtab standing there like that bothered her. It was not clear how long she had left the poor girl waiting in the rain.

Mahtab put the boxful of pastries on the kitchen table and looked for a platter. She knew where everything was. She chose a plate. She placed the pastries on it. She turned the cooker on and put the kettle on. Rana darted here and there. She didn't know what she wanted to do.

She told Mahtab, 'Don't get exhausted. Sit down. Tea's nearly ready. I had only just turned the cooker off. Sit. I'll pour tea.'

Mahtab said, 'No. You sit. I'll pour tea.'

The water in the kettle was making its usual noise as it came to the boil. Mahtab took the tray and placed a couple of glass tumblers and saucers on it. The water boiled so Mahtab poured the tea and brought it over. Rana was sitting in a comfortable chair in the sitting room and looked up at Mahtab as she approached with the tray. Mahtab was dainty and slim with large light brown eyes and soft dark brown hair. She looked like someone Rana once knew. If Malek had seen her she would definitely have said, 'This child is delicate and fragile.' She now understood why seeing Mahtab always made her anxious. Mahtab was the sort whom one couldn't tease much. They were there one moment and might not be there the next. Rana knew other people who had such an unreliable quality; those whose memory was the only thing that was left behind.

Mahtab said, 'I tried to call you a few times but you didn't pick up. I was passing by so I thought I'd drop in to see you and ask how you are.'

'I was downstairs when you knocked. I'd gone to open Uncle's windows to ventilate the room', and then Rana noticed Mahtab's blushing face, the unsettled look in her eyes, and her hands with their intertwined fingers. Mahtab was lying. Abtin must have asked her to call on his mother. Poor Mahtab; she had to put up with holding a conversation with the elderly, mad mother of the man she loved, but who didn't know what he wanted. Rana continued, 'We must change the furniture; down there it looks so worn. I have left out the items that belonged to Uncle for Abtin to remove from the house. Not to sell. No. Better to give it away. It's better that way. Perhaps someone else could make use of it all. Once it's gone you'll have enough room and then you can arrange the house however you wish.'

Mahtab said, 'It's too early for that. We have not made a decision yet.'

Rana looked at her. She had the same anxious look in her eyes that Zari had had. She was lying. It was Abtin who had not decided. He could not make up his mind. Soon he would have delayed so long that Mahtab would get fed up and leave.

Rana said, 'It would be better if the decision was made soon. It's not such a difficult one to make. Everything's ready. There's not much of Uncle's stuff left. I have placed whatever was worth keeping in Uncle's black suitcase and brought it upstairs. We'll empty the storage space downstairs as well so that you can have that too.'

Mahtab said, 'You needn't have rushed. We have plenty of time. Besides, Uncle's things wouldn't take up much room. They could have stayed downstairs.'

Mahtab was being polite and patient; she didn't want to upset anyone. But she was wrong. Those who did not wish to upset anyone often did so in the end. Rana resented not knowing what to do. She knew how such situations could end, when decisions were taken in haste – the wrong steps led to irreparable human errors.

Mahtab went on, 'I thought we could go out for a stroll this afternoon. It's such a pity that it started raining ...'

Rana said, 'Did Youssef tell you that I wasn't feeling well?'

Mahtab asked, 'Youssef?'

Feeling somewhat abashed, Rana continued, 'I meant Abtin. Did Abtin say? No doubt he's worried again.'

Mahtab said, 'No, he hasn't said anything to me.' She then got up, went around the room, and stood before the photographs on the table. She picked up Great Auntie's picture and looked at it intently. Then, turning to Rana, she said, 'She looks so like you.'

Rana visualised Malek frowning and telling Zari that Rana did not remotely resemble Great Auntie. She smiled.

Mahtab said, 'Did I say something untoward?'

Rana said, 'No, not at all.'

'But the girl in this photograph looks very much like you. Is this your Auntie Malek's picture from her youth?'

'No. It's a picture of someone who didn't have a name.'

'How could anyone not have a name?' Mahtab sounded puzzled.

'It happens. Some people end up with no name, or their names just get lost. It's a bit like knick-knacks that get lost among the larger household items.'

Mahtab forced a smile. She couldn't understand a word of what Rana was saying. 'In any case, with or without a name this looks like a picture of you,' and she placed the frame containing the photograph back on the table. She turned to Rana and said, 'Wouldn't you like to have a little haircut?'

Rana stroked her hair, which was tied back. She said, 'I can't be bothered.'

'But you need to be in good shape for Uncle's memorial service. My hairdresser ...'

'Did Youssef tell you to say that as well? He's given you many orders, hasn't he?!'

'No, no. I'm going to my hairdresser tomorrow anyway; I thought you might want to ...'

'No, love. I don't want anything.'

Mahtab was not going to stop lying today. Abtin must have told her not to let his concerns be known to his mother. But she kept saying Youssef instead of Abtin. She was making a lot of mistakes like that lately. She was not sleeping very well either; she kept waking up during the night and dozing off during the daytime. Her reveries would not give her respite; the people came and went but she could no longer decipher what was reality and what was the product of her failing mind. Yesterday – oh God, if it were truly yesterday and not any other day! It *was* yesterday; she could swear Auntie had spent the entire afternoon sitting next to her. She had repeatedly referred to Abtin as Youssef. Abtin wanted to know, just as Mahtab did, who Youssef was. Everyone wanted to know; even Rana. Perhaps even Youssef was searching to understand this as well ...

* * *

Youssef's trip dragged on. At first, he wrote regularly and his letters brought excitement to both households. In them he described the places he had been to and the people he had met. His letters were read tearfully in isolation but when read in the company of others everyone was left feeling happy, which brought much relief. But the period between the letters slowly became longer and longer until, eventually, there were no letters. After that, in the months and years that followed, news about Youssef was heard sporadically. The only thing that Rana knew for certain was that he was well, that he studied hard and that he had not encountered any major problems. Once, they heard that he had become quite unwell, but by the time they had managed to find out more about his illness, he had already recovered. The distance was just too great to foster and maintain any real intimacy.

There had been some changes in Auntie's house as well. The aunties had died one after the other and within a short space of time, as though they had struck a pact between themselves. But before they died, they whipped up one last incident. In the final days, when they were both unwell and in bed, they had begun to imagine that they had each given birth to twins; sometimes it was twins and sometimes it was quadruplets. Occasionally only one of them claimed she had mothered children and occasionally it was both. To begin with, the elder of the two imagined she had just given birth. Her conviction proved contagious so the other one also began to have the same delusion. The elder of the two had even gone as far as choosing names for her children.

The imaginary births made life complicated for Sarvar; both women were convinced – and insisted – that Sarvar had taken their babies to the village and left them in the care of a wet-nurse. They kept asking Sarvar for their babies. One day, Sarvar was so fed up with their questions that she wrapped up a couple of pitchers in swaddling and presented them to the aunties as their babies.

Sarvar's trick kept the aunties content for a few days but unfortunately, as Rahman was sweeping the room one day, one of the pitchers fell onto the floor and broke. From then on, the aunties became more agitated and increasingly unwell; they needed help with even the simplest of tasks. They were in pain, did not eat and could not sleep; they worried constantly about their babies. Finally Auntie went to them one day and reassured them that she would take the babies from Sarvar and raise them herself. The women finally calmed down.

They died shortly thereafter and within a week of each other.

Mehr seemed to spend more of her time with the dead than the living by then. Whenever she came to visit she had plenty to say about the world of the dead, yet she seemed quite unaware of what was going on around her amongst the living. Zaeem was better off now that Taj *Khanoum* and her children lived on his estate. Taj *Khanoum* took every opportunity to take care of the old man: he was rarely seen wearing worn shirts that had not been washed and he did not often leave the house with his gardening hat still on his head. But, despite the changes, he had not given up his eccentric style of dressing. He always wore his tailcoat, stripy trousers and top hat, and carried his silver-handled walking stick.

Auntie always said, 'Zaeem has at least a thousand sets of the same clothing; a thousand sets! And a thousand walking sticks that all look the same ...'

Auntie herself walked with great difficulty, the pain in her legs bothering her. Malek's hair was greyer than ever. Taj *Khanoum* had now become one of the visitors frequenting Auntie's home on a daily basis. Rana was not her old self either; she had become used to life without Youssef but it was akin to a life without dreams. It had been hard during those early months and years but eventually she had got used to it, or at least that's what she thought. She was now a maiden whose future had to be decided, although she wasn't planning to make any decisions herself quite yet. She didn't seem to favour a particular field of study and she wasn't thinking about getting married either. The suitors came and went but she didn't like any of them: one was too short and one too tall; one was boring and one couldn't sit still; one was too quiet and another so talkative that she lost her patience with him. Everyone was growing increasingly concerned. It seemed that Rana was not considering marriage at all.

'She'll soon be past her best. We need to think,' was Mehr's line of thought.

Auntie responded, 'So what if she is getting older? Let her be past her best. Perhaps she will lead a better life, a different life.'

Mehr, who was always against the idea of marriage, scowled and said, 'Surely not! She has to get married in the end. Every girl must get married in the end!'

Auntie said, 'Why? Because then what happens?'

'There's no "then".'

Malek, who wanted to remain neutral, explained, 'Auntie *Khanoum* wants to say what would happen next; would she be happy or would we still have to worry about her.'

When it came to the subject of happiness Mehr sighed and said, 'Well, she won't be happy. No one is made happy by getting married but that is no reason to stop Rana being the next, is it?' Then reverting to her usual self, Mehr continued, 'She needs to get married; otherwise we won't be able to stop people talking behind her back. Perhaps she'll get lucky and her husband will die young. And, if not – God is great – he might be sent away through his job and she won't have to see him that much.'

Zaeem, who was losing patience, said, 'How about finding her an exiled husband, Ma'am, someone who would spend his entire life away from this place?'

Mehr wasn't paying any attention to Zaeem's tone at first because she seemed to be in her own world. She responded, 'Not a bad idea. Not a bad idea at all! That way she's married but doesn't have to be bossed about.' Then, though, she continued,

'But then what would one do with his family?' She turned to Zaeem and asked, 'Do you think they are going to send them into exile with their son? That would be even better.'

'Good grief!' muttered Zaeem, not expecting such a response.

'Let's stop this,' Auntie said. 'Actually it's not the right time for Rana to get married. Let her be. Everything has to be done at the right time.'

Whenever they talked about Rana's future, Taj *Khanoum* was the only person who never said a word. She liked Rana very much and had wanted her to become her daughter-in-law, but Youssef was far away and no one knew when he would return.

Auntie didn't like anyone to talk about Rana getting married; she seemed to share Rana's views. Malek felt that Auntie made up Rana's mind for her most of the time. Youssef was the only young man with whom Auntie could find no faults. Despite his distance, she kept an eye on him; she made sure that he did not run out of money and that he stayed focused on his studies. She would not let him work; she wanted Youssef to concentrate only on studying. She said, 'He must study long and hard so that when he returns we can find him a suitable position. Then he can look after his mother without having to yield to his father's force.' She would then smile and say, 'And he can decide to marry whichever girl he likes.'

Everyone knew that as far as Auntie was concerned the girl Youssef liked most was Rana. Rana, too, had thought the same, once upon a time, but now she was not so certain.

Despite her concerns about Rana's future, Auntie still didn't want Youssef to return quite yet; she remained frightened of what Vaqar might do. Malek could not understand the basis for her fear: Vaqar had washed his hands of his wife and children. He never asked after them. When his offer of a job for Youssef had been rejected they didn't hear from him again and it was as though he was content in the knowledge that no one would ask anything more from him. Auntie, however, believed that there was more to his distant posturing. She said, 'Malek darling, the goat's waiting for the day when he can seek revenge; and he *will* take his revenge. He knows that Youssef is the light in our home and he will not rest until he has done something to harm him. We must make sure that we keep Youssef far away from him; quite far away. This is the only way.'

Malek said, 'Youssef is his son. No matter how nasty and evil he is he'd surely never harm his own child. As long as no one asks him for money everything will be fine; he's not fussed about anything else.'

Auntie would sigh at such times, rest her chin on her walking stick, and say, 'He holds Youssef accountable for his wife and children leaving. He resents him just like his own father resented him; in turn, Vaqar resented his father just as Youssef resents Vaqar. Hatred is this family's only legacy.'

'But Youssef was in the right.'

'It no longer matters who is right and who isn't. I just hope some good comes out of it all in the end.'

After these exchanges Auntie would fall silent and stare off into space with her chin still resting on her walking stick. Malek would busy herself with something and both women would pretend that they didn't have a care in the world.

The general assumption was that, until Youssef returned, Auntie would not consider marriage for Rana. But one morning, as she was coming down the stairs, she called out, 'Sarvar! Make sure the reception room is in a good state. Send Rahman shopping. We have some visitors coming this afternoon.'

Rana asked, 'Who?'

Auntie said, 'Rana darling, don't arrange any outings today. I want you to be at home.'

Rana asked again, 'Who is coming?'

'Sadeq, Shirin *Khanoum's* son; he's back in the country. They've asked if they can come and pay their respects. I've said yes.'

Malek asked, 'For Rana?'

Auntie laughed and said, 'Malek darling, I don't believe anyone would ask to call upon you or me. There's only one maiden in this house, isn't there?'

Rana scowled, 'Auntie, who on earth is Shirin *Khanoum's* son? I really don't like playing these ridiculous courting games. I don't want to be present when they come.'

'It needs many suitors to come calling before a girl can decide who to settle down with. If you keep turning them all down, it will look as though we are saying that we don't want you to get married and then they will stop coming altogether.'

'Well, we don't want me to get married, do we?'

Malek said, 'These are respectable people. Their son is quite pleasant as well; I met him before he left to go abroad and study. There is no harm in them coming to visit.'

Rana muttered, 'I wanted to go and buy some material this afternoon.'

Auntie said, 'You can do that tomorrow. Now then, go and sort yourself out rather than standing here moaning. They'll have some tea and pastries and will be off. If you don't like them no one is going to force you to get married, but don't pull faces either.'

'What about my father? He's got to be here.'

'You know that he's away,' Malek said. 'He won't be back for some time.'

'In that case they should wait for his return!'

Auntie said, 'It can't wait. In any case, no event of major significance is going to take place immediately; nothing is going to happen yet.'

Rana scowled, 'I am not going to offer anybody tea!'

Auntie smiled and said, 'Oh don't worry, Sarvar will take care of that!'

Auntie's decisions were always sudden and often took everyone by surprise, but this one was particularly strange; it was the first time that Auntie had actively encouraged someone to seek Rana's hand in marriage.

Malek seemed calm as she occupied herself with her household chores. Rana spent the rest of the day in her room brooding; she didn't even come down for lunch. Auntie was in an upbeat mood. Sarvar was more confused than anyone else.

The guests arrived around five: Shirin *Khanoum* came with her husband, Mr Atabaki, and their two daughters and their respective husbands. The first thing they mentioned was that their youngest daughter and her husband were abroad on holiday, something that came up a few times during the conversation. The last person to enter the room was a young man, who was clearly their son.

Rana whispered to Malek, 'It's more like an invasion!'

'Is it really so bad that they all wish to pay their respects?' Malek responded. 'They've dropped everything to come here and demonstrate how much you matter to them. Is there any reason why you should complain?'

When she arrived, Shirin hugged Rana and embraced her in such a way that it was as if she had found her long-lost child. Her daughters greeted Rana in a similarly pronounced manner, accentuating their pleasantries. The men were becoming impatient because they wanted to sit down. Auntie led everyone towards the reception room. The guests sat down and they exchanged more courtesies and engaged in small talk. Rana chose to sit down on a chair as far away as possible from the group and, just as she had threatened, she remained firmly seated and didn't offer round the tea tray. Sarvar brought the tea tray in and offered it round to everyone. Mr Atabaki's son, too shy to look beyond the tips of his shoes, mustered enough courage to pick up a tumbler filled with tea.

Malek glared at Rana, prompting her to get up, pick up the plate filled with pastries and offer it around the room to their guests. Mr Atabaki's son looked at Rana as he helped himself, gave her a faint smile and mumbled something that was probably a thank you, following which, Rana quickly pulled the dish away. Malek glared at Rana, which she chose to ignore and quickly carried on offering round the pastries. She then placed the plate back on the table and returned to her chair.

There was nothing wrong with Atabaki's son; he wasn't extraordinarily handsome but he wasn't bad looking either. He was well groomed but was so thin and pale that he looked as though he had just left his sickbed. He constantly looked at the tips of his shoes, leading Rana to think that his shoes must be hurting his feet. After they had gone, Auntie said that the lean look was a trait from Shirin's side of the family, but she could not come up with any explanation for his continually staring at the tips of his shoes throughout the visit. Rana put the latter down to awkwardness and an intrinsic lack of confidence.

Everyone was engaged in a conversation; conversations which were varied and unrelated. The chatting continued until Shirin turned to Auntie and Malek and said, 'I am impressed at how much Rana has grown up ... she is quite a young lady now. She looks so beautiful as well.'

'You're very kind,' Malek offered in response.

Auntie didn't say anything but glanced at Rana, and Rana was surprised at the glance because she thought, for a moment, that she saw a twinkle mixed with mischief in her eyes. She still didn't know what was going on in Auntie's mind but one thing was for certain: nothing was as simple as it appeared.

In response to a question that Rana didn't hear, Atabaki said, 'Yes, the situation is not so good. We have to see what transpires. We have to sort everything out, everything.'

Mrs Atabaki interrupted her husband. 'The most important thing is to sort out the children's future.' And then, turning towards her husband, she continued, 'Don't you think, darling?'

As though suddenly remembering why they had come over in the first place Atabaki said, 'Yes the children. Sorting out their lives takes precedence over everything else.'

'And we're here for that very purpose,' his wife continued. 'Sadeq hasn't been back long. He's completed his higher education abroad and is working now. The only matter left to deal with is to bring my last wish to fruition.' And then she sighed in such a way as if to suggest that she had waited for a thousand years to realise her wish. But Sadeq's expression made it clear that he did not share his mother's ambition. Darling Sadeq kept his head down and, rather than taking any notice of his mother's words, counted the number of flowers in the pattern on the rug.

The Atabakis' eldest daughter said, 'My brother is blessed: he has no flaws; he is quite an accomplished person; he is fully qualified; and he is engaged in a good post. He just needs a good wife from a robust background!' Her husband nodded in approval.

Malek said, 'It sounds as though, God willing, the studying is over.'

'Yes, he passed his exams with distinction as well,' was Atabaki's response. 'His college has asked him if he would stay and teach but his mother couldn't bear being so far away from him any longer and asked for him to return.'

'They were very insistent,' Mrs Atabaki offered. 'If he had stayed he would have become Dean next year. Think of it; he could have been Dean of the whole university. But he's a family-minded man with principles and he didn't like the loose morals in the West, so that's why he has returned. And now, God willing ...' and she sighed again.

Sadeq lifted his head momentarily and said, 'Not actually the Dean but it was still a good position in any case. I could have stayed but mother missed me ...'

Mrs Atabaki interrupted her son, 'Who said I missed him?' She then turned to Auntie and said, 'He did want to return.

Actually, Sadeq said that there was no way he was going to marry a shallow Western girl. He said that he wanted to marry an Iranian girl from a decent family. That's why he came back. Isn't that so, Sadeq darling?'

Like a puppet Sadeq responded, 'Yes, yes, for that reason.'

Rana asked, 'Just for that reason?!' And she was about to say something else when the doorbell rang. Sarvar walked into the room with a tray to clear the tea tumblers.

'Who was that, Sarvar?' Malek asked.

'I don't know. Rahman went to answer the door.'

Everyone stopped talking for a moment. No other visitors were expected.

In order to break the silence, Malek said, 'Rana dear, do offer round the pastries again.'

Rana got up and was about to pick up the plate when Zaeem entered. His appearance, not to mention his peculiar attire and his silver-handled walking stick, changed the atmosphere a little. The guests exchanged meaningful glances with each other but Zaeem did not take any notice. He swapped hearty greetings with everyone, following which the air in the room became awash with small talk again.

Atabaki returned the pleasantries saying, 'What a coincidence! We haven't seen you for some time.'

'Well, it's a busy life and we live far away from our friends,' Zaeem responded. He then looked at Sadeq intently and asked Atabaki, 'Your son? We were under the impression that he was still away.'

'Yes, he was; he's just returned.'

'Great! Wonderful! The last time I saw Sadeq he was a child playing in your father's house.'

Sadeq smiled.

His father was quick to say, 'That was a long time ago. Sadeq's a grown man now.'

Atabaki's eldest son-in-law nodded in agreement, saying, 'Yes, a man. A man who …' but his wife's glare meant that he stopped there.

Rana thought he had not grown that much and that thought made her laugh. Auntie glared at her and Rana swallowed her smile.

Auntie said, 'Well, Mr Zaeem. You haven't been around much recently; it is so nice to see you again!'

'Yes, forgive me. I've been busy but I visited one of the offices today and thought that I should drop by to see how everyone is, before going home. I didn't think you would have visitors and such wonderful guests as well. Tell me, Sadeq dear, what were you studying?'

'Agriculture,' was Mrs Atabaki's quick response, 'and now he's going to turn the estate in Jafarabad into outstanding gardens.'

'What a coincidence! I have a lot of experience in agriculture as well!'

Everyone knew that Zaeem's experience and knowledge of agriculture didn't extend beyond experimenting with the flowerbed in his front yard. They also knew that he liked expressing opinions on things that he knew little about. Auntie shifted her walking stick. Malek was feeling so anxious now that she kept making rapid movements to remove invisible threads from her skirt. Rana was delighted because she knew that as long as the uninvited visitor stayed in the room no one was going to discuss the issue of marriage.

'Sadeq has made a few discoveries,' was Mrs Atabaki's proud proclamation. 'They wanted to keep him at the college. The Dean sent letters expressing his concern over what would become of their gardens if Sadeq left. But my poor darling returned home because of us.'

Atabaki's eldest daughter said, 'My brother has always been successful in every field that he has chosen to pursue.'

'He was always top of his class in all subjects!' added the middle daughter.

'You know,' said Atabaki, 'however successful one is outside one's own country, one is still a foreigner. One's homeland is a different thing. My son can use his knowledge and experience on the estate in Jafarabad.'

Zaeem turned to Mr Atabaki's son and asked, 'What are you planning to do in Jafarabad?'

As though suddenly brought back to life, Sadeq responded excitedly, 'I want to create an outstanding garden. The fruit outside Iran is bred much better so if we use the new methods that I have learnt, we can make proper use of the land. Over there they graft different species of fruit and ...'

Zaeem interrupted him and said, 'Are you looking for new methods? I mean new ways of grafting?'

'Yes. We must relinquish our outdated methods. I actually did some experimental work with this very technique while I was away.'

Atabaki interrupted. 'Sadeq's become quite an expert in grafting. This is what he studied.'

Zaeem said, 'Goodness! What a coincidence! I have to tell you, Sir, that I did the very same thing a few years ago and made considerable progress with it. Quite considerable progress, actually!'

Auntie, who was clearly getting impatient with Zaeem, said, 'Where, in the garden next door?'

'Oh Madam, you do like teasing me! Obviously not!' said Zaeem good-naturedly. And then he turned to Sadeq and continued, 'In Marzanabad; on my late father's estate. Yes, we had a gardener who came from central Iran. He was a big man, very stocky. But his knowledge of gardening didn't go beyond what he had grown up with in his village. One day he would flood the garden with water and then he wouldn't water it at all for a month. One day he would feed the garden with so much compost that the leaves on the trees would wither and grow yellow. And then it would dawn on him that perhaps he shouldn't have used so much compost. Every day he would follow a different course of action but he wouldn't listen to anyone's advice.'

Auntie said, 'There are a few of them around!'

Malek cleared her throat and smiled, saying, 'Her ladyship is referring to me. Yesterday she kept reminding me to put on enough layers before going out but I didn't listen ... I think I've caught a chill as a result.'

Zaeem said, 'Do keep warm, Malek *Khanoum*. Have some mint tea. Hopefully you'll recover soon.' He then turned to Sadeq and said, 'Yes, as I was saying. So one day I decided to pull my sleeves up – as you know, I did study agriculture but I ended up working in a different field – anyway, I pulled my sleeves up and ...'

The impatient expression on the faces of Mr and Mrs Atabaki, their daughters and their sons-in-law prompted Auntie to turn to Sarvar, who was standing in the corner of the room, and say, 'Bring some more tea.'

Zaeem said, 'Yes, some tea would be great. A weak one for me please.' And then, as though oblivious to Auntie's efforts to quieten him, he continued, 'Yes, as I was saying, no matter how much the man protested, I did not take any notice of him. I said I would throw him out. Since he was frightened of losing his job, he became quiet and moved to one side. I pulled my sleeves up and got going! Sir, I grafted tomatoes to watermelon.'

'You grafted tomatoes to water melon?' Sadeq asked, looking bewildered.

'Yes! And do you know what became of it? ... I ended up with tomatoes the size of watermelons.'

Atabaki asked, 'Tomatoes the size of watermelons?!'

'It was spectacular!'

Atabaki's middle son-in-law smiled and said, 'Spectacular indeed!'

Both sons-in-law were silenced by a signal from their wives. All eyes were now on Zaeem. Clearly delighted to be the centre of attention, Zaeem said, 'But that's nothing. My mother loved jam that was made from the rind and skin of a watermelon. But the size of the watermelon often caused her difficulty. She wished it were as small and round as an orange so that she could hold it in her hand and peel it more easily. Well, she was my mother and I loved her so I decided that nothing was impossible and I grafted a watermelon to a walnut.'

'A water melon with a walnut?!' was Atabaki's son's remark.

'Of course it took a lot of thinking about but I managed to breed a watermelon the size of a walnut: small, round and cute. At first mother said, "They're too small", but then she made such a jam! Bless her; she always remembered the grafted water melon as long as she lived ...'

The Atabakis' faces were quite a sight now; they didn't know what to do. In an effort to change the subject Malek started coughing so much that Mrs Atabaki asked if she had developed whooping cough. But nothing worked; Auntie's glare, Malek's coughs, Rana's relentless giggles, the puzzled look on the guests' faces, they all just made Zaeem more determined to continue with his senseless tales.

Hoping he might be able to change the subject, Atabaki said, 'Bravo Mr Zaeem ud-Dowleh, you said it so well. No one could be as caring and loving as a mother. One has to appreciate the blessing. A mother ...' but Zaeem didn't let Atabaki finish what he wanted to say.

'A mother is of course very dear,' he continued, 'but we're talking about the importance of new methods; new ways. This country needs new ways. But this is nothing, my genius in grafting ...'

Without paying any attention to Zaeem, Auntie told Mrs Atabaki, 'Please help yourself to the fruit.'

Mrs Atabaki looked unhappy and said, 'I don't eat much fruit. My doctor advises me against it.'

Atabaki said, 'My wife feels bloated after she eats fruit. But what she cannot help eating is cucumber …' Just the word was enough to prompt Zaeem to start talking again.

'Yes, the cucumber; everyone likes it but, alas, one has to ask one's stomach to eat it. Have you ever wondered why?' And then, without waiting for a response, he went on, 'Because the cucumber is not bred properly. You may have noticed that the cucumber grows on a bush. It grows lying on the earth. If we increased its height, if we turned the bush into a tree, for example a plane tree …'

Auntie interrupted. 'Then it wouldn't be a cucumber …'

Zaeem said, 'Not at all. If you were paying attention to what I was saying, you'd see that it is quite possible. It's like the grafting of a watermelon and a walnut. I've done it myself. You see, the plane tree is just tall; it has no other qualities. But I have grafted the cucumber to a plane tree and managed to breed a cucumber tree; quite tall as well. A tall tree which had cucumber hanging from it …'

This was clearly too much and, with a nod from Malek, Rana sprang up, took Zaeem by the hand and led him outside the room. 'I'm so glad you mentioned all this,' she said, 'because I don't know what's happened to my jasmine. There are no flowers any more. You know so much about flowers and plants; you must attend to it immediately and tell me what to do …'

Though he could never resist Rana's requests, Zaeem said, 'Okay, Rana darling, but not now. Perhaps some other time but now you have guests, so it's not a good time …'

Rana ignored his pleas and continued to lead him to the door, saying, 'This is the best time. I'll forget later or I shan't find you. This is the best time. It's perfect …' and she managed to pull Zaeem away from the reception room.

Once they had left, a sudden silence descended in the room. No one knew what to say or how to react.

Mrs Atabaki was the first to break the silence. Looking irritated she said, 'Grafting of the cucumber with the plane tree! Unbelievable! What nonsense! He talks as though we're fools.'

Malek said, 'Good Heavens! Of course not! He was talking about his own experiences.'

Auntie said, 'Mr Zaeem ud-Dowleh has a habit of exaggerating a little. But this is not a bad thing. In any case, everyone's entitled to their say.'

Atabaki ignored his wife's scowl and said, 'Yes, everyone should have a say.'

Malek asked after Mrs Atabaki's youngest daughter and son-in-law, who were away. The subject of travelling and sightseeing meant that everyone had become more convivial by the time Zaeem returned to the room with Rana.

Auntie asked, 'Have you managed to sort out the problem with the jasmine, Mr Zaeem ud-Dowleh?'

'It wasn't a huge problem. In her enthusiasm to make it grow faster, Rana has just watered it too much, so I asked her not to.' And then he turned to Sadeq and continued, 'Yes, Sadeq dear, let's go back to what we were saying. We were interrupted by the jasmine. We used to have a mango tree in our garden ...'

Auntie snorted and said, 'A mango tree? Here? In Tehran?'

'No, not here; in the south,' was Zaeem's bashful response.

Atabaki couldn't contain his surprise. 'I didn't know you had also lived in the south!'

'Yes, a few years ago. But, of course, not for long ... What can one find in the south, except mango? Lime obviously. I thought of grafting lime to mango. Can you imagine, Sir, what a fruit would result from that?'

'Oh come now, Mr Zaeem ud-Dowleh!'

'I am not joking.'

Trying to proceed with caution, Sadeq suggested, 'You can't graft mango to lime.'

Clearly insulted, Zaeem asked haughtily, 'Why not? A great many things are possible in this life that may not occur to your Westernised mind, just like breeding a crab apple without a core. A crab apple is tasty but the core is annoying. I've been working on this. It won't be long now before I manage to produce a variety without a core. Do you know what that would mean? It would mean a revolution! It would mean a miracle! But the likes of you who spend time in the West, you think you know it all, but you don't know a thing! You think that whatever you were told in the West is correct. You don't know ...'

Mrs Atabaki lost her temper and said, 'He certainly knows more than you or I.'

Zaeem, who was not prepared to tolerate anyone questioning his dream of breeding a crab apple without a core, retorted, 'Perhaps more than you. Not more than me!'

The visit ended unhappily: the Atabakis were scowling, as were Auntie and Malek. The only profoundly happy person was Rana. The sisters of the groom-to-be tried to change the subject. Sarvar kept offering tea and pastries and Rana was still not prepared to lift a finger to help. She graciously sat still and ignored the scowling adults – she was laughing inside. At that point, the door opened and a young man stepped into the room; a man whom Rana thought she recognised but couldn't be sure. She could see that there was something familiar about the line of the face; something which reminded her of a little boy who used to be her playmate but who had changed a lot since then. Her playmate was now a tall grown man with a tan and straight hair that had been combed back. He wore a smile that Rana had never forgotten; a smile that revealed two neat rows of large white teeth which were bright enough to be reflected in his eyes.

Youssef had chosen the worst or perhaps the best time to make his entrance. Following his arrival, the ceremonial visit fell into disarray. The household members were so excited to see him that they lost their gracious veneer. When Rana realised who he was she let out a loud scream, which was hardly becoming for a respectable young lady with prospects of a good match. Auntie embraced Youssef and gave him a peck on the cheek that suggested she had been waiting all her life for such a moment. Malek was trying to introduce Youssef to the Atabakis when Zaeem just remembered that he had actually come over to bring news of Youssef's return. The Atabakis left looking irritated and hurt. They thought that they had been made to look like fools.

Everyone was so excited to see Youssef that no one bothered to see the guests out properly. Worst of all, Rana had completely forgotten about them and was bombarding Youssef with a barrage of questions about all the places he had been to, all the things he had encountered and all that he had done.

Youssef had arrived without prior notice. Or at least that was what Auntie kept saying afterwards. But Rana wasn't so sure; she wasn't even sure that Zaeem turning up in the middle of such a serious visit wasn't more than mere coincidence. Later on she came to the conclusion that Auntie had placed her puppets exactly where she had wanted them on her stage, just like an artful choreographer.

After he had arrived, Youssef realised that Rana had reached an age where she could make her own decisions about her future and might easily slip through his fingers. But it didn't matter. Nothing about their feelings had changed. They had arrived at a destination predetermined by fate.

Youssef's true challenge lay elsewhere and this was what Auntie most feared. Everyone so rejoiced at seeing Youssef again that they did not think of anything else beyond that moment. To them the melancholy years of separation were over. Vaqar had been consigned to the past, a forgotten past. No one thought about the vengeful old man who was sitting and lying in wait for the day when he could ambush Youssef and exact his revenge. Vaqar was not someone who could ever forgive and Youssef was not someone who was going to give in. Youssef's return signalled that the game had just begun for Vaqar.

Chapter 11

The stone prison cell was riddled with worms.

The worms were wriggling around on the floor, up the walls and even on the metal bed frame adjacent to the wall. Rana was trying to get rid of the worms but it was impossible.

She stepped out of her cell. The worms were there as well. They were strewn across the cobbled area outside. She struggled to clear a path through them. She had to find someone to help her to destroy the worms so she climbed up the stairs. Above, on the veranda, a woman was sitting behind a desk and she was jotting things down in a large accounting book. Rana approached the woman and asked her for help. She asked her if she could have permission to move to a different cell. The woman said that it was not possible.

She said that the worms had taken over the entire area, both inside and outside the cell. The woman lifted her head for a moment, glanced at Rana and suggested that using pesticides might get rid of them. If she wanted they could let her have the kit but Rana couldn't fumigate the area alone. The woman was sorry but there was no other way. Rana asked again if she could change her cell and the woman shook her head and returned to writing in the large book that lay before her. It was pointless. Rana climbed back down the stairs determined to look for another cell; she did not doubt that she could find one. This was a big place; it was surrounded by the sea and there were cobbled paths that criss-crossed one another. The cells were situated on either side of the paths, with gaps between. Everything was made of stone; the cells were made of stone just like the cobbled paths.

She picked one of the paths where there was a cell facing her. She could not see any worms there so she moved towards it until she suddenly noticed that she was very close to the sea. The waves rushed towards the cobbled path where she was standing. The big grey foaming waves broke across the path where she was and poured through the gaps between the buildings that contained the cells. The path led nowhere.

She turned away and tried to find a different route. Before her, lay a cobbled path covered by foaming waves that gushed across the stones. She didn't know where she was or which way to turn; she had lost her way. It was not possible to find a shelter in the vast stone structure and she screamed with fear but her voice was lost in the thunderous waves and amid the loneliness of the stones ...

When she woke up she still felt terrified. The stones and the cobbled paths and the cross always reminded her of Moloud. She remembered all the calamities that innocence could bring about.

Vaqar's office was situated at the end of a dark and narrow cul-de-sac. A muddy brook flowed down the middle of the narrow road and the houses on either side were so close that if two people came out of their houses at the same time from both sides of the road, it looked inevitable that they would collide. The houses didn't give the impression that they were solidly constructed; there were numerous cracks in the walls and the paint was chipped in many places. At the top of the road a wall had become so bloated from damp that one feared it might collapse at any moment. The only thing that seemed strong and stable was the cobbled road itself. The cobbles were so in harmony with their surroundings that it seemed they would still be there long after the houses had collapsed.

The only sign that there was an office was a brown worn-out wooden door, which would remain open for the clients after Vaqar's arrival. Inside, there were a dilapidated desk and a few discoloured Polish chairs, one of which was behind the desk. There was also a dark metal heater, encased in a cylindrical frame, attached to the wall over the top of a long crack, which gave the impression that it connected the heater to the ceiling. The room was dimly lit and smelt of damp. Vaqar was sitting behind his desk writing something on a piece of paper; his desk was lit by a sunbeam that penetrated through the window behind him. He placed his pen on the desk and called, 'Salman!' Moments later a waif-like boy, eleven or twelve years old, appeared at the threshold. Vaqar said, 'Where were you?!' and without giving him a chance to answer handed over an envelope to the boy. He gave him Auntie's address and instructed him to deliver the envelope immediately.

The boy's name was not Salman, but as far as Vaqar was concerned all the gophers who worked for him were called Salman. Every now and then a new boy would arrive to deal with the cleaning and with delivering items. The only thing that mattered to Vaqar was that the boys were obedient and ready to work very hard for the lowest wage. There were always families who found that their everyday expenses outstripped their income and these were Vaqar's prey. They were prepared to accept any sum of money without complaint. And he used the slightest disobedience or bother as an excuse to let his latest gopher go, because he knew that he could easily replace him with a new hungry boy; he never kept anyone for a long period of time. He said it suited him because he didn't want any nuisances or useless busybodies. He believed that when people stayed somewhere long enough their tongues would grow long. He didn't need staff and he didn't want anyone to find out what he was up to. He dealt with his own accounts and left everything else for the boy, whom he always called Salman. And those who occasionally passed by Vaqar's office knew that they would always find a new Salman each time; a little taller, or a little shorter, with green or brown eyes, dark or fair hair. But the Salman would possess the same characteristics: he was always illiterate so that he did not read the accounts or strike a deal with the clients; he was always hungry so he always worked beyond the normal hours because he was always terrified of losing his position to the next Salman.

The boy ran all the way to Auntie's house. Rahman opened the door to see a pale-looking boy, gasping for breath. As soon as he had passed on the letter to Auntie he pulled himself together and briefly told her about the state of the messenger. Auntie shook her head in disappointment and told Rahman that before he left he should take the boy to the kitchen so that he could eat something and then give him a good tip.

Auntie sat down and examined the envelope for a while. Rana and Malek had gone out to visit Taj *Khanoum* so the house was quiet. But the envelope seemed much larger than it was; it swelled in her mind like a balloon, until she could think of nothing else. She knew that Vaqar was not the sort of person who would trouble himself to write a letter for no reason.

She tore the envelope open and took the letter out. Vaqar had written the letter with the utmost care, in his uncharacteristically fine script; Vaqar's handwriting was unlike all his other attributes. The contents of the letter were unexpected as well. There were no threats, no bitterness and no poison. The hard-hearted Vaqar had disappeared and in his place there was a caring father, lonely and remorseful, who was asking Auntie to mediate and return his darling son to him. He was saying that in his remaining years he wanted to spend his fortune on his family and, since he knew they could not simply forgive him for his many errors, he wanted to demonstrate his goodwill by taking Youssef under his wing. He wanted his son to be near him so that he could learn about his father's assets and understand the details of his work. He was concerned that after his death his family would not know about a certain part of his wealth and would thus lose it. Of course, he was going to transfer the ownership of part of his assets to his family anyway but it all depended on Youssef being by his side. He could no longer bear people blaming him for what had happened. He wanted to show everyone how much he had changed; that he was a reformed character. But he needed Auntie's assistance ...

Auntie read the letter again and again. It was unbelievable that such a compassionate and kind letter had been written by the person she knew Vaqar to be. She was still pondering the letter and its contents when Rana made a noisy arrival, followed by Malek. Thinking the letter was from her father, Rana picked it up and began to read it; then Malek read the letter. The three of them were quiet for a while. Later Malek said, 'Who brought the letter?'

Auntie said sarcastically, 'Salman.'

Rana asked, 'Which Salman?'

Malek said, 'It's a long story,' then turned to Auntie and asked, 'What are you going to do?'

Auntie said, 'I don't know. I really don't know. I don't know what he's got in mind.'

Rana said, 'Perhaps nothing. Perhaps he has changed. Youssef has returned. He has studied. Maybe he just wants his son to be near him.'

Auntie said, 'Maybe.'

Malek asked again, 'What are you planning to do?'

Auntie said, 'I want to have lunch. It's time,' and then she looked at their bewildered faces and asked, 'Are you not hungry? The *muezzins* have chanted the hour as well!' She then folded the letter and put it back in its envelope, 'And it is best for this to stay there for now,' she pronounced. Then she called out, 'Sarvar! Where is lunch?'

For three days no one mentioned the letter. No one mentioned it to Taj *Khanoum* or to Youssef. It remained in its envelope and, just like that, it was forgotten about. And if Moloud *Khanoum* hadn't worried so much about saving the souls of the family members there would have been no further trouble.

Moloud came over in the afternoon on the third day after the letter had arrived. It was a quiet afternoon; they had no visitors and none were expected either. Taj *Khanoum* and the children were in their own home. Youssef had gone to attend to a task with Zaeem and they were not expected back until late. Moloud arrived unannounced. She sat down, placing her heavy black patent-leather handbag on the adjacent chair; the heavy bag was in contrast to her fine wrist. She looked at Auntie anxiously and sighed, 'I never expected such a thing from you, Ma'am.'

Auntie, who always took what Moloud said with a pinch of salt, casually turned to her and asked, 'What's wrong?'

'Jesus Christ says love thy neighbour. Forgive them their trespasses. Christ was merciful; he said, "Let any one of you who is without sin be the first to throw a stone." "The lost sheep will return to the herd." "We must love them and forgive them." You want to tell me that you have forgotten the story of the lost sheep?'

Rana and Malek were surprised to find Moloud there and were anxious because they couldn't understand what she was saying. But Auntie, who seemed to have understood, looked at this fine-featured woman who insisted on saving the world and shook her head, saying, 'Moloud *Khanoum,* I follow the Prophet Muhammad. He doesn't say that one must forgive with impunity.'

'Don't say that. God's messengers came to forgive, to save the lost souls, to guide people, to spread mercy and compassion, to ...'

Auntie didn't let Moloud finish. 'Why have you come? What's happened? What are you so worried about?'

'I never expected you to adopt such an attitude. I didn't think that you would obstruct the righteous remorse of a broken-hearted old man who seeks forgiveness.'

'And you believe him?'

'Of course I do.' And she put her hand in her handbag and took out a bundle of banknotes, before continuing, 'Look! He has given these to me to help the orphans. The Lord's light has enlightened his soul. When he was giving me this money he was crying. Tears were running down his cheeks and, believe me, believe me, I saw Jesus Christ in every drop of his tears. I saw ...'

Rana couldn't bear it any longer and, quite unusually, interrupted Moloud, asking, 'Who? Who was crying? Who has remorse?'

Before Moloud could respond, Auntie said, 'If I am not mistaken, the remorseful person you are talking about is Vaqar us-Saltaneh. And with all this money that he has given away it is as though he has committed suicide rather than shown remorse.' She turned to Moloud. 'Is that not so?'

Surprised that Auntie had read her mind, Moloud said, 'Yes. Yes, the very man. The poor man doesn't want anything but forgiveness. And Jesus Christ says one must ...'

Malek interrupted her. 'You mean to say that it was him who came to you?'

'He came this very afternoon. He said that he had sent you a note but that he had not received a response. You have no idea how he felt. He bitterly regrets everything.'

Auntie said, 'So he gave you money and he was remorseful. That's very strange; some miracle, surely.'

'The world is full of God's miracles. Every day a sinful servant begins to walk on the right path. I beg of you to help this lost and separated lamb so that he can rejoin the righteous herd.'

'Well, I don't know about lamb, dear Moloud *Khanoum*! Of course there's no objection to him joining a herd. There are a great many herds. No doubt he already belongs to a herd.'

Moloud, who failed to appreciate the humour, said, 'Yes, remorseful is God's lamb indeed, and he must be allowed to remain among the righteous. And even though he has been most sinful he must now be forgiven.'

'Suppose this old bull has become a lamb and been forgiven. What then? What does he want?'

'His son; he wants his son. He wants his family back.'

'What is he prepared to give in return?'

Malek asked, 'Don't you think, dear Moloud *Khanoum*, that this change of heart is unimaginable for someone like Vaqar us-Saltaneh?'

'No, it's not really. Miracles do take place every day. God's light has shone in this man's dark heart and awakened him.'

Auntie said, 'Are you sure this is God's light and not the light emanating from a kerosene lamp conjuring a new trickery?'

Moloud, who seemed vexed, now said, 'You've become weak in your beliefs. Suspicion has darkened your heart. One must ...'

Auntie mumbled, 'I have to get hold of a kerosene lamp.'

Moloud, who didn't catch what she meant, said, 'What do you need to get?'

Malek said, 'She must open Hafez's lyrics and see what he has to say about her fortune ... you do know that Auntie seeks Hafez's opinion at such times!'

Auntie's face broke into a smile. She raised her eyebrows slightly and looked at Malek good-naturedly, then told Moloud, 'What do you expect us to do? Actually this does not concern me at all, does it? It wasn't me who asked him to drive his wife and children to the edge, was it?'

'Of course it wasn't. But you, only you could encourage Youssef to go to his father's office and to work with him.'

'Work with him so that he can name him Salman.'

Moloud was surprised and said, 'No, he didn't talk about a change of name. He just said he wanted his son to be with him.'

Malek said, 'Dear Moloud *Khanoum*, how could you ask Youssef to go and work in his father's office? Don't you know what his father's job is?'

'Yes I do. He's a businessman.'

Auntie said, 'The business of people's blood.'

'What do you mean?'

Malek said, 'It means he lends people money and charges them a high interest. How could Youssef work with such a man?'

'Don't say that. People make up stories about him.' Moloud pointed to the bundle of banknotes and went on to say, 'Which money-grabbing man helps the orphans? No! Vaqar us-Saltaneh is a good human being who has developed a bad name because of his terrible temperament. And in any case, I don't know anyone in this family who has such a superior job to offer that Youssef should be so dismissive of his father's invitation.'

Auntie said, 'There's always a first time in every job,' and then, as though tired of the fruitless discussion, she sighed and said, 'Allow me to talk with Taj *Khanoum* and Youssef. Let them decide. They are hardly children. They need to decide for themselves.'

'So do I take it that you'll help?'

'Yes; certainly, anything. Just let me speak with them. Perhaps they will comply but with certain conditions.' She then pointed to the platter of pastries and said, 'Take a baklava. Rana has made these. They are superb.'

Rana, who didn't know how to make pastries, gave Auntie a bewildered look. Auntie smiled and said, 'Don't be shy. You don't have to be so secretive.' Then she turned to Moloud, saying, 'Rana makes wonderful pastries, just like Malek *Khanoum's* mother.'

Moloud chewed the baklava she had in her mouth with delight and then swallowed, saying, 'Rana darling, this is delicious. You must give me the recipe.'

Rana looked at Auntie furiously but she had to keep Moloud engaged, chatting about friends and family so that she did not ask about the baklava any more. And at least the tale of rescuing the lost lamb was never mentioned again.

However, the most innocent among them had opened the door to the worst monster, the monster of forgiveness, forgiveness for a spirit that had no purpose other than destruction.

Chapter 12

The small green plastic tree, with its dated decoration, was a lamentable sight. Rana didn't know what to do with it; should she throw it away or leave it in storage as a memento? Uncle had bought the tree for Abtin and from then on it had sat on the small table in Abtin's room. To begin with it had been covered with glitter but it had slowly lost its magnificence and it now resembled a dry Christmas tree in a forgotten forest. Still, no one could touch it while Uncle had been alive. He referred to it as Moloud *Khanoum's* tree. The small tree had remained in its place during the past year, even though Uncle was long gone, and every time Rana went to throw it away it felt as though Uncle had appeared before her and was sorrowfully shaking his head saying isn't it a pity? And Rana would change her mind. Moloud *Khanoum's* tree sat in the corner of the room and waited for a Christmas that was not supposed to arrive.

Moloud loved Christmas and observed it to the full: she decorated a tree, placed presents under it, offered pastries and confectionery to her visitors, and served a light supper for those who stayed on into the evening. She didn't have any children of her own and her husband had passed away many years before so Auntie always made sure that the whole family went to visit her so that she did not feel lonely during her most beloved celebration. In a way, because of Moloud, Christmas had come to be a much-respected part of family tradition.

It took Rana some time to get used to Moloud's Christmases. Her Christmas tree was small and modest; every year, she would take the decorations out of a chest and then return them back there at the end of the festivities. The tree and its decorations became more and more jaded every year: the gold trim of the angels' wings and gowns had faded in many places; the silk-covered baubles had threads of different lengths hanging from them; the edge of Santa's walking stick was chipped; the star that sat on the tree top had lost its shine. The presents didn't look too enticing either; there were always rubbers, pencils and notebooks wrapped up in wrinkled paper with drawings depicting biblical scenes featuring Christ and his disciples which had to be coloured in. The pastries and other food were not much better either. For some time, and in order to avoid exotic food, Moloud had omitted sugar, salt and fat from her diet and she imposed the same constraints on her guests.

At her guests' insistence, she would always sit at the piano and play festive tunes. Her fingers were rigid due to her arthritis so it took a lot of effort and time for her to press each key. For this reason Rana never recognised the tune she was playing. What she did play was a collection of disconnected and haphazard notes. Every note would resonate in the space left by the previous note falling silent. But when she stopped playing she would turn to her guests and, with a gentle smile, she would apologise for not being able to play well, as though she were a skilful musician who, despite utmost modesty, was aware of her gift. Auntie encouraged her more than anyone else and Rana had learnt, early on, that praising Moloud for her piano playing was an important part of the occasion, a ritual that had to be observed.

Years later, when Rana remembered Moloud's piano playing, it reminded her of putting up with eating a particular food that one disliked just to avoid offending a kind host. But now she knew the name of the tune; the tune that she had played was the music of affection turned to nightmare and one that made everyone succumb to chaos in an atmosphere filled with apprehension.

It was the dream of a music that did not exist and Moloud's fingers had scattered its notes in space.

Following Moloud's intervention it was no longer possible to keep Vaqar's request from his wife and children. Auntie went to pay Taj *Khanoum* and Youssef a visit first thing the next day and explained everything; she told them about the letter, about the regret it expressed and about Moloud's mediation on Vaqar's behalf. When she had finished talking, no one spoke for a few moments. It was as though everyone had stopped breathing. Youssef finally broke the silence. He said, 'Perhaps I ought to go and see him.' His tone didn't sound like that of a lost soul but rather that of a sacrificial lamb.

Taj *Khanoum* said, 'No, I shan't let you.'

'Perhaps he has truly changed?' Youssef persisted.

'I don't think so,' said Auntie.

Rana said, 'So what is to be done?'

'In my opinion,' declared Auntie, 'we must forget about the whole business and pretend that it never happened.'

Malek said, 'What if he genuinely means well?'

'Impossible,' said Taj *Khanoum*.

The discussions continued. Youssef believed reconciliation with his father could ameliorate the family's financial situation. His mother would not have to see his father; it would only be himself and the children who would visit him from time to time. Malek, for whom appearances mattered a great deal, pondered the idea of reconciliation; certainly the dust would settle as far as the rumours were concerned. Youssef was a savvy and experienced young man and he would not have to spend long with his father either. But Taj *Khanoum* declared that she feared

Vaqar more than Satan himself and that she did not want her sons to deal with him under any circumstances, no matter what degree of wealth it might yield.

Auntie concluded, 'Taj *Khanoum* has expressed it so well; Vaqar us-Saltaneh is more terrifying than Satan himself. Do you know what the best way is to deal with Satan? ... Evasion! One must never enter into any direct dealings with Satan. We'll forget about him.'

And that was what happened. They forgot about Vaqar's proposal. But Satan has a fearsome memory. He stores Man's every flaw in his memory and keeps it there, ready for the day when he will go off to hunt; hunt for the fresh souls of the innocent and the optimistic.

Despite the undesirable developments during their bride-seeking visit, the Atabakis did not give up; they kept sending messages hoping for a positive response. But they kept being told that the girl's family was not yet ready to commit to a betrothal and needed more time to reflect. The tale of the afternoon when the Atabakis had come to seek Rana's hand in marriage, and Zaeem had arrived and made his extraordinary claims of success in the field of agriculture, fed many an afternoon tea and evening dinner for some time afterwards. But Auntie didn't believe that they should put the prospect of such a match out of their minds completely quite yet. Rana had to make up her mind; good people deserved to know whether they were coming or going. Whenever they got together as a family, and particularly when Youssef was present, Auntie would remind Rana that the Atabakis still needed a response. Youssef would remain quiet at such times, while Taj *Khanoum* gave him anxious but hopeful glances. Rana would change the subject by injecting humour into the situation and Auntie would emphasise that a response must be given, although it was not clear who she was addressing: the Atabakis or the individuals around her who lived in a state of confusion?

Youssef was Rana's dream. The intense light that held her gaze wouldn't let any other man's image remain in her mind. Atabaki's son was no less a rival to Youssef for Rana's affections but, in her mind, he was just an outline, a briefly drawn outline that could never be the start of a beautiful piece of work – he was just a sketch that one could tear apart and throw away. The permanent and flawless image that Rana harboured in her mind belonged to Youssef and Youssef remained silent.

In the end, on a day when everyone was present, Auntie laid the law down: Rana needed to grow up and give the Atabakis an answer. Rana scowled and said that her answer was clear but Auntie emphasised that a girl could not stay in her home for ever. Rana needed to make a decision about who to marry sooner or later, but she didn't say who she had to decide upon. When she spoke, she looked at Youssef, who was trying to avoid Auntie's watchful eyes.

Auntie's stance did the trick: Taj *Khanoum* made an eager visit to Auntie and Malek the next day and said that Youssef wished to marry Rana. She said that he had discussed the matter with her the night before. However, she also said that his unfortunate financial circumstances and uncertain future were a matter of concern. As far as Auntie was concerned there was no need for concern; she would soon find Youssef a suitable job. She was certain that he was a responsible fellow and, in the meantime, she would support them both. Malek, who was well aware of Rana's feelings for Youssef, could not contain herself; she was thrilled at the match.

Rana learnt the news later than everyone else. Although she had long been waiting anxiously for such a moment, she didn't rejoice. Something was not right; if Youssef was really earnest in his intentions, he would have spoken to her personally. She knew that Youssef was quite apprehensive about getting married; he had said on a number of occasions that his parents' life had taught him that marriage yielded nothing but misery.

Youssef was frightened of something that seemed absurd to most people; he was frightened of becoming a family man and then slowly turning into his own father – cruel, dominant and scheming. Without an alternative image of his father to consider, he was frightened that one day he would look in the mirror and see his father, an unbearable creature who had brought misery and ruin with him. And what could he do when that happened? What would become of the lives that depended on him? At such times, Rana tried to reassure Youssef that there were no similarities between him and his father, and Youssef would nod his head and fall silent but remain unconvinced.

The others were unaware of the young people's concerns and began to make arrangements for the wedding. First, they sent a message to Nasrullah, who was away travelling. Nasrullah responded that he couldn't get involved for now but said that he considered the match auspicious and that it was generally the ladies that had to be in agreement over the arrangements. Thus, he gave his permission for them to continue organising everything until he arrived back home. There were a number of issues to be dealt with. The bride and groom knew each other and both families were already well acquainted so the engagement was only celebrated privately. It was decided that there should not be much delay between the engagement and the wedding. Mrs Rassouli was given the task of making the wedding gown, which was to be made from white silk and have a long train that swept the floor. Zaeem assisted as enthusiastically as if it were his own son getting married and took care of sending out the invitation cards.

Mehr had been finding it increasingly difficult to get around because of her asthma but when she heard the news she managed to get to Auntie's house, where she announced that she had discussed the event with all the dead relatives and that each of them was pleased with the match. Auntie said, 'Thank goodness that we have the blessing of the dead as well,' and Mehr pointed out that, in general, marriage had to be discussed with the dead. Everyone nodded in agreement and smiled out of politeness, and Mrs Rassouli, who was busy putting the finishing touches to Rana's gown, struggled to control her laughter and, in the process, pierced her finger with the needle and stained the skirt with a large drop of blood.

Malek was troubled by the blood stain. For a moment she remembered Auntie's red hair and her bewildered expression. Auntie consoled her and told her not to be so superstitious; the stain could be removed with a little cold water. But Malek remembered Auntie's tears during Marjan's wedding and became so anxious that she had to excuse herself and leave the room, only returning once she had calmed down.

Malek's anxiety was not unfounded. The next day Moloud, who had been missing for a while, called round. Her small diamond earrings set in their gold frame were dangling from her ears. She was smiling as usual but there was a deep sorrow in her kind eyes. She said that she had heard the auspicious news and that although they had ignored her request for Youssef to visit his father – made in good faith – she now really wanted Youssef to pay his father a visit and tell him about the wedding. As far as Moloud was concerned this was a modest request from a father who visited her once or twice a week looking depressed and asking after his family. Moloud said God was merciful and his servants should practise that same forgiveness. This time Moloud's meddlesome innocence won the day: everyone, even Youssef and Taj *Khanoum*, agreed that Youssef should call upon his father and that doing so would not cause any problems. Youssef didn't want anything from him. He was just going to give him the wedding news. Malek said that, in any case, Vaqar's participation in the wedding reception would stop the rumours. It was only Auntie who maintained her silence: she did not agree or disagree with the planned course of action. She kept quiet and it was decided that Youssef should pay his father a visit at the first opportunity.

Chapter 13

Rana had now put everything that had belonged to Uncle in one place.

She still had three more days, which gave her time to think about which items she wanted to send to storage and which to give away. Before anything, though, she returned Uncle's unused medicine to the dialysis department for other patients to use. She forgot to mention that they shouldn't tell the patients whose medicine they were using – learning that they were taking medicine that had not been effective for another patient wouldn't be welcome news, particularly if the patient had previously undergone treatment with it three times a week. Uncle had been the same: the death of every dialysis patient caused him to question the efficacy of his own treatment.

Giving away the unwanted items was the most difficult part. When someone departs, he leaves behind every ounce of himself in his belongings. Giving away any item was like throwing away a part of him. And this was very much the case with Uncle, whose entire life could fit in a suitcase. Rana couldn't even bring herself to throw away Uncle's old socks; socks that had covered his feet throughout his abortive search for happiness. So she patiently placed the bric-à-brac in a suitcase and decided to put the suitcase into storage and to let Abtin decide later how to deal with it all.

Rana had to speak with Mahtab to tell her to encourage Abtin to make a decision soon about the wedding. There was a lot to arrange: Mahtab had to buy a wedding dress; she had to choose a ring and necklace; they had to send out invitations to their friends. But before anything else, they first had to choose a date; they had to find an auspicious date for the wedding; a date that would promise future happiness for the young couple. But did an auspicious date really exist for a wedding?

Choosing a date for the wedding was more time-consuming than anything else. One auspicious date was too close and they couldn't arrange everything in time. The next was too far into the future and the wedding would be much delayed. They also had to wait for Nasrullah, whose return date was not clear.

Preparing a home for the bride and groom was the other time-consuming task that had to be dealt with before the wedding. Zaeem insisted that a part of his home should be allocated for the purpose but Auntie wouldn't agree. Auntie's home had three gardens and she had already chosen the building in the middle garden for the bride and the groom. They would live there for now and, once everyone realised that Auntie was not prepared to compromise, the decorators were called in and a new kitchen was commissioned.

Rahman had to oversee the work, which meant that the poor man spent the entire day, from dawn till dusk, standing around in the dust. While the renovation work took place Sarvar had more mouths to feed, which made her so busy that she did not have time to grumble. But it looked as though she had no intention of doing so anyway; she seemed quite happy, for the first time in years. Auntie said pleasantly, 'Sarvar would sacrifice everything for the course of true love,' and Sarvar beamed and blushed, making the wrinkles on her face more visible, and said, 'I just remember Seyed's song. He had such a voice! ... What a voice!'

Sarvar had fallen in love with Seyed's voice. Seyed called everyone to pray each morning in their village and Sarvar, who had been a young girl then, with long plaits and no wrinkles on her face, would use the pretext of sweeping the yard so that she could leave the house and listen to him chant. Sarvar had fallen in love with Seyed and their love endured a marriage. But the duration of their happiness was short. Seyed went out to the woods on a snowy day to gather logs and never came back. Sarvar waited a long time for his return. The people in the village speculated about what might have happened; the general belief was that he had fallen prey to a wolf or a bear. The woods were near the border and there had been a rumour that foreign soldiers had dragged him across the border. Some said Seyed had been injured and, suffering from hypothermia, been rescued by foreign soldiers. Years later, after he had been presumed dead, there had been reports from people who had seen a man across the border who looked just like Seyed. The man's dark skin stood out among the rest of the people, who were of fair complexion; they said he was a man who had forgotten his identity and just wandered around aimlessly. Soldiers told the tale of the wandering man, but they could not understand a word that the soldiers said because the 'colourless' soldiers spoke the language of *jinns*; a language that no one understood. All these tales, though, only caused more anguish for Sarvar. Sarvar hated blond and pale people and would still go outside first thing in the morning, hoping she would hear Seyed's call to prayers. The dawn and its cool breeze brought the sound of Seyed's chanting to Sarvar. Finally, in order to escape the dawns and Seyed's chanting, she went to live in Auntie's house.

And now it was perhaps the first time in years that love had come knocking on the door again. Although Sarvar knew that Miss Rana loved Master Youssef she was perpetually concerned and melancholy about it. She saw something in Youssef that reminded her of Seyed; perhaps it was his docile nature or his silence or his kind smiles. Whatever it was, it bothered her; such people, those who led a peaceful existence by your side, could one day leave you just as suddenly as they had arrived. Then it wouldn't matter whether wolves had taken them or foreign soldiers whose language you couldn't understand. What mattered was that you would lose them; just that; and even the dawn wouldn't bring back their chanting. When Sarvar thought about these things her eyes filled up with tears and she started to rub the silverware she was preparing for the wedding so hard that if it had been porcelain it would have broken into pieces, and if it had been material it would have torn.

The preparations for the wedding were endless and the cost was astronomical. Although Auntie had kindly agreed to absorb the expenses, it didn't stop Youssef feeling embarrassed. He saw his mother doing her embroidery until the small hours, in an effort to earn a living and he knew that he was still not in a position to earn a wage. He knew he could not build an appropriate life for a girl like Rana. Perhaps that was why he arrived one day and announced that he was thinking of going to see his father. Everyone went quiet at the declaration. They knew that Youssef had to see Vaqar; he had promised Moloud that he would. What danger could there be in that? Vaqar was a helpless old man who said that he wanted to compensate for his evil deeds – no one but Moloud really believed the lie but they had to give him a chance. Up to that point Youssef had used any excuse to avoid making the visit. Now, however, with the wedding date fast approaching, he had to go and see him and at least deliver an invitation to him in person.

Youssef left one day, just as Seyed had gone off to collect logs all those years ago. It was always the way; cold and snowy days prompted one to do things that were long overdue and resulted in one either falling prey to the wolves or spending the rest of one's life wandering through foreign lands, among people whose language was unknown.

Sarvar remained in her room for an hour before the late afternoon prayers started and fervently prayed.

Chapter 14

Rana found Uncle's wedding invitation amid the pages of the book of Hafez lyrics.

Uncle had never parted with his Hafez. It had always been by his bedside even though he seldom opened it. Rana, however, had managed to find out why a man who did not like poetry much never parted with his copy of Hafez. On the now-yellowish invite the gilt outline of a bride and groom was still visible, the two of them standing side by side and with their bodies slanted as though responding to a gentle breeze. On the back of the invite she recognised her aunt's slightly childish script, *always together in all dreams,* and she had been right: she was with Uncle in all the dreams though not in real life.

Auntie said, 'Whatever you want is within your grasp. Sometimes you just need to look carefully before you can find it.' And once, when Rana got stuck trying to solve a maths problem, Auntie had told her, 'Every problem has a solution. Keep reading the problem until you find the solution.' Rana had believed what Auntie had said and, since then, her life had become a search for happiness. She continually reviewed her problems in her quest to find solutions. At a time when she could find no reason to live; when she had become stuck and unable to find a solution to the simplest of problems, no matter how hard she tried, she still repeated her mantra. *Every problem has a solution.*

She found Abtin at a time when she could not go on living. She had lost purpose and hard as she tried she was stuck, even when it came to the simple issues in her life. There was a hospital near Rana's house. There was a gap between the hospital's walls and the house next door, over which the slate roof of the house extended, as though roofing the gap. The homeless adopted the protected space as a temporary shelter. It was a kind of nest; a nest for the doves that had been left behind in winter. For a while a man afflicted with leprosy sheltered in the gap. He slept and begged from there. But the man had died some time ago and no one else had taken shelter there since. As people approached the spot, which they called the leprosy house, they hastened their pace as though frightened that a frail hand might reach out to them or that they might hear someone moaning for help. Rana, too, walked past the gap quickly but one night, when it was cold and had been snowing, she was returning home from a dinner when a car's headlight had shone into the gap and revealed a small and knotted body. At first she thought she had seen a stray dog that had sought refuge there because of the cold. But as she got closer she identified a small head hiding amid a pair of twisted arms and legs. She always shuddered at the thought of what might have happened had it not been for the car lights passing the house of leprosy at the same time as she had. One wouldn't normally look into every nook and cranny in search of the forgotten or those afflicted by leprosy. And perhaps it was better that way because one could not give shelter to all the lost souls.

Rana had bent over what looked like a small ball. In the dark she couldn't see it very well. She called to it but instead of a verbal response she heard a moan. She stretched out her arm and the human ball recoiled. It was a child; a toddler. Without thinking about the consequences, Rana stretched out both arms and picked up the child. She covered the body with the corner of her coat and took the child straight to the hospital.

Inside the hospital the nurses responded to her calls for help and it was in the dim lighting there that she first saw his face. It was blue from the cold, and when the doctor arrived and removed the child's clothes, Rana saw a bruised and bloody body. The child was still in the hospital when they informed the police. No one had reported a lost child. Rana visited the child every day until, finally, she felt that she couldn't let him go. She adopted the child and became the mother of a boy that no one wanted.

Abtin knew that he wasn't Rana's biological child but he didn't know the real background story. Rana had told him that she had found him amongst the injured at a hospital following a terrible earthquake which had killed his parents. She didn't want Abtin to find out that he had been left to die on a cold winter's night. She didn't want to fill his heart with hatred for parents whom he did not know. She knew what hatred did to people. If she told Abtin the true story now, her son would put it down to the delusion that her illness had brought about. The thought made her smile. Whatever problems resulted from her illness, it had the advantage that she could shield her son from the tragic truth for ever. Rana feared the truth. She was always terrified of it. It was the truth that had made her life with Youssef evaporate, the truth about a hatred that arose from the depths of time; the hatred felt by all sons whose fathers had left them out on cold nights to die; historical hatred where the reason had been lost in the sands of time; silly hatred which caused unavoidable suffering. It was good not to know that they had left you to die because you could live and love without allowing the past to destroy your future in its entirety. But no one gave Youssef the opportunity to forget. The wedding was a pretext to remember the hatred, and its recall brought nothing but destruction in its wake.

Before going to his father, Youssef called upon Auntie first thing that morning. They spoke in private for some time. Auntie didn't allow Rana to be present. Rana scowled. She went up the stairs scowling and remained in her room until their meeting was over. But it was fruitless and, in any case, it was not her place to say anything. After the conversation was over, when Youssef was leaving, Auntie called Rana to come and say goodbye.

Moloud was there as well. In fact it was she who had promised to bring Vaqar his son, and now she had to be there during the first encounter between father and son to orchestrate the reconciliation between them. Moloud had been in Auntie's house all morning. When Rana came down the stairs Moloud was sitting on a Polish chair. Her small feet were suspended in the air. Her head was tilted to one side and she had her eyes closed; from between her half-closed lips there came the hiss of her noisy breathing.

Auntie looked at Moloud and mumbled, 'The sleeping angel!'

Malek touched Moloud's shoulder gently and called, 'Moloud *Khanoum* ... Moloud ...'

She didn't have to call her a second time. Moloud opened her eyes, smiled, sat up straight, and then, while trying to climb out of the chair, turned to Youssef and asked, 'Shall we go?'

Auntie said, 'Do! It's getting late.'

As Youssef was setting off to see his father, his expression was that of a soldier who was going to the battlefield; his face looked harsh and drawn. He gave Rana a wan smile at the door, which bore no sign of happiness. The rest of them didn't feel any better than he looked. Even Auntie, who saw Youssef off, made him pass under the Qur'an to receive blessing and protection.

Those who passed them in the street saw a tall young man walking alongside a short ageing woman who barely reached the young man's waist; the woman's left foot dragged behind her slightly, her gold encased diamond earrings dangled from her ears and she wore a sincere smile on her face. The innocent picture of a matinée stroll bore no relation to the serious business awaiting the young man and the ageing woman at their final destination.

After they had left, Auntie returned to the sitting room. She sat in her usual place, rested her chin against her walking stick and started thinking.

Malek asked, 'Are you worried?'

Auntie looked at Malek and said, 'Shouldn't I be?'

'Perhaps it's not important,' said Malek. 'It's just a visit.'

Auntie sighed and repeated, 'Just a visit!'

'Perhaps he is truly remorseful. Perhaps he really wants to make amends for his bad behaviour.'

'Only the simple-minded Moloud believes such nonsense. I don't believe it for one moment and Taj *Khanoum* doesn't either.'

Malek said, 'Perhaps he wants to change the way he lives.' And when she encountered Auntie's glare, she went on, 'Don't be so hard. There can't be any other reason for seeing Youssef.'

'Yes there is. He has, no doubt, heard about the wedding. He wants to find out what's going on here.'

Malek hesitated and stared at Auntie. 'What purpose would it serve?'

'If you don't know what your enemy is doing how can you plan to defeat him?'

'You're so hard.'

'Vaqar us-Saltaneh hates Nasrullah Khan. It is impossible for him to allow his son to marry his enemy's daughter.'

Malek said anxiously, 'He's not in charge of Youssef. He can't do anything.'

Auntie nodded her head, 'You'll realise one day that he's been in charge of all of us. You don't know the man, Malek darling. He has always managed to take his revenge on anyone he has held a grudge against.'

'But Nasrullah Khan doesn't concern himself with the man. He won't cause any problems for him.'

'Nasrullah Khan has always been contemptuous towards him.'

'Perhaps he's forgotten that now.'

'Vaqar us-Saltaneh doesn't forget ... and he won't let us forget either.'

Malek mumbled, 'God help us in that case ...'

Auntie was quiet, rested her chin on her walking stick and focused on the far distance.

Auntie sat there until lunch time and didn't turn a single page in *The Count of Monte Cristo*.

Chapter 15

The young Russian sailor saw death in the sea.

Late one afternoon as he leaned against the ship's railings and was bending towards the water, he saw it: the mournful and deformed face of a drowned man beneath the surface of the water. The red light of sunset was reflected in the sunken eyes, and the movement of the waves made his mouth look like it was open in an ugly sneer. The eyes were staring at him from the depths of death and the young sailor knew that this was the end. The older sailor had said that whoever sees the face of a drowned man will meet an untimely death. He had to leave the sea, otherwise he would leave with the water, only to return one day as a warning sign to other sailors.

He looked away once the sun had set fully – it was dark and the red flame in the dead man's eyes was extinguished.

The young officer went to the mess. He did not go back onto the deck until the next day. For the rest of the journey he did not look into the sea from the railings, and every day, in the late afternoon, he would lock himself in his cabin. When they reached the next harbour he took his bag and alighted onto dry land. He took refuge in a country where he did not know the language of its people – he had fled the ship where his compatriots were.

The young sailor remained in the harbour. Slowly he put the idea of returning to his country out of his mind. In order to return he would have to cross the seas, and to cross the seas meant he would have to face the drowned man, and he knew that he would not survive seeing him a second time.

The young officer remained there and grew old, and the fear of crossing the seas swallowed all his dreams.

Nasrullah, Rana's father, had once told her the story; he had heard it from the Russian naval officer in person. He said that when he was telling his story one could still see the fear on the naval officer's face. Rana had asked about the fate of the man. Did he have a fiancée in his home country? Was there a mother, a sister, a father or a brother? Was there anyone waiting for his return?

Nasrullah had shrugged at the questions, saying that the sailor was left only with fear; fear turned into his fiancée, mother, sister, father and brother; fear turned into his country and into the grave. Nasrullah Khan had said that if one allows fear to take a hold then one is just as dead on land as if one had been drowned at sea ...

He had said all this to Rana but he had not mentioned anything about the moment when one looks into a dead man's eyes. Nasrullah had always ruled his own destiny and had never seen a drowned man's face in the waters of any sea and knew nothing of destiny's warnings ...

For a while, Youssef stood silently before the man whom he had once called father. Vaqar's dark and sunken eyes were staring back at him, also in silence, but there was a smile on his face which resembled a sneer. The face confronting Youssef had deep lines and was more haggard than he remembered, but although his visage was cold and showed no feeling, the rapacity of the face had not diminished. However, the chill that Youssef had always felt in his presence remained; it was a chill that penetrated deep into one's body even on the hottest days of summer. It was this chill that stopped Youssef from stepping across the threshold; it was as though all his toes and fingers had frozen, rendering him unable to move.

Moloud, however, did not feel the chill: although she was tired from the journey, she went through the door looking cheerful. She entered Vaqar's office and sat on the first chair she saw. Youssef had no choice but to follow her in.

And now, as he stood facing a man he didn't know how to address, he did not know what to say.

Moloud turned to Vaqar pleasantly and said, 'Here you are! Here is your darling Youssef.'

Vaqar opened his arms. He embraced Youssef, who self-consciously pulled away from him. Then, gripping his son's shoulders with both hands, Vaqar shook him slightly and looked at him intently. He said, 'You've grown into a man,' and just for a moment Youssef saw a twinkle in the depths of the dark eyes; a scarlet twinkle like the sun when it reflects off the sea as it sets; a quick and passing flash caused by an inexplicable and momentary anxiety.

Then it was over. He let go of his son's shoulders. The light in the eyes died; the sun set; the sea became dark and a permanent cold shadow engulfed the world.

When he looked again, Vaqar was his usual self: calculating, polite and distant. This was the father he knew.

Vaqar asked Youssef about the years he had spent abroad; about his education, his work and the job he was planning to engage in. The father's formal questions and the son's short responses were interrupted by Moloud's not-so-brief explanations, which diluted the formality of the dialogue. Vaqar asked about his other sons' situation but did not mention his wife's name. Moloud told him about the wedding. Youssef looked for his father's reaction with anxiety. But Vaqar met the news pleasantly. He said he was happy with the match. He emphasised that Youssef needed to think about the future more seriously. In the end, as Youssef and Moloud were leaving the room, he asked Youssef to come and see him again, the next day, so that he could talk to him about business matters that had been delayed by their separation.

Just that!

Moloud and Youssef returned to Auntie's house at noon. Rana announced their arrival since she had spent the entire morning tending the flowerbed out the front as an excuse to hover in the garden while she awaited their return.

As soon as they arrived, Moloud said to Auntie, 'You don't know how happy the poor man was,' and then she turned to Youssef and continued, 'Don't you think? Did he say anything nasty? Did he do anything evil? Nothing! He did nothing except to show happiness.' She then turned to Auntie once again and said, 'He asked Youssef *jan* to go and see him tomorrow to discuss the rest of the business. That's all!'

Auntie nodded. She called Sarvar to serve lunch. Auntie was quiet over lunch. Malek tried to make her talk a few times but, whatever she asked, she received only the briefest of responses in return. Auntie's mind was clearly elsewhere. Youssef looked irritable as well. The scarlet twinkle that he had seen in his father's eyes, or that he imagined he had seen in his eyes, did not give him peace. Just for a moment it was as though he had seen another man in the depth of his father's being; an anxious man whom ... perhaps he even loved.

After lunch Youssef said he wanted to see his mother and left. As always Moloud fell asleep in the chair in the middle of the conversation.

Malek told Auntie, 'Thank goodness it went well.'

Auntie said, 'It's just the beginning.'

Rana said, 'Didn't Moloud *Khanoum* say that he was happy to see Youssef? That's all. So why are you uncomfortable?'

As she was getting up to return to her room, using her walking stick to help her, Auntie said, 'Exactly because of this!' And then, without saying another word, she went towards the stairs.

Youssef went to see his father again the next day and the day after that and all the days that followed. He would get up in the morning and leave, returning late in the afternoon. He didn't say much about what went on between him and his father; he just said that an inventory of his estate was being drawn up. He said that his father insisted on his attendance while this was being done so that, in the event of his death, someone would have a complete picture of his assets.

Auntie, who was angry at Youssef's regular absences, grunted, 'God bless Mr Piran's inventory! If I am not mistaken, Vaqar us-Saltaneh has mixed up the country's treasury with his own estate.'

Rana wasn't happy either; Youssef had changed. It was as though he had forgotten about the wedding. He wasn't attending to all that had to be done and he would give a nonsensical answer when he was questioned. Only once, when Rana protested, did he say he couldn't spend the rest of his life among women. And when his mother complained to him that he was spending his entire time with his father he would say that there were tasks that only men could do; he couldn't hide under the skirts of the female members of the family and forget about his responsibilities just to avoid the squabble between his parents.

It was exactly at this time that Nasrullah sent a telegram saying that he couldn't get back in time for the wedding and asking for the date to be postponed. Malek felt uneasy. Nasrullah was always away when he should have been home and often missed important things. She remembered Marjan, her sister, dying as she waited for her husband to return, but although she consoled herself that she was fretting unnecessarily, she was still in a bad mood as a result of the news. This was a wedding and not a death. Late one afternoon she saw Great Auntie by the flowerbed that Youssef and Rana had made. Great Auntie was standing there with her feet bare and with her hair looking unkempt. She was stroking the flowers as tears rolled down her face; just like the night that her father's library had caught fire and burned down. Great Auntie turned to Malek, shaking her head and lamenting tearfully, and then disappeared.

This was ominous; the most ominous sign possible – even worse than Mehr's bad dreams. Malek became ill from anxiety. She didn't leave her room for two days. In the end Mrs Rassouli managed to get her out of the room by asking her opinion about the wedding gown, which was not yet quite ready. As though a seasoned detective, Mrs Rassouli kept asking Malek lots of questions until she could no longer dodge the episode with Great Auntie.

Mrs Rassouli asked gently, '... the same girl as in the photograph?'

'Yes, the same girl as in the photograph.'

Mrs Rassouli sighed and said, 'Poor girl! Come, Malek *Khanoum* darling, don't be sad. It is wrong. The dead person grieves for her own wedding. You need to make an offering. It'll be all right.'

And Malek decided that Great Auntie was lamenting her own wedding, so she made some offerings and said some prayers, but she remained anxious.

Malek had just left her sickbed when Rana came back from Taj *Khanoum's* house looking as though she was about to burst into tears and saying that she was not prepared to look at Youssef again for as long as she lived.

They had had an argument.

Just like all young couples.

But this time there was a small difference; Youssef had spoken strangely. He said that Nasrullah Khan had intentionally not come back so that the wedding would be called off; that Rana's father did not consider the groom worthy; that Nasrullah had never liked him or his family and now was doing this to belittle them. And he said that if his mother had remained with his father his family would not have become homeless and he would not have had to tolerate the contempt of a man who had always held a grudge against his father.

Auntie listened to all that Rana said as she sobbed. She did not interrupt or advise her, nor say anything to calm her either. She waited until Rana had finished crying, had made her threats saying that she did not wish to see Youssef ever again, then she nodded and said gently, 'Rana darling, didn't I say I was worried about this? Didn't I say that the best way to deal with Satan was to avoid him?' Then she looked at Rana's surprised expression, sighed and went on, 'Don't go to him for a few days. Let me have a think.'

The sun's red flames set in the drowning eyes. The world became dark. And the one who ignored the warning of the sea took steps towards annihilation.

Chapter 16

There was no news of Mahtab.

She had not called or visited since that rainy day when she had come to see Rana. Abtin was brooding, so Rana knew something must have happened, but Abtin would not discuss it. She had told Abtin that Mahtab needed to be at Uncle's memorial service but Abtin kept making excuses, saying Mahtab was busy at university. He said she had to sit an exam; that she had to go somewhere. He made every conceivable excuse but Rana had just shaken her head and said she wanted Mahtab to be there. That's all. Abtin had to call upon Mahtab; he had to put aside his pride and beg her, to convince her to come no matter what.

Abtin thought of himself as proud and stubborn but in reality he was a fool and a coward. He was frightened of life and knew only how to escape. Yet, he loved Mahtab; much more than he realised then. Perhaps other women would turn up in his life later but he would never love them with the same sincerity and passion with which he loved Mahtab. Rana knew that life without Mahtab would be a life without dreams for Abtin. She knew that in the absence of Mahtab's love there would be a void in his life; a silent black void that would take over his entire being and destroy him. She knew that what would be left of his soul would be a ruin, and Rana was tired of living in ruins.

Taj *Khanoum* didn't talk to Youssef for a few days; the mother/son relationship had been reduced to distant and formal greetings. Every time Taj *Khanoum* looked at her son she saw the superficial kind look that masked another gaze in its depths; the same cold and calculating gaze of a man whom she had tried to forget over the years. The longer Youssef spent with his father the more like him he became.

Auntie said that that was the downside of innocence; one could easily be conned. One could easily walk in Satan's footsteps and, if you were not rescued, you could easily slip away. She said that Moloud's innocence had cost her her house and was the reason for her being homeless. And Youssef's innocence ... She would sigh at such times, rest her chin on her walking stick and gaze at the wall in front of her, as though she was waiting for someone to tear it down and arrive to fight Satan and to restore innocence.

Sarvar was irritable as well. Every night she dreamt that Seyed was wandering through a jungle that was filled with enormous blond foreigners. Seyed looked like a tramp and kept asking Sarvar to come and rescue him, but she couldn't. Her feet felt heavy. She kept walking but never arrived where he was; the path was interminable and her legs did not have any strength left in them. Sarvar would wake up at dawn with her face wet with tears and she knew that she would never again hear Seyed's call to prayers.

With Great Auntie appearing in her dreams, Malek recited every prayer she knew at night; then she would make offerings with whatever she could think of to try and cast off the bad omen.

Rana was far too furious and hurt to say a prayer or make offerings. She just didn't want to see Youssef, even though she would stay up every night in the hope that he would appear at the door. Her inner struggle meant that her skin had become fragile and there were dark rings around her eyes. Mrs Rassouli said that the bride must take care of herself, otherwise it would be impossible to apply makeup for the wedding and then the gown would not look so beautiful. She said if Rana didn't take care of herself, she would stop sewing. And she meant it. But Mrs Rassouli's threats were pointless; Rana was not prepared to hear about the wedding.

The brooding all around him drove Youssef closer to his father and Vaqar fanned the flame of Youssef's negative outlook and systematically directed his suspicion towards those who, according to his father, had ruled over him for years. Vaqar told his son that what had happened to Maryam was simply the result of a misunderstanding. He said he never thought his beloved little daughter had been seriously ill. And, unbelievably, as he spoke Youssef saw his father's eyes well up with tears. He said that Taj *Khanoum* had never consulted him about household issues and that whatever he had done had always been for his wife and children so that they could have a better life. He said that he had done wrong; he had made huge mistakes but everyone made mistakes. He said that everybody else had intentionally ruined their lives and destroyed their reputation because he was richer than everybody else; because he had not wasted his father's wealth; because he was an eyesore as far as they were all concerned. He said that Auntie had always wanted Youssef to be hers because he resembled the sons she had lost. But, of course, as far as Vaqar was concerned there was nothing wrong with Auntie's affection for Youssef. The fact that she wanted to own someone else's son, however, was not appropriate. He said that Auntie preferred it if Vaqar's family always remained in her debt financially because then she could demean them by showing everyone how caring and kind she was. What other purpose could there be for her bestowing such benevolence? And to demonstrate his own good intentions Vaqar told Youssef to choose any one of his assets that he desired and he would transfer it into his name whilst he was still alive. He went on and on and on in this vein ... And although Youssef doubted him at first he slowly began to believe him. As every doubt was removed and every belief explained, he became more and more distant from his mother, Auntie and Rana. He eventually reached the point where he doubted everyone. He saw an evil intention and purpose behind every kindness and attention that was given him.

Every time they met, Vaqar filled Youssef's mind with more tales about the family's devious intentions and Taj *Khanoum's* naiveté. It was he who planted the negative seeds of thought about Rana. He said that Rana was the bait being used to trap him with people who did not love him but who wanted to rule his life. From being his favourite childhood friend, Rana slowly became the rope that was to hold him captive.

Vaqar never said that Rana was not a nice person or that she wasn't worthy of Youssef. On the contrary, he said that Rana was a lovely girl who would make an exceptional wife. Alas, she was the daughter of a conceited and foul-mouthed man; he said Nasrullah was a man who had left his sick wife to die alone as she waited for him to return to her. He was a man who had seldom visited his daughter all these years and yet claimed that he was a good father. The reality was that Rana had effectively been brought up on the charity of others. She had frequented homes and eaten lunches that had been given to her out of compassion. This type of person, someone who had been raised without true affection, might perhaps leave Youssef one day just as her father had left her mother. Perhaps she would leave Youssef and allow their children to be raised in other people's homes and with other people's charity. Just as she had been brought up and then ... Well, Vaqar didn't wish to plant seeds of pessimism but what about the tale of the madness that runs in their family? Apparently her mother had been mad. It was true that she had died of a disease but the rumours said that she had lost her mind long before becoming unwell. Even if one did not trust the rumours, her aunt's madness was also public knowledge. Worse, they were all perfectly well before they got married. It sounded as though there was some festering tumour in their soul that opened up after marriage. Could Youssef put up with a neurotic and sick wife for the rest of his life? And if Rana didn't go mad, what about the legacy that she could leave for her children; children, who would be born healthy, grow well, and then, as adults, when they reproduced, perhaps end up insane. Youssef would be left hanging from a rope that he had created for himself.

Every time they met, Vaqar would reveal a few things; a sentence here, a sentence there. During each visit he would gauge Youssef's patience and tolerance. He was always careful to inject just enough poison in his mind to make him suffer but, at the same time, to keep him alive. Vaqar was gradually killing his victim with poison, like an expert criminal.

Youssef closed down his feelings; no matter how hard the elders tried to reconcile him with Rana, it was hopeless. Every time he saw Rana he saw the suffering and misery in her face, just as his father had described to him. Great Aunt's photograph was always on the table and no one in the family resembled her as much as Rana. Youssef made a connection between Rana's anger and rebellion and the mad look on the face of the girl in the photograph, and thought that perhaps Rana would truly become insane after marriage. Wasn't she already behaving in an illogical and irrational way? Youssef hadn't done anything. Nothing had changed. He had just said that he was upset because Nasrullah didn't give their marriage enough importance. If Rana quarrelled with him now because of a father whom she barely saw twice a year, then where would they end up once they were married? As for Auntie, why, in fact, was Auntie so kind to him? He couldn't take a dead son's place, could he? He couldn't and he wouldn't want to. He had no intention of making himself a nuisance or of being in their debt for ever. He wanted to stand on his own two feet and not be at all needy. He wanted to be the man that he had to be; a proud man and the ruler of his destiny. But what would he have to sacrifice in the process?

Every day, Youssef increased his distance from everyone else. Every day Rana withered a little more. The day Mrs Rassouli announced that the wedding gown was ready the wedding was already on its deathbed. And the day that the news reached them that Nasrullah was coming home was the day that the dying betrothal drew its last breath.

Chapter 17

The sound of the telephone ringing brought Rana to the sitting room.

It was Simin; Auntie Mehr's niece. Her children had been living in Europe for some years now. After her husband's death she had spent most of the year in Paris where her youngest daughter lived. Now she had just returned and wanted to see Rana sometime during the next few weeks. She sounded quite thrilled. She said to Rana that she had a great deal of news about the family. Rana made an excuse, saying that someone was knocking on the door so she had to go, but before she put the phone down Simin said that she was coming to see her later that same morning.

When Rana put the receiver down she wished she'd thought to say that she would not be in. Simin could come the next day to Uncle's memorial. It was easier to tolerate her in a gathering, but now she had to put up with spending an entire morning alone with her. That wouldn't be easy but at least it was easier than going to her house. Simin loved antiques. Despite being almost permanently absent from Iran she had done nothing to reduce her collection. Whenever Rana went to her home the excessive number of objects made her feel claustrophobic. Her reception room was filled with a number of items, both large and small, which she had acquired from her travels all over the world. And still, after every trip, the collection continued to grow. Every table and chair, every dish and statue, every picture on the wall, each had a particular history that Simin insisted on sharing with her guests, 'I bought this mirror in Germany. It's pre-war and I found it in a small old antique shop.' And she would point to the small mirror on the wall, which had ripples across its surface, and every time Rana looked at it she thought she could still see the face of the original owner, who might perhaps have been killed in a bombing raid or in a concentration camp. Simin would then point to the porcelain statue of a girl with a long skirt gathered at the waist. 'I found this in a shop in the little alleyways in Venice. It was lying on top of a pile of bric-à-brac. As soon as it caught my eye I realised what a jewel it was. The shop owner explained that it depicts a girl who's waiting for her lover to return.' The statue's painted face revealed an expression of permanent wondering, as though she knew she had to keep watching the road.

Simin's reception room resembled a collection of ghosts; ghosts that had each been stolen from different parts of the world. They didn't understand each other's language and were condemned to await their fate in that dimly lit and sad-looking room.

Their fate was not very different from each other's: every plate and statue broke into pieces. Eventually, every item in the room would become obsolete and be of no use. These changes would occur gradually, so no one would notice until much later.

A moment of inattentiveness here and a precious plate was chipped; a sudden impact there and a crack would appear. The most sincere promises and agreements were trodden upon and, in the end, everything – all the plates, the people, the promises and the agreements – would get ready to depart for the afterlife ...

The news of Nasrullah's imminent arrival was received at a time when everything was disintegrating. Youssef had never said he regretted his decision but his behaviour became colder and more indifferent by the day. At times, for brief periods, he would become his old self again, only to revert back to the stranger later on; no one knew what to do with the remote stranger. Rana, who wanted to call a halt to everything, left her final decision until after her father arrived home. Nasrullah was due back at a most critical moment; at a time when everyone was avoiding speaking to one another and when no one knew what to do. Taj *Khanoum* tried to compensate for her son's negligent behaviour by being ostentatiously affectionate towards her future daughter-in-law, but it was of no consequence. Every day Rana witnessed Youssef become more distant. If Nasrullah had arrived now he would have found an anxious and confused maiden rather than the cheerful bride that he expected to see and he would never have conceded to the wedding. They could try and pretend that everything was as it should be; they could say that Rana was just as anxious as any other bride and that her pale complexion and the dark rings around her eyes were the product of all the excitement she felt about the wedding. But they also had to think of an explanation for the way Youssef was behaving.

Auntie, who had for some time now been keeping herself to herself, became more aware of the situation. One day, before Nasrullah arrived, she decided to have a word with Taj *Khanoum* and Malek. Whatever was the content of their conversation, the atmosphere changed. The melancholy air that had engulfed them for the past few weeks lifted. The arrival of the father of the bride was a good excuse to organise a number of social gatherings, one after the other, thus preventing Youssef from visiting his father as frequently. The father-and-son encounters became limited to once or twice a week. The other days Youssef had to undertake chores related to the wedding; endless chores: from attending to the renovation works to the building that would become their home after they were married, to making a list of the names of the guests, or doing the shopping, not to mention the multitude of tasks, both large and small, that no one had even thought about yet.

Amid all this, and in an effort to ensure her son was at home more often, Taj *Khanoum* pretended that she did not feel well. Taj *Khanoum's* illness didn't have any particular symptoms, but its development necessitated that Youssef should not stray far from her. Whenever Youssef wanted to go and see his father, Taj *Khanoum* became quite lethargic, or her vision darkened, or she thought that her heart might stop beating at any moment. But if Youssef was with Rana or busy attending to the renovation work on the house, all the symptoms of her curious illness would miraculously disappear. It was an old trick but proved to be an effective one. Youssef at least realised that mentioning his father was sufficient to see his mother's condition deteriorate.

Youssef didn't seem unhappy with the situation either. He became less irritable and anxious. What he saw around him was in contrast to his father's tales about the family. Rana seemed to be revived; she had regained her colour, she started smiling again and there was no evidence of an unruly or wandering expression.

By the time Nasrullah arrived everyone felt that the marriage had been resurrected.

Nasrullah was his usual self; well groomed, neat and good natured. He had a warm and friendly encounter with Youssef, asking him for nothing other than his daughter's happiness. Rana was elated and her father saw the same determination that Marjan had shown at the time of her marriage. The thought of Marjan and all that had happened during their life together upset him a little but this was a different tale; a new tale and one, no doubt, with a happy outcome. The elders sat together on the very first day and decided on a date for the wedding. Nasrullah couldn't stay for long so it was decided to have the nuptials ten days hence, followed by a wedding reception the week after that. The decision about the date transformed the recent melancholy atmosphere. Everyone was busy with their own particular tasks.

And it was Youssef who informed Vaqar of the date of the wedding. He was sure that the news would make his father happy.

Perhaps Youssef shouldn't have told Vaqar about Nasrullah's arrival and the wedding date – something that was pointed out later by many, friend or foe. When Vaqar learnt about the wedding date it must have sounded a warning that the game was nearly over and that it was time for the final attack, a move that he had long been planning.

From that moment on, everything moved quickly, like an avalanche. It was so unexpected and without warning that no one remembered exactly what happened. Everyone had their own version of events and none of them was the same.

Two days later, Nasrullah stormed into Auntie's house, looking fired up. He did not resemble the composed and sophisticated man they all knew.

Malek asked Sarvar to bring Nasrullah a glass of cold water. Auntie invited him to sit down. Fearing her father's fury, Rana was looking at her father curiously. Nasrullah could not speak properly because he was so angry. He would only occasionally mumble, 'Unscrupulous man ... I'll show him ... bastard ...' and he completely ignored the presence of the ladies.

Eventually, amid a torrent of angry and incoherent words, Nasrullah managed to say that Vaqar had sent word that he should leave his son alone; that if the whole family thought it could steal his wealth they were mistaken. No one could extort any money from him. Youssef had nothing and would never have anything, so they could not make their rootless and homeless daughter an heiress. Vaqar had spoken of Nasrullah, Rana, Marjan and even Great Auntie in such a way that Nasrullah's fury brought him to the point of insanity. He had also said that Rana had conceived a child with Youssef and that was why they were in such a rush to stage the wedding. Worst of all, he had come in person to see Nasrullah and had talked openly and in the presence of his colleagues. So many people had witnessed his insults that it would be impossible to bring the episode to a close.

Nobody ever found out exactly what Vaqar had said to Nasrullah; he was far too angry to remember every word. All those who had witnessed the exchange claimed that they were so shocked by what they had heard that they could no longer remember the details, although later, despite their shock, they proved more than able to recount the episode in great detail. Insult was added to injury, every time it was retold.

Calming Nasrullah down became impossible. He said that there was no way he was going to permit the wedding to take place. Even when he was told that it was not possible to cancel it at such a late stage because everything was already done, all the arrangements had been made and all the guests had been invited, he announced that it did not matter: the wedding celebrations would go ahead but the groom would be someone else; anyone but that bastard's son; anyone like Mr Atabaki's son, for example. What was wrong with him? He was educated; he had travelled abroad and his parents were respectable people.

Nasrullah slammed his fist on the table saying, 'I'll be damned if I do not have my daughter wed Atabaki's son. I am going to speak to him in person, right now,' and he left. When he returned an hour later, he announced to everyone's bewilderment and disbelief that the Atabakis had gladly welcomed the proposition. Malek knew that they would do so. Nasrullah was a wealthy and influential man, and everyone thought Rana was also Auntie's heir. The match was advantageous to the Atabakis in every respect and they were people for whom such arrangements never depended on matters as mundane as love.

The world turned upside down. Just like that, in a moment.

The tale of Nasrullah wreaking his vengeance on Vaqar passed from person to person for years to come. In the versions that followed, the date of the betrothal was brought forward to the very evening of the dispute. Rumour had it that Nasrullah had brought in a cleric that evening and married his daughter off to Atabaki's son so that he could put an end to the marriage tale. But the truth was different. Rana shed many tears while Malek and Auntie tried to mediate, but it was to no avail. The pregnancy slur was not something that Nasrullah could tolerate. As far as he was concerned his daughter could become anyone's wife but Youssef's. Otherwise the disgrace would remain with them for ever.

The wedding took place as planned and with all due pomp. The bride was the same bride but the groom was someone else.

During the ceremony Rana resembled Great Auntie more than ever; she looked bewildered and dazed, as though she was attending someone else's wedding. She didn't know anyone present and didn't want to either.

The ceremony was over. But Rana's state of shock remained. And calamity lay ahead.

Chapter 18

Not many people attended Uncle's memorial. Many had forgotten about him during his years of solitude.

When people spend too long anticipating someone's death, the death itself becomes quite simple; they are often more surprised to learn that the person is still alive. When one hears about a change in a patient's state of health one asks, 'Oh, he's still alive, is he?!' And if the patient's family leaves him before he dies, his death seems even more imminent and acceptable. At least that was Rana's way of thinking; she knew Uncle only had a few good friends who were genuinely sorry to see him go. The rest didn't count for much.

Rana had just finished sorting out the sitting room downstairs when someone knocked at the door. Who could that be at this time?

It was after the second bell when she remembered; it was Simin. Rana had completely forgotten that she had said she would call in the morning.

She hurriedly ran her fingers through her hair and opened the door. It was her; she stood on the doorstep with open arms and she was beaming widely, revealing two neat rows of teeth in good order. Simin was always the same, larger than life.

Rana took Simin to the room downstairs, which she had made ready for the memorial gathering. Perhaps it wasn't the right thing to do but she wasn't in the mood to go up the stairs again. Simin preferred the first floor as well. Her slender figure, golden hair and a face that had been lifted a few times could not cover the pain of the arthritis in her joints. The youthful appearance was just a mask for an old woman to hide behind. But it didn't matter. As long as she did not want to change Rana, her ways did not matter.

When she saw Uncle's photograph, Simin became tearful. She carefully dabbed the tears from the corner of her eyes so that her mascara and eyeliner did not smudge or run down her face. Rana could never understand how Simin could apply makeup so meticulously when her eyesight was so weak. Abtin had suggested, 'Auntie Simin applies makeup to her face from memory.' Be that is it may, her efforts to escape old age were her own business and no one else's.

Contrary to Rana's expectations, it was a good visit. Simin talked about her daughters and what they were doing; about their husbands and children; and about the rest of the family who had for some years now adopted a different homeland. Some were doing quite well, some were in good health and a few, like Uncle, were no longer around.

Simin also gave an account of all the marriages and divorces. She delivered her news about the children, who Rana found it difficult to picture as adults, and spoke of so many divorces that it was hard to believe. Some couples had formally divorced – a few had resorted to a phenomenon that they called geographical divorce. As far as Simin was concerned this latter option was much more sensible; people got rid of each other without making any noise. But what she did not say was that her eldest daughter had resorted to such a divorce.

Rana had just served the second round of tea when Simin remembered the most important item of news about Vaqar's son: Youssef's mysterious death.

'... He was found in his own home,' she said. 'He died with his hands tied and his face looked bewildered; not a single injury on his body either …' And then, when she noticed Rana was not listening, she said, 'Rana … I'm talking to you, Rana …'

Rana had been nodding out of politeness since the middle of Simin's previous sentence, because her mind had become diverted by the thought of tomorrow's guests: perhaps it would be different; perhaps a large number would turn up. What would she do then? Perhaps it would be better to order dinner from outside …

Simin said again, 'I'm talking to you, Rana …'

Rana now returned to Simin from the middle of tomorrow's event. She was abashed. 'I'm so sorry. I suddenly …' And then she offered Simin some pastries.

Simin said, 'You know I don't eat pastries … but as I was saying …'

Rana said, 'Yes, you were saying.'

'He was found in his home. His father's home …'

Rana asked, 'Who was found?'

Simin said, 'Oh my God, Rana, you're driving me mad! I am talking about Vaqar us-Saltaneh's son!'

Rana asked with surprise, 'Vaqar us-Saltaneh's son?!'

'Stop it! Do you mean to tell me that everyone knows, except you? I swear you're becoming as mischievous as your Auntie Malek.'

'I've been quite tied up with Uncle's affairs in the past week. I've received no news about anyone.' She didn't want to tell Simin about her forgetfulness or her medicine.

'I was saying that they found him! In the same house! Think about it!'

'In which house did they find him?!'

Simin was losing patience, 'Oh my God! In his father's house! His hands were tied to a chair. And it was not clear what had happened to him. No injury, no marks; he had died, just like that.'

Rana suddenly grew pale. Like that. It was not possible.

She asked, 'Which son?'

Simin said, 'Are you teasing me? You know; Youssef! Who else lived in that house after Vaqar us-Saltaneh?!'

The house of doom; the house he hated; the house whose inhabitants he resented.

Rana shook her head vehemently, saying, 'It's not possible.'

'It's very strange. But their stories were always strange ... Just imagine, the same house in which his father's bloated corpse was found. He died in the same house ... after all these years ...'

'It's a lie. Youssef was not there.'

'Of course he was. After his father's death he took over all his assets and began to live in the same house as well.' Then, as though pleased to see Rana in a state of shock, Simin continued, 'And he died there too. That is stranger than everything else ... Tell me, don't you believe in divine retribution?'

As though in a dream Rana said, 'Youssef was not there. Youssef drowned. He drowned himself. He walked into the sea. He had dressed as though he was going to a dinner party; he wore the same suit that he had purchased for our wedding. Youssef walked into the sea and never returned ...'

'No, love! You're in a muddle. It was Zaeem ud-Dowleh's friend who killed himself in that way and no one ever found out why. Zaeem ud-Dowleh used to recount the tale to everyone. You do remember his temperament, don't you? He must've really spiced up the tale. How his friend really died heaven only knows.' Then, as though remembering an amusing secret, she laughed and said, 'Youssef did kill someone but not himself ...'

Rana rose so abruptly that the tea tumbler fell, along with the plate of pastries. She said, 'That's impossible. Youssef died years ago; in the sea. Youssef didn't kill anyone. Youssef couldn't kill anyone ...'

When Abtin arrived, Rana was sitting in a corner, hugging her legs, punching her knees and mumbling to herself; the only words that Abtin could distinguish were 'sea' and 'Youssef'.

The physician had warned Abtin that she might experience episodes of intense crisis. But he had not imagined that it might become so bad. He gave Rana some tranquillisers and contacted her doctor, who prescribed as much rest as possible. His tone suggested that he had expected this to happen.

Simin had only left once Rana had calmed down a little but before she did so she shed a good many tears. Rana had been fine. They had chatted happily – about ordinary topics – until she had broken the news of Vaqar's son. The news had shaken Rana so much that it resulted in the state she was now in.

Simin did not tell Abtin that Youssef used to be Rana's fiancé. She didn't tell him that they had been supposed to get married, until ...

Rana could not participate in the memorial gathering the next day. Abtin went to the cemetery by himself. He washed the lonely and strange gravestone. He placed a few flowers on it and was home in no time. Mahtab had stayed with Rana, who was quiet. Since her attack of anger the day before she had not said anything else; she had just sat staring into space. Her face was without expression. No chagrin, no fear. Nothing!

From late afternoon onwards Uncle's friends began to arrive, one by one. Abtin and Mahtab attended to the guests and told everyone that Rana had suddenly developed a fever and could not attend.

That night, having bid farewell to the last of the guests, Abtin placed his arm across Mahtab's shoulders and said, 'Thank God you were here.'

Mahtab wanted to say that he couldn't take her presence for granted but Abtin's face was so drawn and tired that she could not bring herself to add to his burden.

She did not say anything. As she cleared away the glass tea tumblers and plates she said to Abtin, 'Check on your mother; she might need something.'

Abtin said, 'Do you think she'll get better?'

Mahtab said, 'Certainly. She'll certainly get better. It's always the way. The crisis comes and goes.'

'What if it doesn't? What if it doesn't go? What if she stays like this?'

'It's too early to say. She was tired, very tired. Besides, we don't know what happened yesterday.' And then she said, 'Go on. The medicine has made her drowsy. Let her rest. She'll feel better by tomorrow,' before adding, firmly, 'Definitely, she'll definitely feel better tomorrow.'

When Abtin switched the light off and closed the door, Rana had still not closed her eyes. She was looking at the ceiling; she was staring at an image that nobody but she could see.

The wedding guests were still arriving at Auntie's house when Youssef left. After wandering the streets for a while he found himself standing outside his father's home. It was dark now. The door had been left open, ajar. Vaqar was attending to some clients in his home. These people had found themselves in financial difficulty and didn't wish anyone to know about their troubles; people came and went through the door as quietly as shadows and lived in a state of heightened anxiety in case a passer-by recognised them.

The house was quiet and dark, just like any early evening. The only light was coming from Vaqar's study on the second floor. Youssef headed up the stairs. He flung open the door so abruptly that it banged against the wall. Vaqar, who was seated behind his desk and busy with the accounts, lifted his head slightly and saw Youssef.

Vaqar said, 'I expected you a lot earlier.'

* * *

Youssef returned home at the crack of dawn. He went to his room quietly and fell on the bed. He didn't leave the room for a week and when he did finally emerge, he was no longer the Youssef that everyone recognised. He was a cold zombie who never smiled again.

Vaqar was discovered in his study a few days later. They said his corpse had bloated. His tummy had swollen and flies were buzzing around the body. The coroner, who was a relative, said that the death was as a result of electrocution. The officer dealing with the case, also a relative, said that it was possible that his reading lamp had been faulty and that he had been trying to repair it but, since he did not know much about electrical repairs, he had inadvertently electrocuted himself. The evidence he cited was that the lamp had fallen off the desk and landed beside him. No one considered the cut to the corner of his open mouth to be significant. According to the autopsy the cut had probably occurred because the victim's head had hit the edge of the desk as he had fallen to the floor. In other words, it was determined that Vaqar had brought about his own death. No one mentioned that the timing of the incident coincided with Rana's wedding. No one asked where Youssef had been at the time of the incident. Though no one doubted how Vaqar's death had occurred, the only one who could have been guilty was Youssef. Auntie made Nasrullah and Mr Sardari use all their influence to ensure that the case was closed as quickly as possible. Only Mr Sardari mentioned on the first day to Auntie, 'What if he's guilty? We can't turn a fact into fiction, can we?!'

Nasrullah responded, 'What exactly are the facts? It was always likely that someone would kill that man anyway.'

Auntie said, 'I just know one thing. It was Vaqar us-Saltaneh who murdered Youssef.' And then, after the case was over, she never mentioned Youssef's name in Nasrullah's presence again.

After Rana's wedding, Youssef was not prepared to continue to live in Zaeem's house. The case had only just closed when he took his mother and brothers and returned to their own home. He took over his father's estate. He raised his brothers. He brought Mrs Rassouli to live with them and to keep his mother company. And he never set foot inside Auntie's house again.

The day after her wedding, Rana became like a candle whose flame had been extinguished, and she disintegrated completely when she heard the news of Vaqar's death. She wouldn't speak, eat, comb her hair or even change her clothes. She would spend the entire day sitting in a corner and staring into space with the same bewilderment and apprehension as the girl in the photograph. Malek had seen it before. It was she who asked Auntie to speak to Nasrullah. Regretting what he had brought upon his daughter he decided to annul the ridiculous marriage. Rana's divorce was just as fast and as sudden as her wedding had been. Once Nasrullah had settled the divorce affairs on his daughter's behalf Mrs Atabaki went around saying, 'As soon as their girls get married they go crazy. Her mother's aunt was the same. They are well before the wedding but as soon as they get married ... My poor darling boy,' and she would sigh and then wipe away invisible tears.

It was the rumours of family insanity that prompted Nasrullah to send Rana to Switzerland with Malek, under the guise of continuing her education. Rana's university was in reality a sanatorium, where she was taken care of for two years. The story of Youssef's drowning was born in Rana's mind during that period. She mentioned it to Malek one day when they were sitting in the sanatorium's garden. When she talked about Youssef drowning she looked calm. So calm, in fact, that Malek couldn't bring herself to tell her the truth. The man who had really drowned himself was someone whom Rana had never met, and he might even have stemmed from Zaeem's imagination. But among Zaeem's many tales, Rana borrowed this one and for the rest of her years Youssef had drowned in a sea that did not exist.

After Malek had gone away with Rana and Youssef, Taj *Khanoum* and the children returned to their own home. Auntie's house became even more melancholy and lonely than ever before. Mehr had become bed-bound so could not leave her home; Moloud used the permanent pain in her legs as an excuse to avoid the place. This seemed quite wise as far as Auntie was concerned because she was not so sure that she could tolerate her for a long period of time. Mr Sardari would (very rarely) find an excuse to visit Auntie. Mr Zaeem ud-Dowleh also paid a visit from time to time and would spend an hour with Auntie, during which time he would ask after Rana and Malek, read Malek's letters, and then say, 'It's a bad year, Madam, a bad one.'

Auntie would nod in agreement and then they would both remain quiet.

When Youssef asked Mrs Rassouli to come and live with them as his mother's companion, Mrs Rassouli sought Auntie's opinion. Auntie did not think that there was anything wrong with such an arrangement; neither woman would be lonely. Mrs Rassouli could not keep sewing for the rest of her life; her eyesight had already grown weak by then and when she bent over the material her neck ached. Auntie thought she could rent out her small house and spend her retirement with Youssef and Taj *Khanoum*.

Auntie said, 'Anyway, the last chapter of one's life is always quiet; quiet and bitter. No one stays with us.'

'It is not a good chapter. It isn't good at all.'

After Mrs Rassouli had left, Sarvar came to clear the plates away. Auntie leaned on her walking stick, rose with difficulty and walked towards the stairs to go to the floor above.

Sarvar said, 'Where are you going, Ma'am? It isn't night-time yet. Perhaps you'll have another visitor.'

'No Sarvar. I don't think so.'

'Shall I ask Rahman to clean the fireplace and get a fire going?'

'What on earth for?'

'In case someone comes.'

Auntie was slowly climbing the stairs when she said, 'It is not necessary. Just close the blinds, draw the curtains in the reception room and shut the door. I don't think anyone will visit again for some time.'

And by the time Auntie reached her room, Sarvar was just drawing the curtains.